RESTORATION HEIGHTS

RESTORATION HEIGHTS

A Novel

WIL MEDEARIS

HANOVER
SQUARE
PRESS

HANOVER
SQUARE
PRESS

ISBN-13: 978-1-335-21872-8

Restoration Heights

Library of Congress Cataloging-in-Publication Data has been applied for.

HanoverSqPress.com
BookClubbish.com

Printed in U.S.A.

For my mother

RESTORATION HEIGHTS

"...perhaps, in the worst case, there is no comprehensive natural order in which everything hangs together—only disconnected forms of understanding."

Thomas Nagel, *Mind & Cosmos*

ONE

You know Reddick. He's that white guy on the subway, past thirty and showing it, jeans and boots splattered by work that was never intended to be permanent, that was tolerable enough while he waited for the big break that never came. Patience hardening in his bones like concrete. Resignation passing as stoicism. He stands in the door of the northbound G, third car from the front, eyes down, headphones on, clinging to a rhythm you can almost make out. From Bed-Stuy to Long Island City all the stops exit the opposite side, he is neither disturbed nor in the way, he has claimed a space, found a comfort that lies somewhere between habit and ritual. You barely notice him. These guys are all over the city.

So is Harold, hustling for a swipe of your MetroCard. Middle-aged, black and sturdy, it isn't obvious why he's waiting outside the turnstiles as you exit, why he can't drum up the fare. There is nothing in his face to explain his reliance on your charity. In the armor of his quilted sweatshirt, his tangerine hard hat—you expect to see men like Harold on the afternoon train, nylon cooler between his spread feet, slumped body wasted by the day's work.

He caught Reddick maybe eight or ten weeks ago, before the holidays—a wordless transaction, each man accustomed to his part, actions polished smooth as pearls by countless practice, by years of commuting. They were wearing the same boots. Reddick swiped him in again two days later, then three times the week after Thanksgiving, a series of small coincidences, their schedules momentarily in sync. The contact expanded with each instance—first a nod of recognition, then small talk, and finally gentle, shallow questions; two surfaces content to brush against one another, without expectations.

A few weeks later they crossed paths on Nostrand Avenue—a final coincidence that each took for granted—and talked for half an hour, bound by their tiny plot to defraud the MTA, one fare at a time. That was when they finally traded names, offered sketches of their histories. Harold grew up in Bed-Stuy but moved into his mother's house in Hunter's Point when she passed. He worked construction, fortifying the army of gentrifiers pushing east into his old neighborhood, buttressing their territory with bland condo towers, conspicuous redoubts of murky brick and cheap metal looming among the old stone houses. Reddick worked freelance, moving crates and hanging other people's art on other people's walls, the time spent in his own studio withering from neglect. He usually blew off painting to play basketball. He rarely felt guilty about it anymore. A shared awareness of failure bridged the gap between their ages. Afterward their morning conversations became routine, even when someone else swiped Harold in, a few stolen moments, brief dispatches on the surface facts of their lives.

Reddick left early that Monday, to tell Harold about the girl in the alley. It was a longer story than they typically made time for. He had seen her on his way home from the bar, just after eleven, in front of his shabby building. Tapping at her phone, coiled on the hood of a dark sedan, she had been surrounded by snow—the uneven slate sidewalks encased in white, the stoops enveloped in buttery swells. He caught the scene catty-corner, framed by the towering skeleton of unfinished construction rising from the adjacent block—with the empty street, the half-buried car, she had seemed like the final survivor of some climate apocalypse. Her breath formed ribbons of condensation, fainter than the trails of her cigarette. When she looked up he saw the inebriation on her slack face—a house party refugee out to escape a crowd, to have a smoke. She watched him dig out his keys, wrestle with the frozen lock. It occurred to him that she might be locked out—he turned to offer the open door but she stared through him, oblivious to the gesture. He left her outside.

He returned with garbage, a straining bag in each hand, clear plastic stretched around a bulk of dusky glass, of empty bottles. The girl had been reabsorbed by her phone. He carried the bags to the gated alley on the side of the building, set them down in a shallow trench to fumble for his keys. There was an unlocked door in the back of the alley that opened into the rear of the building; he didn't use it because his apartment bordered the front stairwell. The key ring was caught on the lining of his jacket—he tugged viciously, the thread snapped, the keys tumbled through his numb fingers and thumped into the snow. He put the bags down and bent to pick them up.

He hadn't heard the footsteps until they were on top of him. He spun and raised his arms—a large, violent motion. It was the blonde. She didn't acknowledge his overreaction, just stood, panting from her sprint, fogging the air between them. He swore and reached down for his keys and swore again.

"You can't just run at a stranger like that," he said. "Not alone. Not at night."

"Sorry," she responded, her voice so flat it was unclear if she knew what she was apologizing for.

He was embarrassed and it irritated him. "Who knows what I might have done?"

"You're a nice guy."

"And you could tell that from over there?"

"I'm good at people. At reading people, I mean." Her eyes began to focus on his face, slowly, as if recovering a lost habit. "Only I thought you were someone else."

He stopped himself from pointing out her inconsistency. It didn't matter, not in her current state. She had lapsed into a world of moment-to-moment truths.

"Do you live here?" she asked.

"Yeah."

"It's like, a really great building." Her voice was nasal and high, the ends of the words tapering into each other in a way that flouted the integrity of their borders, that threatened their meaning. It was the voice men do when performing a specific type of twentysomething white girl, a voice that didn't quite fit her face. He wondered if she always talked that way. He wondered if she was doing it for him.

He unlocked the gate. "It's alright."

"I'll come with you."

He looked at her, and then into the alley. The darkness waited for them to give it shape. He stepped aside and followed her in.

"We should, like, hang out," she said.

"Okay." The gate rattled shut behind them, the lock clicked into place. The motion sensor triggered and the lights came on, revealing the narrow, dirty walls, the rows of cans, plastic and tin. Several bags had already been sorted and were heaped in a corner, crusted with snow. She continued talking without saying anything. He opened a bin beside her narrow hips.

"So we should definitely hang out, then," she repeated. Her phone began to flash—not just the device, but the case as well, garish and emphatic. She brought it unsteadily to her face and began to pluck at the screen. She was small, with a head that seemed slightly oversized, a narrow face with the high cheekbones and large eyes of an actress. Her lips were thin and never quite seemed to meet. Lifeless blond hair fell from her knit hat, the ends brushed her collarbones. She wore leggings beneath her skirt, long sleeves but no coat—she hadn't intended to stay outside long. Her fingers shimmered with meaningless rings. He tried to imagine her sober, in the daylight, but couldn't fix her into place. She seemed to slip between possibilities.

"I have to send this text," she said, concentrating. "But you could probably, like, kiss me when I'm done."

He looked to see if she was joking.

She laughed with her entire body, bowing at the waist, taken with her own audacity. "I mean if you, like, want to. You know, whatever."

"How much have you had to drink tonight?"

"Me? Look at you with all those bottles."

"Those are from last night. We had friends over to watch the game."

She wrinkled her nose at "game"—she found sports either dull or repugnant. "So you have a roommate?"

"Yeah."

"Is he home?" Her smile revealed her motivation—it was precisely the recklessness of her actions that seemed to thrill her. He was a prop, the ground she was stringing her high wire over.

"No."

She returned to her phone. Both of his bags were in bins and they were standing, alone, closed doors on either side. It would be easy to let her wreck herself against him—more than easy, a relief. He stepped toward her and touched her arm.

"I think you should go home." He wasn't certain he would say it until he heard the words.

"Home?"

"You've had a lot to drink."

"Yep." She smiled. "Probably too much. But I earned it."

Her phone erupted again and she returned to it. He started to walk past her.

"Wait." She put her body between him and the gate. "You're leaving?"

"Yeah." He looked over her head at the empty sidewalk, the empty street. "You should go home."

"That's it, then?"

She wore her petulance loosely, provoked by disappointment that barely seemed to reach her. It wouldn't take her long to stumble upon another wild impulse.

After a moment he sighed. "Look. I'll get you a car."

"Ugh."

"If I get one will you take it?"

"Maybe I should."

"The thing is, I would need my phone, which is upstairs, in my apartment." He couldn't take her up there—he didn't trust his resolve if she decided he was worth one more shot. "Will you wait while I get it? Or can we use yours?"

"Hold on." She was interrupted by more gaudy flashes. This time it was a call. She trudged away from him to answer it, into the deep shadows at the rear of the alley. He felt her attention shift with inebriated finality. If he walked away now she wouldn't notice, might not remember the encounter at all—but an obligation had formed, however much he resented it. If he could just get her back to the party he could find her friends, make her their problem. He waited near the gate.

The back door opened, spilling amber light onto the pale snow. He could see an arm holding it, white skin, thick and masculine. She turned toward it and seemed to recognize the owner. She hung up and went inside. The door shut behind her. He stood in the alley alone for several minutes, but the night continued as if she never existed.

"If that had happened to me?" Harold said. "To a brother? I'd be in jail already."

Reddick had spun it for laughs—exaggerated his surprise, her intoxication, the absurdity of her unprovoked offer.

"I was just trying to take out my garbage."

"You don't know who she was or where she went?"

"No idea. I just wanted to take her back to her friends."

"That was the right move. Nothing good would have happened if you kept talking to her."

"It feels like I avoided some kind of disaster."

"I remember when a white girl wouldn't have walked down that street at night. Now they just following men into alleys?" He shook his head, rendered mute by the magnitude of this transformation. The alarm sounded—Harold's train rumbling into the station below them. Reddick reached back and swiped him in. They slapped five across the turnstile.

"My man," Harold said. "If this is the kind of shit you get into I'm going to bring you out with me sometime."

Reddick left the station and made the huddled, hurried walk through frozen Long Island City to the Lockstone warehouse. He punched in and joined the rest of the art handlers as they prepared to load the truck for the Seward job, all of them still on morning time, smoking cigarettes off the open dock and sipping noisily from paper coffee cups, nibbling at bodega pastries. The warehouse floor was large and open as a chapel, the crates lined up like pews. He gave the crew the same take he did Harold, played it for comedy, until he got to the anonymous arm at the end, the way the door cracked the space open and consumed her.

"Wait," one of them asked, "you didn't see who she left with?"

"No. She was gone and I just went back up to my apartment."

"Dude, that's really sketchy."

Another handler interrupted. "I hope that chick is alright."

Reddick frowned. "What do you mean? I didn't leave her alone. I'm sure they just went back to that party."

The other handler shrugged. His name was Allen; he was thick-necked and short, an oil painter who made winding, precise abstractions, memories of a three-week mescaline binge he had during his final summer in Wisconsin. "Look, you don't know that guy. You don't know if *she* knew that guy. Don't you remember that chick in Coney Island, from a couple years ago?"

"Maybe?"

"You should. It was all over the news. There was a whole hashtag thing about it. This drunk girl leaves a party with two dudes, tells her friends she's going for a walk on the beach. They don't know the guys but, you know, it's a party, so everyone just assumes everyone else is cool and no one thinks anything of it when she leaves."

One of the crew flicked his cigarette off the dock. "I remember this."

Allen continued. "Yeah, it was bad, man. They tried tossing her into the fucking ocean when they were done, like idiots. A couple of Russians, dumb as shit. The chick was an NYU student—I think one of her roommates was from Coney Island or something, is why they were down there. Her body washed up the next morning, a little farther down the beach."

Reddick took a drink of his coffee, went back over the alleyway scene in his mind. Something about the way it ended had spooked him, but he hadn't followed the sense to any grim conclusion.

"Really fucking bad, man," Allen repeated.

They stood quietly until one of the other handlers grunted, slapped Reddick's shoulder. "She's fine, dude. It's Brooklyn, if you worry about every drunk white girl you run into you'll be on Xanax by the end of the month. You'll probably see her next weekend, and she won't remember a thing." The rest nodded, grateful for the scrap of optimism. He continued. "Adults can take care of themselves."

The group dispersed and began to load the truck, hauling the art into the back in crates and commercial bins, securing it with bungee cables. They packed blankets, hand tools, rolls of Tyvek and dollies, working until midmorning. After they finished Reddick lingered near the cab, itchy to leave, as Allen made one final pass over their inventory. They had spent the past week shoveling snow around the warehouse, a team of seven up to their knees in powder and ice, digging out two of Lockstone's four loading docks, the client parking lot, the sidewalk around the sprawling facility. They were sore from the work and anxious to be away, on a job. Reddick eyed the cars parked across the street, imagined he saw a girl sitting on top of one of them, saw her disappear in his mind's eye with a stranger. Piles of shoveled snow curled like waves around the bumpers, distant traffic throbbed like the sea.

"Let's do this." Allen slapped the side of the truck, startling Reddick from his daydream. He opened the passenger door, then walked around to the driver's side. "You're not still thinking about that chick, are you?" he called through the cab.

Reddick climbed onto the bench seat. "No," he lied.

TWO

The Seward family underwrote the New York art world—their name beside your favorite painting, revered by curators and directors, cited in provenances. They rehung the walls of their Upper East Side townhouse regularly, flaunting prized acquisitions or plucking favorites from the depths of their Lockstone vault, succumbing at times to the gravity of the neighboring Met by syncing a wall or room to a special exhibition—assuming that the relevant works weren't on loan already. The breadth and depth of their collection allowed for quirks of hubris. The current installation was the largest Reddick had been part of in his six years at Lockstone. It was scheduled for the entire week and covered all five floors—a dozen paintings, a handful of smaller framed drawings, and a few assorted wall-hanging sculptures, plus crating and storing all the work that was currently on display. Five of the paintings were for the front gallery, two more for the dining room downstairs, the final five for three rooms on the second floor—including the parlor, which was set aside for the collection's newest addition: a small, stern Richter whose acquisition had prompted this rearrangement. The fifth floor was left unplanned, to be improvised from the leftovers.

Lane and Dean were already on-site. Lane was Lockstone's manager. Alert with preppy optimism, twenty years younger than the man he replaced, he had been introduced to the crew two years ago, during a gritty job packing a collection of dense, precarious sculptures. He had shown up to the client's apartment in chambray shorts and linen Toms—Allen had nearly crushed a finger when Lane couldn't wedge his toe beneath a lopsided crate. But his white-bread smile soothed their clients, and the company's owners adored him. Relations between Lane and the crew eventually settled into a wary truce—he stayed out of their way as much as possible, and in return they tolerated his supervision.

Lane had picked Dean up and driven straight to the Sewards' in order to prepare the space for the crew's arrival. They had mapped routes through the house—rugs were removed, plastic runners edged the walls and snaked up the front staircase, moving blankets wound like scarves around the banister. Dean had been Reddick's roommate since their final year of college—a decade plus and counting—but he'd lately been sleeping in his Bushwick studio several nights a week. His intricate balsa wood sculptures consumed his time, drove him to choose the ratty couch in his studio over the late-night G ride home. The hard work was slowly paying off; his sales had increased yearly and his practice nearly covered his expenses. He needed only about twenty hours a week at Lockstone to make up the difference. His parents paid his share of their rent but he and Reddick never spoke of it. His studio was a few blocks from Lane's condo, which made him the convenient choice to accompany the manager that morning—but he also tolerated Lane's blithe cheer better than the rest of them, so they were happy to let him go.

The handlers changed into plastic booties and nitrile gloves, their snow-drenched boots quarantined alongside their coats in the outermost foyer. Dean waited in the gallery, gawking at a pensive Rachel Whiteread mounted on the rear wall.

"The thought of this being in a box for the next year depresses me," he said when they joined him.

"Just hang it in your studio, then." Allen eyed the sculpture's soft geometry, its chalky surface. "I'm sure they won't mind."

Dean ignored him, took off his glasses to wipe the lenses, his exposed eyes pink and tender. "Everything go okay this morning?"

Allen shrugged. "Your roommate nearly screwed some girl on a pile of trash but otherwise, yeah, regular morning."

Dean looked at Reddick, who rolled his eyes.

"It wasn't exactly like that." He started the story again, details trimmed. He barely had time to hear Dean's reaction before Lane came in, broke them into teams and got them started.

Dottie, the family's house manager, oversaw the work. Dark-haired, exhausted but precisely assembled, she carried herself with impatient authority—no matter how succinctly Reddick addressed her she gave the impression that he was absorbing too much of her time. She came off as basically a Seward, the vast desert between her and the family collapsed by the crew's distance from either, miles of social landscape swallowed by foreshortening. She conferred often with Mrs. Seward, who was the primary architect of the overhaul, dissecting issues of placement or spacing, at times pushing back against her employer with a lack of deference that Reddick found surprising—although there was often a moment, some signal of tone or inflection that he couldn't detect, when Dottie would capitulate. Mr. Seward was not involved; he could speak eloquently about his family's collection at charity dinners or museum galas, but seemed indifferent to the arrangement of the art in his home.

Their only son, Buckley, was a few years older than most of the Lockstone crew, with heavy eyes and a narrow chin that jutted like a drawer pull from his compact face. He wore a sweater over his collared shirt, and had walnut hair that was wavy and thick to the base of his skull. The family called him Buckles. He greeted the crew briefly when they arrived, near eleven, and Reddick didn't see him again until two hours later.

Reddick and Allen had paired off to hang drawings in Mrs. Seward's third-floor office. She gave them instructions herself—Dottie was busy with the gallery downstairs—then stayed to make a call while they worked silently. There was a portrait of her on the wall behind her desk, a large Schnabel that Reddick wanted to linger with but couldn't get close to with her in the room. It wasn't part of this installation. She was speaking with an accountant or financial advisor, sorting through a pyramid of open folders and splayed papers, discussing the wedding gift she had planned for Buckley—one of their Italian villas, a small one near Florence. She worried about the tax benefits of writing it off; the gift must be an act of generosity, she said, not financial manipulation. The eavesdropping handlers fought to keep their faces neutral.

Her son entered the office. She hung up when she saw his pale, distraught face.

"She still hasn't called." Buckley's voice was deep and commanding, shoring up his willowy presence. He was struggling to keep it even, to mask his concern.

"Oh, Buckles, I'm so sorry. I'm sure she has some reason we haven't thought of."

"That was a fine response last night, when it was only dinner. But it's been almost twenty-four hours."

Mrs. Seward considered it. "You're right. This isn't like her."

"I called Tony, and he seemed concerned."

"We can send someone down to her apartment. You could go yourself."

He looked terrified of the idea but he nodded. "Yes. Yes, I should do it."

Mrs. Seward caught Reddick listening and flicked her eyes at him, quickly enough that her son didn't catch it. Reddick glanced away.

"I'll have Dottie call for the car," she said.

After Buckley left his anxiety infected the staff. A cough-like name moved through the air, *Hannah*, soundtracking the staff's routines. The art handlers broke for lunch—when they returned a pandemic of unease had saturated the house.

They split up and went back to work. When they got to the parlor, Reddick remembered that Dottie had wavered on whether or not to hang the Polke—the connections to Richter seemed too obvious—and postponed her verdict until they returned from their break. He went upstairs to get her. There were service areas on the first three floors, orderly hallways with teeming sideboards and austere worktables linked by an enclosed stairwell. He interrupted Dottie and one of her assistants eating lunch on the third, in a kind of converted break room. They were having the same conversation as the rest of the house and he came in midsentence, Hannah's name hanging in the air like a ghost.

The crew had pieced together a theory from the snippet of conversation that Allen and Reddick overheard—there wouldn't be a better time to confirm it. "Is it Buckley's girlfriend?"

Dottie's stare said it was none of his business. "His fiancée."

"She's missing," offered the assistant. Dottie tried to cut him off but he protested. "I'm sorry, Dot, but this is how rumors start. They can see something is wrong. You're better off just telling them."

"Look, I wasn't trying to pry."

"Of course you were," Dottie said. "But he's right. It's better that you know the truth, or who knows what story might work its way around." She placed her fork neatly beside her plate, slid her chair away from the table and squared her shoulders to Reddick. Her attitude, her tone, assumed the authority of a dean lecturing a wayward student. "Buckley's fiancée, Hannah, didn't show up for dinner last night, and he hasn't heard from her today. Those are the facts and I expect you to be discreet with them."

The assistant sighed. "God, I hope she's okay. Poor Buckles."

"That's awful," Reddick offered.

"It isn't anything, yet," Dottie snapped. "Don't make judgments before you know what you're talking about. Now, did you need something?"

He asked about the parlor, and after she clarified her intentions he left to report to the rest of the crew. He was almost to the stairwell when he remembered that he had left his level in Mrs. Seward's office. He thought of the Schnabel and doubled back, both to save himself a trip later and to steal a quiet moment with the painting. The room was empty, the portrait untended behind the desk. Reddick eyed the long canvas. Mrs. Seward looked at least twenty years younger, her angular silhouette carved by wild thrusts of oil and resin. The surface was uneven, lurching from translucent washes to an impasto so thick it bordered on geological. Reddick thought about how much material it took to build up those areas—he was numb to the prices that art sold for but not to the infinitely smaller costs of making it. It would burn a week's paycheck just to paint that dress. Drawn in by the texture he moved closer, until he was almost leaning on the desk.

"Do you like Schnabel?"

He jumped and turned to face the speaker—Mrs. Seward. The transition was dizzying—from image to flesh, from decades past to the present. He anchored himself on the details of her appearance. Her coffee-brown hair was flecked with gray, pulled back into an ample, haphazard bun. She had a hard, handsome jawline that it must have killed Buckley not to have inherited, and large eyes set deep in a web of wrinkles so fine they seemed drawn in graphite. She walked toward him, moving with the loose comfort of someone whose equanimity hadn't been threatened in years, perhaps decades. He was inexplicably nervous.

"I came in to get my level and—it really grabs you, doesn't it?"

"Differently when you're the subject." She smiled and crossed her long arms at the wrist, a gesture meant to relax him. "But yes, it does. Are you an artist?"

"We all are. I mean, except for one. But he's a musician."

"I've always assumed that most of you were. To treat the work well you must have some reason to care for it. Do you show?"

"Not…not in a while."

She was too polite to acknowledge his hesitation. "Well, just keep working. You never know what might happen."

"Oh. Thank you. I—you know. You never know."

She smiled again. He had a sense of the power she could

put behind it. "I believe that I left my phone up here. On my desk, probably. Would you mind?"

She gestured behind him. He turned around and saw the heel of it peeking from beneath a stack of folders. He slid it out carefully, to avoid an avalanche, and his thumb inadvertently pinched the home button. The screen flashed awake. He glanced at the image it revealed.

"Thank you." She held out her hand but he didn't pass it to her. "Young man." Her impatience was hemmed by courtesy. He caught the inflection in her voice that meant the discussion was over—it was easy to recognize when you were the target—but he didn't let go.

"Young man, would you please hand over my phone?"

She seemed perplexed by his disobedience, and Reddick was suddenly unsure if her radiant authority was merely a bluff, if there would be no consequences for ignoring her. But he couldn't stop looking at the image on the screen—at Buckley smiling behind a dining room table, clasping the hand of a thin blonde woman who reason insisted must be his missing fiancée but who nonetheless looked exactly like the girl who had asked to kiss him the night before, in an alley, surrounded by garbage.

THREE

"And you are absolutely certain that this was her?"

"Yes. I'm telling you. One hundred percent."

He was in the parlor, on a blocky Bauhaus chair they had moved to the center of the room. Other furniture was pulled away from the wall, tools laid carefully in strategic corners—the work abandoned until Reddick's wild claims were resolved. Mrs. Seward was seated in front of him, leaning into his face, elbows on her knees. Her expression was worried and kind. Her husband reclined beside her with disinterested skepticism, his bored face a worn replica of his son's. Whether he didn't believe Reddick or simply thought that this was a crisis not worth his time was unclear. Dottie paced behind them, playing the part of bad cop with cinematic fidelity. Lane stood in place, straining to keep from sweating.

Reddick only wanted to help.

"It was dark," Lane said, offering a way out, his eyes begging him to take it.

"The lights in the alley came on. I could see perfectly."

"Winter clothes. Hat, scarf. Everyone is so bundled up this time of year."

"She wasn't wearing a coat. She had been inside, was obviously not planning on being out long. Just a hat, and that was pulled back from her face."

"But why was she in Brooklyn alone?" Mrs. Seward said. "It simply doesn't make sense."

"I have no idea. I mean, she didn't really tell me about herself." He thought of her clothes, her voice. "She didn't seem out of place."

The version he offered hit different beats than what he had spun for the crew and for Harold. He omitted her abrupt pass. He didn't need to heighten their suspicion. He felt it already; knew how he looked in their eyes. Just over six feet but reed-thin, shoulders hooked forward in a way they would never have allowed in their own son. A lanky Southerner with rough skin, blond hair and a motley face—lips full but jaw too narrow, eyes too close together. An ethnic background so muddled as to be wholly American, in a way that stripped him of context—without immigrant success or a colonial lineage, just guesses and inferences about who might have been what, marriages by people too poor and too scattered to bother noting which part of the Old or New World they were descended from. He had a Scottish first name that he received like an heirloom from the one person in his family tree that was decidedly not Scottish, who could lay claim to an ethnic heritage that an old New York family might understand—if privately recoil from. His paternal grandfather went by Red, because it was short for Reddick but also because it suited his clay-colored skin. Red was black. Reddick was not. That heritage had slipped through the cracks along with all the others, just another fact of DNA indistinguishable in his mongrel white face.

What did the Sewards see when they looked at him? He supposed it was nothing. He did not figure into their idea of the world and therefore he was nothing.

They could only receive his claims with suspicion. Their encounters with people like him were too circumscribed to do otherwise. Alone in a dark alley with their son's fiancée—sex ran through that scenario like ether. He didn't need to mention it for them to think of it, and if he did—even in denial—the innuendo would harden into fact. To claim he made the moral choice required acknowledging that there was another option, and once that other option was attached to him they wouldn't let him shake free.

He decided that her reckless offer was immaterial anyway. It was enough to know that she was drunk—her vulnerability could be assumed. What mattered were facts of timing and location, hard data that could be used to find her. He was clear about that and quashed the rest.

"How out of it was she?" Dottie asked. "Did it seem as though someone might have drugged her?"

Reddick shook his head. "I don't know. I mean, she was—sorry—but she was pretty loopy. She just seemed drunk to me, but I don't know much about it—being drugged, I mean. She smelled like alcohol. And she was coherent. She knew where she was."

He had asked for the police. They put him off, said they wanted to speak privately first—they were hung up on the unlikelihood of his claims. This fluke encounter, he wanted to shout, could save her life. Just accept your good luck and listen.

Buckley returned from Hannah's apartment. Dottie had texted him when he was on his way back but hadn't given details. That morning's vague concern had tightened into dread—something about the trip had shaken him. He was wide-eyed and flushed.

"Mother, she wasn't there, obviously, but—"

"I think you should hear this."

"There was no break-in or anything like that." His deep voice had lost its commanding edge. He seemed diminished, cowed by the growing crisis. "Would you and Dad— I would like to speak with you both, about what to do next. Privately of course."

"Son, listen."

His mother's command yanked him from his fugue. He seemed to finally assess the scene—his family arrayed in front of the art handler. It was a tableau of judgment, of accusation. Reddick saw Buckley's face shift and knew it was over—he had tumbled from witness to suspect. He wondered why he thought it could have gone differently.

"Reddick," Dottie said, "tell him what you told us."

Buckley listened impatiently. "And where was this?" he asked when the story was finished.

"Brooklyn. Bed-Stuy."

His cheeks paled. "That's impossible. She wouldn't have been out there."

"What's that supposed to mean?" Reddick snapped.

"Buckles, you both go to Brooklyn plenty," his mother said.

"Events at the museum. Drinks in Williamsburg."

"But isn't this near—"

He cut her off, barked, "Mother."

She slashed her eyes at him, and continued, "Near BAM, I was going to say. Where precisely was it again?"

"Off the A, the Nostrand stop."

"Mother, that is nowhere near BAM." He seemed impatient to be done with the conversation, to be alone with his parents. "It's nowhere near anything."

"Except my apartment," Reddick said.

"Look." Buckley turned to him. "I don't mean to come off like that. I simply mean that I know my fiancée, I know where she goes and I know she wouldn't be at a party out there."

His smug dismissal grated. "You don't know where she is right now."

"Look here—"

"Reddick!" Lane barked.

"I'm trying to help you, man. You won't even listen to me."

"I don't think you're trying to help at all. I think you want to insert yourself into this situation out of some perverse desire to become a part of our lives."

"Are you being serious right now?" Reddick said.

"Buckles," his mother chided.

"You're like those awful people who call the police with fake tips, for attention."

Reddick jumped to his feet and yelled that he didn't want his attention, that Buckley was a fucking snob and that if something happened to his fiancée it was his own fault. Lane wedged himself between them. The Sewards tried to calm their son while he fired insults back. Finally Dottie exiled both camps from the foyer, dragged Reddick and Lane down the front steps into the gallery.

"There's work to do down here, right? And we have you booked for—what—two more hours today?" They nodded. "You," she jabbed at Reddick's chest, "don't leave this room. Understand?"

"But you have to call the police."

"It's a family matter and they are going to discuss it as a family."

"You have to find that guy she went with."

"If you can't respect their privacy I'm going to ask you to leave right now. Do you understand? Mr. and Mrs. Seward will do what they think is best. Lane? We will speak with you privately."

The manager followed her up the stairs.

Dean joined him in the gallery. Reddick offered a terse account of the confrontation; afterward they worked in uncomfortable silence. Buckley's hostile disbelief had left him sore and humiliated. Just before four they began to pack their tools. The rest of the crew came down and they loaded supplies and empty crates onto the truck, returning each room to order. No one talked to Reddick beyond sorting out the logistics of the work. When they were nearly done Lane appeared and pulled him aside.

"Have you calmed down?" he asked. Reddick nodded and he continued. "The Sewards have asked me to insist that you respect their wishes. They will consider what you have said, and if they need anything else they will contact you. You are not to reach out to them or to the police, is that understood?"

"I'm telling the truth, Lane. This isn't right."

"This is how you keep your job, Reddick. It would be easier all around if I just fired you. Do you understand? I fought for you. This is the best deal I could get. Tell me that you will do as they say. Leave them alone. Don't go to the police. Okay?"

"Fine."

"Fine, what?"

"Fine, I won't bother them. I won't go to the cops."

"One more thing. Buckley doesn't want you back in the house, so I'm taking you off this job. You can work in the warehouse tomorrow."

"Is there enough to do?" Two full-timers ran the warehouse, older guys who generally didn't like having the freelancers around.

"You'll find something. I have to meet with another client in the city tonight, so I'm not going back. Just close up and punch out after you unload. Let everyone else know."

Reddick walked back to the truck, slipping between crawling traffic on 77th. The streets and sidewalks were shoveled clean, the brutal winter tamed into picturesque lines of white on gray branches and stone facades.

"Well?" Dean asked.

"I'm not fired." Everyone smiled, and some tension drained away. A couple of the guys offered support.

"You really saw her?" Allen asked, crouched in the truck bed.

"I wouldn't have said it otherwise."

He shook his head incredulously. "I thought maybe I just spooked you this morning."

"Maybe you did, but that's not what this is about. I know what I saw." Reddick heard the rough edge in his own voice, the sandy indignation of his questioned credibility. "I am off this job, though. Warehouse tomorrow."

"Yeesh. That's gonna be dull."

"I know. Hey, can I ask a favor? Lane isn't going back to the warehouse tonight, and I could really use a drink. Could one of you clock me out? I want to head downtown and grab a beer."

It was a common request when one of the crew had happy hour plans in the city, and they agreed.

"Want me to come with?" Dean asked.

Reddick shook his head. "I'm good, man. I'll see you at the apartment tonight?"

"Probably. I need to grab a shower."

They finished packing. Once everything was secure Reddick stepped into the street to wave the truck into the gnarled traffic, tapping goodbye on the door as it pulled away.

He returned to the sidewalk and stared at the house, squeezed in a row of limestone elegance. It barely stood out—its grandeur reduced to texture, to the ambiance of fathomless wealth, an image offered to postcards and the wonder of tourists. But it was a home; there were people inside, people whose names and faces he knew and who he could help if they would let him. He had no intention of going downtown. A person was missing. He had to make them listen.

"Are you going to try again?"

The man who spoke was three or four inches taller than Reddick, his large frame draped in a black wool coat that sloped gently over his round belly. He extended a gloved hand. "Thomas," he said.

"Reddick." He shook it, tried to remember if he had seen Thomas inside. "Do you work for them?"

"The Sewards? No, actually—I work for another family, who live nearby. The Lelands." He paused, as if waiting for Reddick to react to the name. When he didn't, Thomas continued. "I have friends on the Sewards' staff. Dottie was apparently seething after the incident you caused, and one of my friends invited me out for coffee, hoping to lay low until she had a chance to cool off. He told me what happened."

"And Dottie was worried about *us* spreading rumors."

"Yes, well—the Sewards, the Lelands, their world is quite hermetic. Incestuous, even, if you're feeling uncharitable. Once you're inside it you quickly find that there's no drama quite like the one happening around you. You end up living their life as much as your own, and you develop favorites." The big man shifted, suddenly uncomfortable. "It's difficult to explain to people on the outside."

"Favorites? Like who, Buckley?"

Thomas nodded. "I know that family well. Buckley isn't a terrible guy. There are things about him…he can't really be himself most of the time."

"He's too proud to let me help him."

"That's not it. It must seem that way but—it isn't that. I'm certain of it. I was told that he was very shaken up. There was something else bothering him."

"Something other than his missing fiancée?"

"Did he seem scared? Or worried?"

"He was scared—of course." Reddick thought of the girl in Allen's story, her gray body sprawled in the loamy shallows. In his mind she had Hannah's face. "But that's exactly why he should listen to me."

"I agree. I'm just saying don't judge him too harshly. You don't know everything."

"Is that why you're here? To plead Buckley's case?"

"Yes and no, actually. The Lelands' house is around the corner, on Fifth—I went back there after our coffee and told Mrs. Leland what I had learned. She was very interested. So much so that she asked me to get you."

"What?"

"I was worried that I'd missed you. She wants to hear your side."

"I'm not sure I should tell this story to anyone else."

"You said you wanted to help. This is how you do it."

The Lelands' house had a guard in the foyer, an older man in a crisp suit, seated at a Victorian desk with an array of laptops. He nodded at Thomas as the pair shed boots and coats. They went inside, to a sitting room, where Thomas instructed another staff member to let Mrs. Leland know that they had arrived. Reddick eyed the dark room. There was a large floral carpet over the hardwoods, and carefully carved furniture, cherry and mahogany, the upholstery on the chairs expanding on themes the carpet introduced—flowers, vines, sinewy arabesques. The contrast with the Sewards' vivid modernity seemed intentional—an argument over the right way to live. After a few minutes Reddick was led upstairs, to a parlor making the same argument.

Mrs. Leland waited for him in an olive wingback. She was a pair of decades older than Mrs. Seward, thick white hair pulled tightly back from her lined, formidable face. She smiled with political precision and beckoned him to sit. He did, and Thomas left. Two members of her staff, young girls, loitered nearby.

"Did Thomas offer you a drink?"

Reddick replied that he was fine but she insisted that he have something. He agreed to coffee and one of the girls scampered away.

"Is that a Sargent?" he gestured at a small painting behind her. It was a portrait of a young girl, smiling impishly, a pale blue ribbon running through her ash-blond hair. Mrs. Leland answered without turning.

"It's a William Merritt Chase. That's my grandmother when she was a child."

"It's lovely."

"We have a Sargent in the rear parlor," she said. "I could have Thomas show it to you when we are finished."

"Thanks. I'd like that very much." The girl returned with his coffee, in a Wedgwood cup and saucer. He thanked her. He thought of his earlier conversation with Mrs. Seward, after she caught him admiring the Schnabel. "We're all artists. Art handlers, I mean. For the most part we're all usually artists."

"I suppose that makes a sort of sense." Mrs. Leland paused for a long moment, peering at him intently. This was easier than he expected, the encounter had a grooved familiarity that settled him. When he told his story to the Sewards he had been an intruder, had forced himself into their private crisis. With Mrs. Leland the relations had snapped back to their accustomed place. She wanted something from him, a service—she wanted him to tell her his story. He knew she would offer something in exchange—assistance, he hoped, in convincing the Sewards to listen. This encounter had the security, the transparency, of a transaction. He might resent his subordinate role but he understood it, a clarity that soothed him.

Finally, "So let's hear it, then."

He told her both halves of the story—first the surreal alleyway encounter and then the Sewards' reaction to it. She listened without interruption. He gave her the same version of Hannah's actions that he had offered to the Sewards, for the same reasons—bleached of sexual interest to keep himself clean.

"What do you make of it?" she asked when he finished.

"I think whoever opened that door for her knows where she is. I think the police should be in my apartment building right now questioning the people who threw that party, compiling a list of everyone who saw her that night. I think they need to be in her apartment, looking for clues. I think if they don't act quickly they're going to squander whatever chance they have of finding her, and all because Buckley is too ashamed to admit that his fiancée was out partying in a black neighborhood."

"Was it a black man who opened the door for her?"

"No. I saw his arm. He was white."

"But the neighborhood?"

"It's…it's mixed, now. It has changed a lot since I moved there."

"Gentrified, you mean?"

"It was better before."

"Better for whom, I wonder?" She didn't expect an answer. He waited for her to continue. "Do you blame the Sewards?"

He hadn't thought that far yet, hadn't gotten past his frustration that they wouldn't listen. But on the surface the answer seemed obvious. There was guilt to go around—a share for everyone at that party who watched her leave, for his own inaction, for Buckley's intransigence.

"I think if she—if the worst happens, they will be partly to blame. Morally if not legally."

"The morality of it matters to you."

"I don't see how it couldn't."

"A righteous crusader."

He suspected mockery, but saw none in her face. Only a detached, probing curiosity. "I don't think so. I just— Is it so much of a stretch to believe in right and wrong?"

She smiled indulgently. "Not to me."

"Can I ask why I'm here?"

"You may. Perhaps I'm a moralist like you. Perhaps I believe in right and wrong, and when Thomas relayed the details of this unfortunate situation I wanted to help."

He answered cautiously. "So you'll call the police?"

"They won't get very far without the cooperation of the Sewards. If you truly wish to act on your principles you will have to do so directly."

"Our principles, you mean."

She kept her face even. "I have met Hannah, on more than one occasion. I know the Sewards quite well. I have seen their temper firsthand. I have seen them close ranks. They are never so vicious as when they are accosted by the truth."

It seemed too vague, too abstract to be any help. "What kind of truth?"

"The versions of it they cannot control."

"So where does that leave me?"

"Here." She spread her hands gracefully. "With me. Where we will try to discover whatever truth it is that has provoked them."

"I just want to help Hannah."

"And I wish to help you. Does that arrangement appeal to you?" He nodded, unsure of what precisely he had just agreed to. "Very good," she said. "Thomas will handle the details. I wish you the best of luck."

She instructed one of the girls to take his cup, the other to retrieve Thomas and have him show Reddick the painting. He returned quickly, and led the art handler toward the back of the house, into another parlor. The windows revealed a spacious rear courtyard, snow cordoned into smooth pools, the edges crisp around a stone walkway and tiered fountain.

"Here is the Sargent."

Reddick moved away from the window and looked at the painting. It was a small portrait of a cherubic boy, a rose shine brightening his pale round cheeks. He seemed to be moving. Reddick moved closer and the image fell apart, reassembled into a map of brushstrokes and slippery pigment, a record of gestures—three to make lips, three more a nose, a dash for eyes, a smear for hair. That the illusion of selfhood could be conjured with so little effort.

"It's fantastic," Reddick said.

"Yes." Thomas smiled. "So was Mrs. Leland quite clear?"

"Not exactly."

"She would like you to look into Hannah's disappearance."

This wasn't the help that he expected—it wasn't help at all. "I'll be fired if I hound the Sewards any more."

"There are other lines of inquiry to pursue. Do what you

said the police should do. Go to her apartment. Ask questions. You live in the building where she was last seen."

"Why doesn't she hire a private investigator?"

"Because she doesn't want a private investigator. We will cover your expenses." Indoors, out of his coat, there was something delicate about Thomas, in his precisely trimmed beard and pale eyes. He had a blue-collar body but a white-collar face. His suit fit him beautifully.

"Expenses? What does that mean?"

"Here is five hundred dollars cash. Save your receipts and if you need more I will transfer it to you." He gave Reddick the money with a small business card on top, printed with his name and a phone number. "Text me at this number and I will send you Hannah's information. Her address, her photo."

"Why do I need that?"

"To show people when you ask about her."

"She wants me to go door-to-door?"

"She wants you to do what you think is right. Keep me updated."

"She wants updates."

"What she wants is simple." He moved closer, until Reddick could smell the saltwater cologne on his notched lapel. He rested a massive hand on the art handler's shoulder. "Find the girl."

FOUR

4 to the C, fighting the rush hour crowd for air. He dug his free hand into the pocket of his jeans to fondle the five one-hundred-dollar bills folded inside. Not because he cared about the money, but because it verified his memory, offered proof that he hadn't imagined the surreal day.

He was headed home to change clothes and then to the Y, to play ball. Mrs. Leland's offer demanded a response from his body. Thomas had insisted he take the cash even though he hadn't committed to anything yet. He walked north out of the Nostrand stop and cut east on Halsey, one of the few blocks in Bed-Stuy where the wide sidewalks had been entirely cleared and salted, past rows of brownstones, their fat banisters and iron fences trimmed white with snow. Less magisterial than the Upper East Side but just as lovely. A few houses clung to their holiday lights, their courtyards sheltering a stray Santa or snowman that had survived the weeks since the new year. Nearly every home posted a sign declaring opposition to Restoration Heights. He could see the fence ahead, the resting claws of earthmovers parked for the winter, the skeletal towers sheathed in plastic, scaffolding wrapped like wire around their lower levels.

It was easy to imagine how it began—on a map of Brooklyn, in some sprawling office, you saw the future. Start with the East River, where the swelling pressure of downtown Manhattan sent a wave to the opposite shore, a rising tide of young, moneyed whites flowing inward along the L and the J, dousing and displacing black and brown communities, encircling the entrenched islands of housing projects or crime or just people who loved too much to sell. It drowned Williamsburg and Bushwick years ago, pushed east and south toward the only logical end point, the convergence of the two train lines: Broadway Junction. Once the borders were marked all that remained was to fill the spaces, paint over the existing lives and businesses with gluten-free bakeries and bicycle lanes, clusters of bars and fair trade coffeehouses. Shops that sell cheese at forty-nine dollars a pound. Delineate and fill.

But there is another train at that convergence. Why limit this playground to the L and the J when the A forms the natural southern boundary. It was already happening, at the edge of Clinton Hill, in Bed-Stuy and Crown Heights. Refugees from overcrowded Bushwick have established base camps, four or five to an apartment, marveling at the space and the architectural detail, funded or only recently defunded by their parents, with professional jobs and professional salaries but with bohemian values and aspirations. Kids whose desires can make smart men rich. The model was already in place. Do to the A what was done to the L. Zoom out from the map, trace this new perimeter—from the water, along the L to East New York, but now touch the A, follow it back west, toward the river. Do you see what that does, the shape that it makes? How it captures and unifies—the bravado of it—how it dares to claim the heart of the borough? It is the masterstroke of a land war, a double envelopment. It allows only one response: abject surrender.

Restoration Heights is your conceptual lynchpin. Two towers on the main property, ringed by commercial space, a small park with an open field, honey locusts and sycamores, 15 percent more units allocated for affordable housing than the ordinance requires—a campus stretching from Tompkins to Throop. Two smaller satellite buildings that follow the same logic, camouflaged by skilled design. Spread them out as a gesture of appeasement, a way to knit the project into the fabric of the neighborhood, to leave landmarks intact in the shadow of the new construction. An olive branch, like magnanimity isn't one more mark of power.

The white kids will complain—another bullshit corporate condominium, destroying the neighborhood—but those same white kids will move in. *I never thought I'd live in a place like this but, ugh, I need a dishwasher. And I hate laundromats. All my friends are here and besides, the design fits the neighborhood, not like those other buildings, plus a doorman.* All the cachet of the neighborhood and none of the hassles. The guilty thrill of being surrounded by blackness without having to live like them. Not separate but unequal.

You still have to get it past the community—local councils, the Historic District. That's why you chose that block, the whole thing was an eyesore, except for the church, and you're keeping the church. Postwar brick townhouses and a massive, sloppy apartment building—it didn't fit the rest of the neighborhood, it represented precisely the sort of additions that the Historic District was created to guard against, so knock it down, give them something that fits, a design that respects the surrounding architecture. Sell it as a job creator. Give it a name that connects it to a community landmark, that summons a false history. Bribe the right people. Steamroll whomever you cannot cajole.

Expect protests. Expect a grassroots coalition to mobilize. Expect hand-wringing, black opposition and white guilt. Expect them to have some successes. Permits delayed, city council votes against you—at least you have the mayor. Expect a hard fight until ground is broken on the first site and even after, when the battle is won but the opposition continues. It's been three years since the first plot of land was bought by Corren Capital—the old buildings are leveled, concrete is poured, the frame is constructed, and still resentment erects obstacles and roadblocks. You have made no progress on the two smaller sites, where the current buildings still stand. You must trust momentum to realize the totality of your vision. It is late fall when some technicality is raised, some ordinance that your cadre of lawyers missed, and you have to stop. Wrap it all up for the winter and blame the weather. It was snowing on Thanksgiving. It promised to get worse, to be hard enough and regular enough to offer a plausible excuse, the worst winter since '96. Save face, don't allow them even this minor victory. Restoration Heights will define Bedford-Stuyvesant for decades to come.

The truth was that it looked like a good place to hide a body. Maybe that's why he came. He stared between panels of green plywood at plastic sheeting rendered almost opaque by weather, at the yawning dark spaces beneath it. Kids must hang out there. He looked for evidence, for bottles or crumpled cigarette packs. It didn't seem that difficult to get inside. Maybe the homeless used it for shelter. Stacks of building materials littered the campus, enigmatic shapes of plastic and metal waiting for spring. Vast areas of rough ground, buried white, surrounded the unfinished towers. It could definitely hide a body.

This was a morbid way to begin. If that was what this was, a beginning. Why assume a body, assume death? The Coney Island girl had anchored Hannah to a violent fate; Reddick couldn't shake the similarities. He had only intended to walk to the fence and look, a half-formed purpose to help him think. He couldn't admit that he had already made his decision. He walked north to Monroe, turned west toward the Y.

It was an open court at seven, after the last group fitness class surrendered the floor. Crowds varied, particularly in the late winter, and informal games took shape around the evening turnout, half-court or full, according to mood and ability. Derek was waiting out of bounds when he arrived, cheering the group through a final round of sprints and jump squats. Reddick didn't understand the class's appeal—an hour sweating through watered-down facsimiles of the drills he had dreaded on his high school team. He slapped his friend five and sat on the floor beside him.

Derek was a Bed-Stuy native who seemed to know everyone. He was a year younger than Reddick, a little heavier, well-muscled and compact. He ran track in college and looked like it. They were both high school threes, slashers who earned starting time getting to the rim, so they weren't natural complements. But they enjoyed playing together and found ways to make it work. Derek's game had more dimension—he could hang outside, feed Reddick the ball on in-cuts while he backed out into open jumpers.

Once the class cleared they took jump shots and layups with bouts of half-hearted defense. The weather kept everyone else at home. They were alone for almost half an hour and Reddick told Derek everything.

"Wait. Buckley Seward's neighbor wants *you* to find out what happened to his fiancée?"

"They aren't neighbors exactly." Swish. "But yeah. Strange, right?"

"We're talking about the same Buckley Seward?"

"How do you know him?"

"Because I work with money. And the Sewards have a lot of it. The bigger question is how *you* know him."

"I told you, they're clients. We manage their collection."

"And also, as of today, find their missing acquaintances."

Reddick grabbed a rebound, shrugged. "Yeah."

"You're an artist. You're not qualified for this shit."

"I'm so not."

"That lady is using you for something."

Derek's shot rolled out and Reddick let it bounce. He had been so consumed with what he should do that he had barely thought about her motives. "What?"

Derek scooped the ball up and dropped a jumper from the corner, then whirled around Reddick to grab it again.

"She's using you, man. I can't tell what her play is exactly, but she has one. If she just cared about the girl she would have hired someone who could do the job."

"I can't do the job?"

"You can do some things. You can draw. You can paint."

"I can play."

"Your three is garbage. But you can play a little bit. You just can't find some missing white girl."

While they talked, two guys came into the gym and began to strip out of their sweats. Reddick didn't recognize either of them. Once the newcomers joined the shootaround the conversation dropped off, their intention narrowing as they moved toward an inevitable two-on-two. One was light-skinned and stocky, with a shy face and a stain of dark hair above his lip. Maybe twenty, but two inches taller than anyone else on the court, his height carried with loose grace. He began the game on Derek. They were used to this—on the rare occasions when their opponents weren't Y regulars they always lined up their best athlete on Derek, lured by his track physique and the loaded preconceptions of his dark skin. The other one was smaller, a few years older, with a pocked complexion, a sprout of tight braids and a sly smile. He started talking immediately, the kind of guy whose mouth was half his game, who counted on flustering you and abusing the holes your frustration opened. He was genuinely funny.

"You look like if Tom Hardy got AIDS," he said to Reddick when they lined up. "I'm playing against sick, skinny Tom Hardy."

He ran with the theme as the game progressed. "Damn, Skinny Tom Hardy got a little quick."

"What's your shirt say, Skinny Tom Hardy? What the hell is a modest mouse?"

"You feeling it, Skinny Tom. Where's your Bane mask at?"

"Skinny Tom having the game of his life tonight, though. You going to tell your grandkids about this night."

"This dude playing ball in a indie rock T-shirt."

There is a type of athleticism that you cannot see in a person until he moves. Acceleration, power, quickness—the cluster of qualities that make someone explosive are not linked to weight or strength or the amount of visible muscle he carries. Three-hundred-pound linemen who can leap over teammates, five-foot gymnasts launching double backflips—it's the same adaptation, a ratio of fiber types within the muscle that is locked in when you escape the womb. Hard work can make slight shifts in either direction, expand the total amount and improve performance, but the basic proportions remain more or less intact. It is a genetic adaptation, and like any genetic adaptation it may be overrepresented in some populations and underrepresented in others. There are tendencies, deeper and more specific than race. A Jamaican sprinter is more like a Bulgarian weight lifter than she is a Kenyan marathoner, in the composition and force of her body, in the skein of fibers and neurons that map her athletic potential. But these are specific truths, and once they are uncoupled from their narrow province they foster an ugly, lazy shorthand. They become fodder for bigotry and stigma. They set false expectations. And when an outlier comes along the level of surprise is more or less a function of the depth to which these expectations have been absorbed.

Which is to say that Reddick isn't always sure how people will react when he dunks.

The guy with the braids went quiet. Pouty. Never mind that his teammate had already buried one after Reddick and Derek got tangled on a pick, never mind that it had come off the rebound, on a rushed shot by Derek that glanced favorably off the glass—he had been dunked on by the white guy. He was pissed. He had built his game on trolling but didn't take well to the other side.

"You let that white boy dunk on you?" It was the first complete sentence they had heard from the younger player.

Braids was petulant. "That shit wasn't on me."

"You were standing right there."

"Man, I didn't even go up."

"Because you saw what was about to happen," Derek taunted.

Reddick was good for one or two explosive plays like that a game, not only dunks, but sharp cuts, leaps and crossovers—feats of athleticism rather than skill. At nine or ten years old, the only white kid on his street in North Gastonia, it was the way he had learned to play. He and his friends just wanted to be Jordan. They would spread their legs in the air, unfurl their tongues and palm matted tennis balls or the undersized toys of infant siblings, pretending the edge of the sidewalk was the free throw line, soaring to glory. Be like Mike. No one told him he was the wrong color, that he was supposed to facilitate or work on his defense. Nobody worked on their defense. It was hero ball or die trying.

On his block he was sometimes singled out, outbursts that were recriminations for a legacy they were all too young to verbalize, but never on the court. There he could disappear. The marks of his difference, his blond hair and pink skin, were rendered irrelevant by shared ambition. There was only one standard by which a player was judged: Could he ball? Once the answer was yes everything else fell away.

He finished first in scoring his second year of varsity, a feat driven by a first step so quick it bordered on arrogance. He noticed the way it chafed a few of his black teammates, a resentment that wasn't quite envy, but something darker, structural. He squirmed beneath what he saw as the unfairness of it—as if he were the vanguard for yet another campaign to stymie black progress. As though he were trying to take something from them. He didn't want to take. He wanted to belong. It never occurred to him that this distinction might not matter.

He had offers to play Division II but went to art school instead.

Being white made him a minority at the Y, like he was in high school, but the disbelief his occasional highlight play fostered was rarely expressed in racial terms—not by the regular, rotating crew of guys that teamed up on evenings and weekends. Most of them had played high school ball, too, were used to being among athletes from different backgrounds. Basketball was pure sport again, released from the web of ambition and status. Until nights like tonight, when new players came in and he and Derek exploited their expectations, and he waited for that hint of resentment, that sense that he was overstepping his bounds—waited for it and dreaded it and worried that he was imagining it, that it was all in his own mind, his own history—and he was back in high school all over again, losing his only faith.

But who doesn't love making plays. Particularly on a guy who has built his game on his mouth. Reddick hung sixteen of the twenty-one points they needed to win the game himself—Derek barely broke a sweat, and by the time Braids was ready to admit defeat and switch he was far too tired to cover a former collegiate track athlete, never mind their ten-year age difference. Derek dropped two uncontested jumpers and a layup and they headed off court.

"Good game," Reddick said, extending his closed fist. The taller kid bumped it. Braids stared at it long enough to make everyone uncomfortable before finally extending his own. They tapped knuckles gently. The defeated pair left first, surrendering the empty court like conquered ground.

"He got a little salty," Reddick said.

"Dunked on by the white guy."

"You know my granddaddy—"

"Nobody believes your blond ass had a black grandfather." They started for the stairs.

"I think he was half."

"Yeah. Half white, and half made-up."

Laughing. "I'm going to find you a photo."

"That's what you keep saying. But I still haven't seen one."

"You want taqueria?"

"Nah. I promised my mom Netflix and takeout tonight."

They clasped hands and bumped shoulders and Reddick started alone toward the basement locker room.

"Hey," Derek called when Reddick was at the middle landing. "What are you going to do about that girl?"

He exhaled and rubbed the sweat from his hairline. "I think I should try and find her."

He repeated that assertion to Dean and Beth Han. The three of them were in Reddick and Dean's living room, drinking beer. Reddick started at the beginning, for Beth's sake, before moving on to Mrs. Leland's enigmatic offer.

"What could that woman possibly expect you to do?" Beth Han made jewelry, and was almost always referred to by her full name to differentiate her from her studio mate, also a jewelry maker and also named Beth, who had a cumbersome Polish surname no one wanted to bother with. Their studio was next door to Dean's. Around the building they were usually addressed in plural, the Beths, and when one had to be singled out it was Beth Han who was dignified with an individual humanity, the second Beth reduced to reflection or description. The Other Beth. Tall Beth or White Beth. Blonde Beth until Beth Han had her hair stripped to the color of bone, complicating even that distinction. Beth Han lived in her studio, without a shower, which meant that she couch-surfed a few nights a week to maintain an acceptable level of hygiene. For the past several weeks all of this surfing had taken place here, on Dean's schedule. There was a burgeoning depth between them that Reddick didn't probe.

"Like I said. She expects me to find her."

"That's not the real question, though," Dean said. "What I want to know is why girls throw themselves at you when they've been drinking."

"Wait, has this happened before?"

"It happened *twice* at U-Arts."

"Totally different," Reddick protested. "I already knew both of those girls."

"You had a class with one of them. The other was up from Baltimore. We were at a house party and she follows him into the bathroom, I kid you not."

"But I had been talking to her all night. Also she was crazy."

"Reddick!" Beth's eyes were wide and her hand was over her mouth. "What did you do?"

"What do you mean? I got the fuck out of there."

"Really? Oh my god."

"Just turned and ran."

"I can't believe you left."

"It was freshman year. The sight of breasts still came with a hint of terror."

"I had no idea we had such power."

"Promise you'll only use it for good."

"Never." They laughed and drank. Beth continued. "So that's one. What about the other?"

"Completely different. It was this girl who I used to flirt with in Figure Drawing. We were drinking in the studio one night, something was definitely going to happen eventually but she made the first move. We dated for weeks after that. Only Dean has ever connected it to the other incident."

"Because you didn't have to do anything." Dean straightened his glasses, tried to look persecuted. "I, on the other hand, feel like I'm always doing the heavy lifting."

Beth cut her eyes at Dean, so subtle that Reddick almost missed it. "Seriously, though," she said. "You're not going to do this thing, are you? It's not your problem."

"I don't know. Maybe?"

"Where would you start?" Dean asked.

He thought about Restoration Heights, about whether her

body could be there, blue and hard beneath the snow. It was too morbid to say out loud but he couldn't shake the image.

"Buckley seemed really suspicious," he said.

"That's usually who it is, right?" Dean said. "When someone is killed it's usually the spouse or partner."

"The husband," Beth said. "The man."

"Women kill their spouses, too."

"Men are usually the perpetrators of violence, is all I'm saying."

"That's good, because I only have male suspects. I'm playing the odds."

"You have suspects, then?" Dean asked.

"Just the one."

"Oh, right. Buckley. The Sewards are a big-time family. There must be a ton of stuff online about him."

"I don't know if we should encourage him," Beth said.

Dean took out his phone. "Let's look him up." He searched for a minute. "He's a Wharton grad. Looks like he was in Philly around the same time that we were, getting his MBA. Here he is at the ICA. I guess he helped put this painting show together?" He turned the phone over so that Reddick could see the screen. Buckley stood on the balcony, overlooking University City, with a glass of wine in his hand. The photo was contrived but he looked sharp and confident, a privileged young man coming into power. Reddick swiped through more of the photos, gallery shots of the work.

"I remember this show," he said. "It was the spring before our freshman year. I had come up for a second look at U-Arts."

"We just missed him, then."

"Didn't Sarah go to Penn?" Beth asked.

"Yeah," Reddick said. "She did." Sarah was a painter who worked in the same building as Dean and Beth. She was a little older than Reddick; they had gone out a few times but it had never moved past drinks. "She would have been there at the same time he was. Maybe she knew him."

"Now you have a witness to question."

"This is not a good idea." Beth laughed as she said it.

"Okay, what else?"

"I have her address." Thomas had forwarded that information, along with her photo, after Reddick had returned from the Y. "I might go check it out."

"Looking for what?" Dean asked. "Signs of a struggle?"

"Remember how shaken Buckley seemed when he got back from there yesterday? Maybe he saw something."

"I don't know. He said there wasn't a break-in or anything like that."

"Wouldn't he say that, though? I mean—if he's a suspect."

"How will you even get in?" Beth asked. "To her apartment, I mean?"

"I don't know." Reddick thumbed the mouth of his beer. "I guess I'll just show up and see what I can improvise."

"You make such detailed plans," Dean said. "That's always been something I admire about you."

"Ha ha. I'll figure something out."

"Alright, so we've got a suspect, a character witness and a scene."

"There's also the people who threw the party," Reddick said. "They may have seen something."

"How will you find them?"

"I guess knock on some doors."

Dean winced. "Don't do that. I live in this building, too."

"I have to do *something*. I could start tomorrow, after work."

"It is kind of exciting," Beth said. "A sort of game."

Reddick's reply was sharper than he intended. "It's not a game for Hannah."

The unexpected gravity of that realization killed their mood. They drank quietly. Dean and Beth skimmed their phones while Reddick stared blankly at his hands. Finally Dean spoke.

"Reddick, you aren't going to do this for real?"

"I don't know." He finished his beer. "Yes."

FIVE

Another early morning, another subway ride. Harold waiting across the turnstile.

They traded daps. "What's up, young brother?"

"Hey, remember that story I told you yesterday? About the girl? Well, it got a whole lot weirder." Reddick told him what happened at the Sewards' house, the coincidence of Hannah's identity and the family's unexpected response.

"See, that's how they treat people. That's what they're like." Harold said. "If you're not one of them, what you say doesn't matter."

"I know how they see me, that I'm just trash. But I didn't think they would discount me completely."

"You never thought that. I would have thought it. I would have gone in knowing they weren't gonna believe anything I said. I've learned to expect that from people like them."

"Well, you would have been right. Because Buckley wasn't hearing any of it."

"So what about the girl? She just gone?"

"Looks that way."

"And you're kind of hung up on her now."

"I was the last person to see her."

"You feel responsible for it in a way."

"Someone has to be. Look I was— This is stupid, but I can't stop thinking about it— You worked on Restoration Heights, right?"

He nodded somberly. "Yeah, I did. Before it got delayed. Not saying those protestors didn't have a point, but that's people's jobs right there."

"Yeah. I'm sorry about that. I was just— Do they ever find bodies in construction sites?"

"Oh yeah. Not really all the time but it definitely happens, I know that. Once a project has been delayed for a little while the city sends inspectors to the site to check things out, you know, make sure nothing is out of hand, and they find some things."

"Bodies?"

"Bodies. Sometimes bodies. Sometimes other things that shouldn't be there. Drugs. Campsites for people that got nowhere else to go. You think this girl is there?"

"I don't know what made me think of it."

"In this weather if she's there she isn't camping. I hate to say it."

"I know."

"Listen, though. You know I grew up around there—I know some people. I mean people that are in touch. If anything shady happened, they know about it."

"I'm thinking this is something domestic."

"It doesn't matter. I'm telling you, if it happened, I got some people that can find out." He seemed revved by his own confidence, as though the stronger he asserted his claims the more he believed them. "After work I'm usually at this spot near Clinton Hill called Ti-Ti's, and I can find out whatever you need right there. If you're really hung up on this just let me know."

Reddick considered it. How would any friend of Harold's know something about this—about Buckley Seward? There were layers of New York between them, fortified strata of class and race designed explicitly to maintain an impassable distance.

"I think I'm good."

"I can see it in your face, Reddick. You can't let go. Let me give you my number. If you change your mind, you text me." He took Reddick's phone to add himself as a contact.

"Ti-Ti's, huh? Maybe I could come down there with you."

"Anytime you want. You might stick out a little bit, though. No offense."

"No worries, man. I'm not sensitive about that kind of stuff. You know my grandfather was black."

Harold glanced up from the phone, his face unreadable and solemn. After a moment he smiled. "Come on, Red. I like you, brother. You don't have to say that."

"It's true."

"It might be. But it don't mean anything. You're as white as every other white dude in Long Island City this morning. Don't make it into a thing."

At the warehouse the annoyed full-timers had no use for him. He wandered the halls, lurked among the vaults, until he found an empty crate to perch on and put his phone to work.

First the Sewards. Twenty-sixth on the *Forbes* list of wealthiest families, their fortune accumulated in the old American industries—steel and oil—enabling the extensive philanthropy that had tagged their name on music halls and special exhibition spaces, on wings and renovations, across the northeast. Old money that had aged well, youthful vigor maintained by a commitment to the cultural avant-garde. Buckley had two dead uncles—cancer and an airplane—and several cousins, but no siblings. He was the sole heir for the New York line.

The Lelands were twenty-third on the same list. The article announcing this ranking was buried on the second page of the search results—the first was all hits for Mrs. Leland's son, a politician. Reddick followed politics haphazardly, on the whims of scandals or elections, and hadn't heard of State Senator Anthony Leland, but the stories painted him as a rising star, a square-jawed Christopher Reeve look-alike going gray with aesthetic precision. His pedigree didn't match his face. By the standards of most families on the list he was nouveau riche—the family was poor until Anthony's grandfather made his fortune. This seemed to complicate Mrs. Leland's claim that William Merritt Chase had painted her ancestor so he sorted for images, found the painting and clicked on it. *Portrait of a Serving Girl.* The subject had worked in the kitchen of the artist's sister—she was the daughter of Irish immigrants who Americanized their surname and considered themselves lucky to land a job waiting on the Anglican upper class. Soon even that tenuous connection was lost, and the painting was just a family legend, a story told over Prohibition whiskey in Hell's Kitchen, until Mrs. Leland's father came back from the war with a lesson about pain—that its ubiquity was an untapped market. He built an opioid empire, and when the painting came up at auction his children bought it, reclaiming their history and adopting a stature their ancestors were denied. They built not only a collection around it but also a way of life.

The question was who resented whom. Did Mrs. Leland believe the Sewards had been unfairly gifted with the life her father worked for—were they too casual with a prize she treasured? Or were the Sewards irritated at being passed on the leaderboard of the point-one percent by a family of relative nobodies? How much did a thing like that mean to people like them?

Perhaps nothing. And any tension between the two families was a side issue to finding Hannah. What mattered was that Mrs. Leland wanted to help—he could put aside her motives.

By noon the full-timers had succeeded in convincing Lane that there wasn't enough work to keep him around and the manager called to send him home.

"You're not suspended, exactly," Lane said. "This isn't meant to be punitive. But we aren't going to need you until next week, when the Seward job is finished."

He was happy to have the time—and Mrs. Leland's cash would make up for the lost hours. He went back to his apartment, made a turkey sandwich and tried to figure out where to start. Her address beckoned—but the thought of going there daunted him. Some of last night's confidence had evaporated with his buzz. He needed to build back up to it. Start with something easier.

What had Thomas said? *Ask questions. You live in the building.*

He carried his plate to the sink, took out his phone and pulled up the photo. Hannah was standing next to Buckley, caught midlaugh. She was hard to place as the girl in the alley. Her hair looked thicker, her cheeks rounder. She seemed unfazed by her rare fortune. What she stood to gain from her marriage was unimaginable. Perhaps she had come in with her own wealth—or perhaps she had gone looking for someone else's and was braced for the shock of its acquisition. But if it was an accident, what pressures did that create? Did she feel liberated or trapped? He remembered their conversation, her ambiguity—was she struggling to stay composed? Would that be enough to make her run?

Buckley, beside her, had the look of a man attached to a luminous mystery. What did a man in his position want from a woman—what could she offer? Loyalty? Discretion? At the very least not to throw herself at a stranger in an alley. Perhaps Sunday night wasn't the first time—perhaps he had started digging and uncovered desires he couldn't tolerate. Could he have been so entitled that he hurt her?

There was no reason to suspect him over anyone else, not yet. She had been vulnerable, an easy victim. It could be anyone in the building.

Reddick grabbed a small Moleskine notebook and a pencil from his studio. He walked to the back of the building, called the elevator and rode it to the top. The sixth floor hallway was identical to his own, faded tile and rust-colored doors, windowsills and corners dusted gray from neglect. There was something institutional in the hollow silence, in the intrusion of his clacking footsteps. He went to the first door, held his breath and knocked.

Nothing happened. He waited and knocked again. Finally he scribbled a note, asking if the tenants had thrown or attended a party in this building on Sunday night, explaining that he wasn't an upset neighbor complaining about the noise but just trying to find someone, and could they email if they knew anything. He walked to the next apartment. This time a man answered. Reddick asked about the party—the man blinked sleepily and said he didn't remember hearing one. He thanked him and moved on. It was becoming easier, he had begun to adapt to his new role. The last two apartments on that floor were empty and he rewrote his note.

He took the stairs down one floor and repeated the process. He got odd looks and unhelpful answers from the three tenants who answered, and left a note on the final door. He hadn't thought the party was this high up so he wasn't discouraged yet—he hoped for better luck on the fourth but it was the same, mostly empty apartments. It was the wrong time of day for this, he should have waited until evening. A woman in 4C remembered the noise and said she was pretty sure it was below her somewhere, possibly directly below her. No one answered at 3C or at the other apartments on that floor. He scribbled out four more notes. On the second and first the tenants he spoke with remembered the party but hadn't paid particular attention, the footsteps and the laughter dissolving into the ambient sounds of a weekend night.

"Sundays were quiet in this building once," a man complained.

Reddick went back to his own apartment. He hadn't even gotten to show Hannah's photo—he had struck out completely, with no plans for the evening other than to follow the leads this search generated. He bundled into his winter coat and boots, grabbed his sneakers and left for the Y.

It was around five, too early for a pickup game, the court quiet in the dead space between the adjacent high school's daytime programs and the evening rec classes. He took shots alone, let his mind go. Between the bounding echoes of his dribble he could hear the breath of a man jogging the indoor track above him. After twenty, twenty-five minutes people began to drift in, gathering for the next class. He tuned them out. When the teacher arrived he picked up his coat and boots and went downstairs. Derek was in the lobby.

"Leaving already?" his friend asked.

"There's a class upstairs. I was just trying to kill some time."

"Come lift with me."

Reddick wrinkled his nose.

"You're such a coward," Derek said.

"Weights are heavy."

"Yeah. That's the whole point."

"It feels like work."

"Work is good for you. Speaking of—you didn't work today?"

"I left early." He told him about being sent home, and about the notes he left throughout his apartment building.

"Your neighbors are going to think you're crazy."

"If I can help. A little, even."

"You need to get the police involved."

"I already told you. It will get me fired."

"Maybe if you kept it unofficial. You know the cop that works out here?" Reddick shook his head. "I'll introduce you. You can ask him."

"Is he here now?"

"He should be. He lifts with Sensei. They're here every night, basically."

Sensei was in his early sixties, about Reddick's height but fifty or sixty pounds heavier, lean and thick as a bull. He had acquired his name from the earnestness of his followers, five or six muscular twentysomethings who followed his lifting regimen with cult-like devotion. Reddick knew him only by reputation until they met at an anti–Restoration Heights rally in the fall. Reddick had gone with Dean, who didn't share his interest in the neighborhood, who just wanted a cheap place to live while he made art. The crowd was 80 percent black. Dean's discomfort had been palpable. Sensei had been standing outside the College of New Rochelle that day, in a pressed button-down and white kufi; they recognized each other's faces from the Y, and introduced themselves. Sensei had helped organize the event.

Dean had spoken favorably of the rally afterward—he always worked to be on the right side of history—but it didn't mean anything to him, it was just one more position to calibrate. He had no emotional stake in the outcome.

Reddick and Sensei spoke occasionally afterward, in the hallway or the lobby of the Y. Their conversations were cordial but brief. Reddick had forgotten Sensei's real name, and he doubted that anyone called him Sensei to his face.

"Come on," Derek said.

They went to the weight room.

Several guys were gathered around the squat rack—Sensei, two friends, and an indeterminate number of acolytes, some of whom were merely watching. Sensei had just stood up with what seemed to Reddick like an impossible amount of weight on his back. His legs shook. Two of the guys helped guide the weight back into the rack. Once it was secure, Derek glided into the group; Reddick waited nearby.

He admired Derek's social dexterity. It was half innate and half learned, his intelligence and easy charm sharpened by a lifetime crossing barriers of race and class. His mother had bought a house in Bed-Stuy shortly after she arrived from St. Thomas. Derek was two. He and his mother were left alone after his father passed; she made do with a cheap mortgage and a tedious job. For ten years they lived in the basement apartment and rented out the rest, cutting corners, haggling with negligent tenants and crooked repairmen. Then she bought the house next door, and three years after that the building on the corner—home to five apartments and the bodega where she once shopped for their dinner among the dented cans and cellophane. Her diligence and triumph were a road map for her son. After he earned his MBA he lingered in South Florida, working at an investment bank but pouring his time into side projects, real estate and other ventures, ostensibly enjoying the beach and the clubs but really, Reddick suspected, just enjoying the work. He came back a year ago with a sizable nest egg and prospects at a handful of downtown banks, all of which he was postponing until he found and closed on a Manhattan apartment. While he looked, he was staying with his mother, in a brownstone a couple of blocks from the Y.

He waved Reddick over. He was standing beside a short, middle-aged man with a round frame, huge through the chest and gut, an easy face and tightly clipped hair circling a bare, glistening crown. Like everyone else in Sensei's crew, he was black. He smiled when Reddick approached. The area around the rack was a slurry of chalk and sweat.

"So you need a cop, huh?" he said.

"Reddick, this is Clint."

Reddick told him about the alleyway encounter with Hannah, and the Sewards' response. Clint listened blankly.

"Let me get this straight. You saw a girl, one time, for two or three minutes—in the dark—and now you're convinced that she is the missing fiancée of some guy you work for, even though that guy says she isn't?"

"I saw her."

"You saw *someone*. And maybe you've gone back in your mind and inserted this other girl's face into your memory. I can't tell you how often this happens."

"It was definitely her."

"Is she actually even missing? I'm saying have they or anyone else in her family filed a missing persons claim?"

"That's one of the things I thought you could help me out with."

"You want me to find out for you?"

Reddick nodded.

"Hand me your phone."

He wiped his hands before he took it.

"So you can access police data online?" Reddick asked.

"Yeah. It's called Google." He showed him the web results and clicked on the first hit, the city website. "You can sort by borough."

"Holy shit," Reddick said.

"It's the twenty-first century. There are resources for this shit. You don't have to bug me." His tone was jovial, teasing.

Reddick took his phone back. "Her name isn't on here."

"There you go." That seemed to answer the question for him.

"But she's still missing. I mean—I was in their house. I heard them say that she was gone. Isn't there anything you could do about an unreported missing person?"

"How exactly could a person be missing if no one was missing her? What kind of sense does that make?"

"But that's what I'm telling you. I heard them say it."

"Look. It's been, what, a day and a half? If they haven't reported her it's because they found her. Maybe she freaked out and went home to her family. Do you know where she's from?" Reddick shook his head. "See, you should know that. They are the first people you should have called. Because I have to tell you—it isn't my thing, but I know—you're talking about a domestic case and it is almost always just that the person left. Our guys show up at the home, there's a bag packed, a bunch of empty hangers in the closet, but the poor husband is too shocked to admit that his wife left him of her own free will. Went home to the family or off with another lover or just wanted some time to think. Sometimes it's the only way to force themselves to have the conversation they need. It's private, and it's got nothing to do with you."

"Except that I saw her."

"Except that you say you saw someone who looked kind

of like her. In the dark. This is New York, man. You understand we have shit to do?"

He let his final point sink in, and clapped Reddick's shoulder.

"No hard feelings, right?"

"What if I find something? Some evidence, something that proves she is missing? Will you help me? Off the record so that the Sewards don't get me fired?"

Clint shook his head. It was clear he believed he had already made his case. "Listen to me. You are not a cop. You are not even a private investigator. You cannot do this."

"But I've already started. I just want to know if I can come to you when I find something."

"You won't find something because there is nothing to be found."

"Can I come to you?"

He sighed, finally softened by Reddick's persistence. "If you have evidence that a crime was committed, it is your responsibility to come forward with that evidence. That's not me promising anything. That's not me endorsing this. That's not me saying I will help you. That's just your legal obligation."

Reddick smiled. "I'll be back, then."

"Evidence, I said. Okay? *Evidence.*"

"Evidence" meant more than what he could learn talking to people who were at the party—Clint's insistence made that clear. He needed something tangible, something that proved she was gone, that erased doubts—his own included. An abrupt breakup didn't explain any of the questions that nagged at him—why Buckley reacted the way he did, why Hannah was dead drunk the night she went missing—but it had the force of being ordinary, the appeal of simplicity. He had to eliminate it—or succumb to it, if her apartment was emptied out, her closets bare. Either way he had to be sure, had to cross it off the list. He walked to the subway.

Rush hour was tapering off; waiting for an uptown express, he tapped the transit Wi-Fi for more research, read the results on his way up. He wanted to see if the facts backed up Clint's confident dismissal. He found an article summarizing missing persons data going back half a decade—around half a million reported cases a year, with about 90,000 individuals listed as missing at any point in time. He was surprised to see an even split by gender, an array of ages. Like most American afflictions it hit the poor hardest. Almost all of the cases were eventually resolved. Kids taken by a wayward parent or relative, adults who wandered away from their homes, addled by drugs or dementia, chasing phantoms. Hard-luck runaways dreaming of a better life, sprung from the cage of a violent partner, an abusive parent. In most cases the cause was explicable, layered into the facts of the person's history—their lives a prologue for their disappearance.

In some cases they were murdered.

He closed his phone, got out and walked northeast, to 90th between York and First. It took a numbing twenty minutes at a quick pace, stabbed by the cold, to reach Hannah's building. He eyed it from the opposite sidewalk, six floors of pale brick in the center of a residential street, not as new or well-kept as the prim high-rises on the corner. An iron fire escape, glistening with frost, snaked up its face. Reddick crossed one possibility off his list—that she had come in with her own money, that she wouldn't have been floored by the ease of Buckley's lifestyle. This neighborhood was what passed for middle class in the city, the residents floating on expenses that would drown much of the country but that someone like Buckley could manage with the cash he left in yesterday's sport coat. Reddick thought of Hannah's clothes, the way she talked—could the girl he met have abandoned the comforts that a marriage to Buckley promised? Perhaps she had never loved him, perhaps it was only ever about his money, and her disappearance was a capitulation to the pressures of this deception. Perhaps she was fleeing the consequences of her own greed. Perhaps she had emptied her apartment, was on the road somewhere, relieved to be free of a lie.

Her number was 4B. All the windows on the fourth floor were dark, their treatments clustered in pairs—it looked like two apartments per level, splitting the fire escape between them. He guessed she was to his left—from inside the building, facing out, the apartments ascending from left to right, like the alphabet—but there was no way to be sure. The shades were up in the left windows; he tried to see inside, could make out nothing deeper than a cluttered sill—a couple of houseplants, a bowl. There were lights on in the apartment below, vague movements flitting behind soft curtains. He wondered if she knew anyone in her building.

The narrow lobby was brightly lit, the shape of its interior clear through the glass door. Reddick saw the elevator open, a man get off. He jogged across the street, caught the door just as the man was leaving.

"You heading in?" the man said. He was white, short with sloped shoulders, wavy brown hair pinched beneath a wool cap.

Reddick tried to look like he belonged. "Yeah, thanks."

"No key?" The man was smiling, not quite suspicious.

"No, I have one, I just—I'm doing Airbnb, and I'm not used to the keys yet. Actually—she didn't say whether she was allowed to sublet or not, so maybe forget I said that."

The guy laughed. "It's cool, man. Which apartment are you in?"

"Do you know Hannah on the fourth floor?"

"The fourth...is she blonde? Kind of a looker?"

"Yeah, you know her?"

"No, I've just seen her smoking on the fire escape."

Reddick shivered. "In this cold?"

"I guess if you gotta, you gotta, right? Anyway, I'm up on six." The guy extended his hand and offered his name, Reddick lied about his own, then lied a few more times. Wherever the guy had been heading he wasn't pressed for time. Reddick nodded along, answered when asked, a plan coming together while he listened.

After a few minutes he made his move. "So maybe I could ask you, what's the deal with the roof? She had a picture of the view in her ad, but she didn't mention how to get up there. Does anyone have access, or just the apartments on the top floor?"

"It's for anyone, definitely. There's a separate stairway up from six. To the left of the elevator. God, if it was just ours I'd never be able to swing my share of the rent. Not that the view is that great."

Reddick shrugged. "I'd still like to check it out—you know, first time in New York."

"I get it, man. I remember when the city was like that—new and invigorating." He sighed, affected a weary knowingness. "It just wears you down eventually."

"I bet. How long have you lived here?"

"Almost two years, actually." He nodded with an air of worn pride.

Reddick glued his eyes to the guy's chest, kept his face level. "In this building the whole time?"

"No. I moved in last spring. Actually—right before the girl you're renting from did. I remember seeing her carry a couple boxes in, and wondering when the movers had brought the rest of her stuff. I work from home and I hear everything up there. Echoes or whatever."

"Well, listen, I'm gonna head up, but I'm glad I ran into you."

"Yeah, me, too. If you need anything, just come up to 6A. And make sure you have that key handy next time. This neighborhood is pretty safe but we still like to keep security tight."

Reddick smiled. "Will do."

The guy left him alone inside the bright lobby. He took the elevator to 4. He had guessed correctly—her apartment was stage right. He knocked on the metal door and waited. Nothing. He knocked again, to make certain, a snare drum tap that he hoped her neighbor couldn't hear. He pressed his ear against the door. The apartment was quiet as a tomb.

He went back to the elevator, rode it to six, took the stairs up to the roof. The wind carved through his jacket. A handful of mismatched plastic chairs were scattered around a cracked table, the ensemble blanketed by snow. High-rises circled the building, pinholed with light, straining toward the tar-black sky. If she smoked on the fire escape often enough for that guy to notice, maybe she didn't bother locking her window. The iron handrails of the fire escape's ladder curled over the lip of the roof; he grabbed them and descended carefully to the first platform. The icy metal rattled beneath his weight. He crept past dark windows until he reached the fourth floor.

He tried Hannah's window gently—it was unlocked. He looked around the block, made sure no one was watching and yanked it open. The bowl on the sill was heaped with ashes and twisted butts. He moved it aside and slipped into the warm apartment.

When Reddick was thirteen years old he had a friend, Alvin, who was in the middle school band. It was a humid

July afternoon, and they were bored; Alvin had wrapped up a summer fund-raiser selling candy the day before, delivering his earnings to the band director's house, a brick two-bedroom near Crowders Mountain, encased by woods. There wasn't another home in sight, Alvin said. He had watched the band director stash his money with the rest, in an overflowing metal tin inside his desk drawer—there had to be like three or four hundred dollars, he insisted, an astronomical sum. They'd recruited Alvin's brother—older, with a license, but bookish and shy—to drive them out. They bribed him with an equal share, told him he could wait in the car while they did all the work.

The boys jimmied the sliding glass back door open by derailing it with a stick. Nothing else went as planned—the desk drawer was empty, the metal tin gone. The band director must have taken it with him that morning, to deposit the money. They discussed looting the place but it turned out that neither boy had a thief's heart—stealing the fund-raiser earnings had seemed victimless in a way that taking the band director's own possessions did not. But they didn't leave. They were snared by the thrill of transgression. They went through the refrigerator, drank his two-liter Sundrop and tossed the empty bottle on the floor, opened drawers in every room, read labels off the army of squat orange medicine bottles arrayed on his kitchen table, invented wild conditions for each one to treat. They sprayed each other with his drugstore cologne. They rummaged through his videocassettes, praying to find an X-rated title. Outside, Alvin's brother squirmed with fear in the sweltering car. The boys left two hours later, intoxicated by their own daring—the house in disarray, the sliding door cockeyed and misgrooved, their pockets empty.

They didn't brag to their friends—they were too afraid.

A simmering panic settled in as they waited for news of the break-in to roll through their school, for suspicions to fall inevitably on them, driven by some mistake, some carelessness of execution. It never came, an absence that Reddick read as an affront to the world's moral order, to the sense of earned consequences enforced by both his mother's emphatic decency and his adolescent boy's notion of honor and retribution. It was a lesson. Punishment does not fall on its own; it isn't a natural law, an inevitable consequence. You can get away with anything if no one catches you.

This lesson worked both ways.

Hannah's apartment was well kept and bland, furnished with chic frugality—an Ikea backbone touched with bespoke flourishes. There were half a dozen prints on the walls, in matched frames. He recognized one of them, an anxious Paul Klee—he had helped crate the original yesterday, in the Sewards' dining room. An ab wheel rested in one corner, below a slumped yoga mat. A radiator gurgled beneath the window. Reddick checked for a thermostat, found nothing—it was probably controlled by the landlord, its baking heat said nothing about Hannah's status. He couldn't risk turning on a light; he waited for his eyes to adjust to the sallow glow drifting in from the street. He listened to his breath, his chest pumping exhilaration and fear in equal measure. The air was dry as old leaves.

A short bar split the living room and kitchen; he swept both spaces calmly, going over each object with forensic attention. He noted the television remote upended on the couch, casually discarded after switching off the TV. The lack of books, mail or magazines—evidence of a tidy life. The unwashed glasses in the sink, the squat boxes of leftover takeout stacked like children's blocks in the refrigerator. He took one out, pried open the lid, was splashed by the meaty smell of lasagna. It looked stiff but edible, maybe a week old. He replaced it carefully, noticed a photo of her and Buckley pinched to the refrigerator door by a magnet the shape of a sunflower. The shot was taken at an angle above them, Buckley's raised shoulder pegging him as the cameraman—a grinning selfie, the two of them not inured by Buckley's wealth from a couple's goofy pleasures. Reddick squinted, tried to read details from the background in the dim light. It was an interior shot, anonymous, whatever occasion prompted the photo lost on him. He padded into the bedroom.

Dark clothing was pooled on the floor, beside her haphazardly made bed. He went to her drawers, thumbed the round pulls through his winter gloves. There were layers to infringement, nuances to the boundaries he crossed as he bulled deeper into the nested dolls of her home and property—what point was far enough, how deep a violation could he justify. He slid the top drawer open. It was full, cramped with airy fabric, sorted and folded, bits of lace hinting at an intimacy that rebuffed him. He shut it and opened the closet, a shallow niche barely deep enough for her clothes; dresses, pants and shirts segregated by type, draped casually over plastic hangers. He slid the closet door closed, returned to the living room.

He wheeled slowly in the center of her floor, viewing it all from a distance, one final pass to see if anything felt wrong. There was nothing here that would have spooked Buckley—only the emptiness, the carefree negligence that argued she might return at any minute. She hadn't packed, hadn't prepared for a trip. He had seen enough.

He went back through the apartment, to make sure he hadn't left anything out of place. The window was shut, the bowl lined up on the sill. He set the latch on the door to lock behind him and looked through the peephole, listened for the elevator. Once he was sure it was quiet he opened the door, slipped into the hall and left.

SIX

He rode his adrenaline to Bushwick, told Beth Han and Dean all of it over drinks.

"I can't believe you did that," Dean said.

"What if you had been caught?" Beth asked. "You could have been arrested."

"I didn't take anything."

"That isn't the point."

"A note on every door? Now our entire building knows, okay, A, you're nuts, and, B, your email address."

"Dean, do you really think that's what matters right now?" Beth seemed shaky, unsure of how to calibrate her reaction. She turned back to Reddick. "That cop isn't going to help you if he knows you literally *broke into* someone's apartment."

"Look, he didn't hurt anything, he didn't get caught."

Dean reached over the table and rubbed her shoulder. She took a drink, sighed and closed her eyes. "Reddick, just tell me that you see that what you did was crazy."

"I was careful."

"That's not what I meant."

Dean turned to Reddick, interrupted Beth before she could get worked up again. "Forget this and paint. Lane gave you, like, a week off. Just lock yourself into your studio and get to work. Order takeout. Pretend you're back in school."

Reddick checked his email as he listened. "I had to do something," he said. "I keep seeing her step into that open door. The back of the alley was dark—she was just a shape back there, an outline, kind of glowing from the light of her phone. And then wham, the door opens and she goes in, and she's gone. I should have—I don't know—followed them. Gone up to the party to look for her friends."

"You don't know what happened, though," Beth said. "That arm could have *belonged* to one of her friends. Why is she your responsibility?"

"She was in trouble, and I happened to be there. That has to mean something."

"I get it," Dean said. "There is a lot of literature about this, you know—ethics and obligation and moral luck."

Beth cut him off. "Which none of us cares anything about."

"Beth to the rescue," Reddick said.

"I'm just saying. It's interesting and it does sort of apply."

"I'm sure it does." She patted his hand and turned to Reddick. "Look, it's not like you witnessed a crime."

"Maybe I did."

"But even if you did, you had no way of knowing. It's just as likely that whoever opened that door was a genuine friend of hers, someone she trusted. Whatever happened to her might have come hours later."

"Which I kind of agree with that cop," Dean said. "Can she really be missing if no one has reported her?"

"Enough with the philosophy."

"I meant that literally."

Reddick stabbed at a bobbing ice cube with his straw. "It isn't just the way she disappeared. I mean, yeah, that spooked me and the image has been hard to shake. But you remember that girl that was killed in Coney Island a couple years ago?" They nodded and he continued. "Well, Allen was telling me about it yesterday."

"Telling you?" Beth said. "You hadn't heard about it? It was literally everywhere."

He tried to recall that summer. It was mostly flashes of painting and basketball, indistinguishable from the months before or after. He remembered the girl he was dating, the maraschino-red bikini she wore to Fort Tilden—he averaged about one listless relationship a year, rushes of sexual intrigue that all fizzled the same way, dwindled into amicable dissolution. Restoration Heights was underway and brooding about the changes it represented had begun to swallow his time. Maybe he had heard about the murder.

"I think I did," he said. "A little."

"I'm pretty sure *we* talked about it," Beth said, "and you just don't remember."

"The point is she had friends there, at the party. And they let her go off with these two guys, these killers, and no one stopped to question it. I've been thinking—no one at that party had a bad feeling about her leaving with them? What if someone did, only they didn't do anything about it because they didn't really know her, or because no one else thought it was something worth caring about. Everyone around them thought everything was fine, so they didn't listen when their guts told them it wasn't. And yeah, I get that it was no one at that party's *responsibility* to intervene, but that doesn't change the fact that if someone had done it anyway, even though it wasn't their responsibility, that girl would be alive. And could you live with that? If you had a feeling and did nothing and someone died because of it?"

"But no one is dead," Beth said. "I get it, her apartment didn't look like she had packed for a long trip—and I haven't changed my mind that what you did was wrong, but Dean's right, what's done is done—and fine, you saw what you saw. But maybe she left in a hurry? Maybe she's planning on coming back for her stuff. You don't know anything for certain."

"It's everything together, though. The condition that she was in that night, Mrs. Leland's support. And if you had seen the way Buckley overreacted to me—tell her, Dean, it was crazy how he just shut down when I mentioned Bed-Stuy, like he was afraid of something."

"It was weird but, dude," he grabbed Reddick's arm, "if you would spend three-quarters of this energy on your painting."

Reddick's response was interrupted by the chime of a new email downloading. He shook free of Dean's grasp and checked his phone. "Holy shit, it's them."

"Who?" Beth asked.

"The people in our building. The ones who threw the party." He scanned the rest of the message. "They're home. They said I could come by tonight."

He stood up and threw cash on the table. "I'll see you later?"

"I don't think so," Dean said. "I'm knee-deep in work right now."

For the first time in what felt like ages, Reddick thought, so was he.

The boy who opened the door at 3C was about twenty, wiry and good-looking. He invited Reddick in, seemingly immune to the strange circumstances. The apartment's floor plan was a mirror image of his and Dean's, which Reddick found disorienting, almost dreamlike. The walls were hung with haphazard drawings and framed posters, a blend of irony and high culture. There were four other kids inside—two girls and two boys, in flannel and faded denim. They hummed with entitled confidence.

One of the girls, her head cradled in a diving helmet of curly brown hair, lit a joint. "So you're looking for someone who was at our party?"

On the way down Reddick had decided which pieces of the truth to use. He didn't mention the Sewards or Buckley by name, just that Hannah was a friend's fiancée, and that he thought she might have been at their party, and that now she was missing.

He showed them the picture on his phone.

"She was definitely here," the girl said.

"She was?" one of the roommates asked.

"Yeah. With those neighborhood guys."

"Oh shit. That's her? I didn't recognize her at all."

"She was talking with that guy, Frank?"

"Who's Frank?" Reddick asked.

"Honestly, I don't know, man." The girl had passed the joint along, and one of the boys offered it to Reddick. He waved it off. The boy continued. "I'm not sure who invited him. He's just this old guy who I've seen around at parties."

"One of the neighborhood guys?"

The curly-haired girl shook her head. "No way. Not this guy. That was the other two. They kind of, uh—stood out, you know what I mean?"

Reddick looked at the room of cherubic faces, their pale skin. "You mean they were black?"

"That's not what I meant. I mean, yeah, they *were*, but, you know, we have black friends."

"Saul is black. He's over here all the time. So is his boyfriend."

"Saul's boyfriend is Dominican."

"Yeah, but he's like, Dominican *black*. That counts, right?"

The curly-haired girl interrupted them. "Anyway. What I was trying to say was that these guys looked like they were maybe from around here. Originally. *Neighborhood* guys, you know."

"Fine. So she was here with three guys. Two black guys and an older white guy. Did it look like she was actually *with* any of them?"

They shook their heads. The other boy spoke up. "I just want to note that we aren't the ones bringing their race into this? Anyway, yeah, I don't think Frank knew those other two. He seemed kind of, I don't know, pissed that they came with her."

"Did they argue?"

"No. I just mean he was sulky. He was in the kitchen talking to some other girls when she showed up, with them. I was getting a beer, and I remember that he seemed put out."

"Did they leave together, Frank and this girl?"

The kids looked at each other for answers. Finally the curly-haired girl said. "They just left, you know? It was a party. No one was keeping track of who went with who."

"Whom," the wiry boy said. The two girls rolled their eyes.

"Okay. So did anyone else that you know talk with them? Get their names, at least?"

"Oh yeah. Trisha was flirting with one of them all night."

"I think she already knew one of them?"

"Who?" Reddick tried to keep up. "Frank? Or one of the others?"

"Now that you say that, I'm not sure his name is actually Frank."

"It definitely is."

"Really? I thought it had two syllables?"

"Well one of those syllables is Frank. He introduced himself to me. Not Sunday night, I mean a few months ago. At some other party."

"Franklin, maybe?"

"Maybe. But anyway," turning back to Reddick, "that's not who Trisha was flirting with."

"Alright, so could you guys hook me up with Trisha? Give me her email?"

The curly-haired girl smiled at him. "I have her number. But I don't feel comfortable giving that out to you?"

"I'm not going to harass your friend. Also, I'm your neighbor."

"Have we actually seen you in the building? We know people here."

"I've lived on the second floor for eight years."

She seemed skeptical of this claim. "I'll tell you what. She works in the neighborhood. You know that specialty food store a few blocks away, on Bedford? She's there most mornings. Go there if you want to talk to her, so I don't have to, like, spill her personal information all over Brooklyn."

Reddick thanked them and left.

He woke up early, was bundled in his winter layers and out the door in fifteen minutes. Claws of hard ice resisted the morning sun. After a short walk Reddick stamped his boots dry and went inside.

The store was boxy and cramped. Soft fluorescents fell on rows of metal shelves, glinted dimly off satin finishes, caught the grain of recycled paper—the packaging, like the store, positioned to oppose the high gloss of corporate grocers. The products advertised an ethos, signaled their virtue so clearly you were desperate to pay the higher price. There was a deli in the rear, and a wooden coffee counter near the front. A few tables were jammed into the window. Reddick approached the counter, which was helmed by a sleepy twentysomething, and ordered a large coffee.

"Trisha?" he asked, after she made change. The girl looked at him blankly for a moment and then asked if he wanted to speak to her. When he said yes she yelled back to the deli.

Trisha came out wearing an apron, a gray thermal shirt and matching beanie over thick waves of barn-red hair. She was nearly his age, tall and robust with a round, affable face. She shook his hand with suspicion and got a coffee of her own. They sat down at one of the tables. He gave her the same version that he had offered in 3C.

"Maybe she wants to get away from your friend. She has the right to leave, you know."

"Of course she does. That's not why I'm here. I'm not trying to get her to go back to him or anything like that. I just want to know if she's okay."

"*You* do? Or your friend?"

"I want to know for my friend."

"This seems a little creepy. I don't want to help some stalker."

The description stopped him. Flashes from the night before—opening Hannah's drawers, her closet. But he thought of Mrs. Leland, her insider's confidence that something was awry, and repressed his doubts. He lifted his jaw toward Trisha, tried to convey the virtue of his resolve. "I'm just trying to help."

"Maybe she doesn't need your help."

"But what if she does?" He showed her the photo. "Do you recognize her?"

She eyed him for a moment as she wrestled with her suspicions, then squinted reluctantly at the image. "Wow, yeah. She looks really different, but that is definitely her."

"They said you spent some time with one of the guys she was with."

"Tyler. But he doesn't know her. He mentioned at the party. She was a friend of his friend, who was also there."

"And what's his friend's name?" He opened his notebook, which seemed to spook her.

"Ju'waun. Look this is really weird."

"Did they leave together?"

"I'm not sure. I left before either of them."

"Did you get Tyler's number?"

"I did. He's a nice guy. I had Monday off and we spent some time together."

"Did he stay over Sunday night?"

"That's none of your business. Really none of this is your business."

"This girl is missing. Vanished."

"So where are the cops?"

"I've done everything I can to convince her boyfriend to call them. It's complicated. But if I can make some headway—if you help me—then the police will get involved. They'll have to. But I could use your help. I need to talk to Tyler."

She measured him briefly. "I don't see what it can hurt—but that's his choice, not mine. Give me your number, I'll ask him and let you know if he wants to talk. Fair?"

It was the best he was going to get from her. "Fair."

Back in his apartment he texted Harold, told him to ask around about Tyler and Ju'waun. *Neighborhood guys.* He wasn't expecting much—all he had were a pair of first names, and he was skeptical that Harold's claims had been anything more than boasts. But Harold responded immediately, said that he would hit up his sources after he got off work.

Reddick needed more background on Buckley, on what he was like when his family wasn't around. He thought of Sarah, who was at Penn while Buckley was getting his MBA, and sent Dean a message to check if she was in the building. She was. Reddick bundled up and left for Bushwick.

He found Dean in his narrow studio, splayed on the couch, drinking coffee and thumbing through a magazine. A pair of tall windows doused the room with pale light. Arranged on a large central table was the willowy armature of a nascent sculpture, framed by scattered pieces of balsa. The walls were papered over with sketches and lined with crowded shelves.

"I dropped in on Sarah and told her you were coming. I didn't say much about why." He laid the magazine on his lap, adjusted his glasses. "Look. I thought about it all morning. Beth is right. You need to give this up."

"I've only just started."

"Which means you haven't wasted much time. Whatever you think you're going to get from doing this, you're wrong. There's nothing there."

"I'm not doing it for me."

"Really? Because no one else seems to care."

He picked his magazine back up and Reddick left. Solvents and varnishes, pigments and adhesives—their fumes as sweet as honeysuckle, as toxic as venom—permeated the vaulted hallways. A circular saw whined somewhere above him. The building was a five-floor beast, one of several massive industrial spaces in Bushwick that had been renovated on the cheap, guts carved into row upon row of high-rent artists' spaces. They were positioned throughout the neighborhood like bunkers, repositories for the ambitions, the rivalries and dramas of the swarming MFAs who labored inside. Craft beer and cold-brew coffee had sprouted on the sidewalks between them, an ecosystem of young businesses that thrived off the flimsy cachet of the new population, the alcohol and caffeine fuel for the young artists' most daring hopes. Just catch one dealer's eye, one time. Never mind that even the existence of these buildings argued against the possibility of success, that no matter how you arranged the numbers there simply wasn't enough money to build careers for the glut of people working inside. Dreams are numb to long odds. And selfish, because each artist must believe that she is the great exception even as that prospect dooms her friends to anonymity. They reveled in the support, the camaraderie, but squirmed with private envies.

Reddick had always worked from home.

"Sarah?" Her door was open, he knocked on the wall and went in. She looked up and smiled. Canny and quick-witted, with auburn freckles and caramel hair, Sarah was one of the first friends he had made in the building, the two of them going out for drinks shortly after Dean moved in down the hall. She was among the few people Reddick knew who had moved to Bushwick before the bars and restaurants, when the cars of the L train shed their last white faces by Morgan Avenue. He enjoyed her stories of the old neighborhood. A copper-skinned black girl, anonymous to the pale youths shuffling past her to the exits, her artistic practice had felt at times like a thrilling secret. Her career had blossomed with the neighborhood; now she showed as often as anyone Reddick knew. Her paintings were large and unruly—de Kooning–esque horses with enormous phalluses, jizzing and fucking in orgies of incandescent color.

She stood up and hugged him and they chatted for several minutes, catching up on the months since they last hung out. He remembered she had started dating someone—it was, he suspected, one of the reasons they hadn't seen each other for so long. The demands on her time had already been high; the zealous painting schedule, the part-time job that helped keep it afloat. Adding a romantic partner didn't leave much room for maintaining already tenuous friendships.

"So your roommate wasn't exactly clear about why you wanted to talk to me?"

"It figures. I think he hates it." They sat down and he told her a little about what he was doing, and why. "Buckley rubbed me the wrong way, and I was wondering if you knew him at school. I gathered he was connected to the art program somehow?"

"Everyone called him Buckles. You want tea? I'm having tea. He was at Wharton, but he was always hanging around the MFAs. He was at our parties, would show up at our studios. You know, we got these guys occasionally, business or prelaw, chasing art pussy or trying to make themselves feel hip or intellectual or what have you. Trying to show the world they're deeper than their suit. Like it was date an art student or get some tattoos, your choice."

"Guys who buy David Foster Wallace but don't read him."

"Ha ha, you get it. But Buckles wasn't one of those. We were just his business. I mean, you've worked for that family, right? Art is what they do. The other stuff makes the money, but art makes their name. So for Buckles, visiting our studios was learning the family business."

"Did he buy student work?"

"A little. Not necessarily because he thought the artist would blow up. Not in a way that seemed overly serious. More just practice. Like to get the rhythms of the transaction down. He honestly didn't seem like that bad of a guy. Nervous and serious and kind of hopeless. He always seemed like he was under a ton of pressure."

"So people liked him, then?"

"He got a lot of that white male pushback, you know? One percenter, bestowing his largess on us hapless bohemians. But a lot of that came from other white dudes, guys trying to hide their own upper-middle-class background behind flannel and beards and critical theory. You went to art school. That's everything. For my part I didn't mind Buckles at all. He was thoughtful and sweet. I don't hold him responsible as a person for the power structures he benefits from. Being an asshole to rich people doesn't make you a revolutionary, it just makes you an asshole. Anyway, he was better than his friend Franky."

"Wait. Frank?"

She shrugged. "He only ever went by Franky. Franky Dutton. Remember how I said there was a reflexive resentment of Buckles because of his background? Well, it's funny because there are also guys like Franky who that kind of stuff should attach to but somehow doesn't. He had all the benefits that Buckles had, plus he was a total asshole, not interested in anyone but himself—but he was hot, and sometimes that's enough. People forgave him everything, at least the girls did, and the more he did things that needed forgiving the more willing they were to absolve him."

He smiled. "Not you, of course?"

"You know me. I flirted back—we all did. But nothing ever happened between us because I knew his rep."

"Because he was just there for the art—for the girls."

"The art *pussy*, Reddick. You prude. Once you've allowed power to dictate language you've already submitted. Warm up your tea? Anyway, yeah, Franky was one of those guys I mentioned, just chasing the scene, but that's not the rep I was talking about. There were rumors of stuff that was a little… dark, you know? Like he enjoyed hurting people."

"And y'all still tolerated this guy?"

"Being sexy goes a long way when you're twenty-three. And they were only rumors. Most of the other girls behaved like I did anyway—just flirting. He was so good-looking that his interest was flattering. I'm not saying it wasn't a little fucked-up but that's how these things go. A few girls fucked him but they never mentioned him crossing any boundaries they didn't want crossed. You know this guy is still basically doing the same thing, right?"

"What do you mean?"

"He's some big shot developer now. Here, in Bushwick. He's done a few buildings, sells them off to management companies when he's done. You haven't seen his signs? FDP. Franky Dutton Properties. He never had to bother with creativity."

"He's here in New York?" Reddick's pulse skipped.

"Living the same life. Going to parties in Bushwick, preying on the creative class. I saw him out recently—it was barely a year ago, probably. With some top-heavy blonde girl. I think she was European or something. At least she seemed closer to his age than what he usually goes for—maybe the competition is getting to him. Bushwick is packed with guys like him now—good-looking white boys clinging to the scene just to prove how different they are from their fathers. No offense."

"None taken."

"He doesn't stand out the way he used to, is all I mean. But he's still around."

"Do you still hear the same rumors? About him hurting people?"

"Nothing like that anymore. Maybe he's cleaned up, or maybe he's gotten more discreet. Now he just seems more sleazy than creepy—always trying to flash his money around, never mind that half the girls he goes out with are probably suckling on some kind of trust fund. From what I hear he likes to take his dates to his properties—he always makes sure one or two stay furnished, to show off."

Reddick pulled out his phone and opened the photo of Hannah. "You ever see him with this girl?"

She shook her head. "Sorry, no. She's cute but probably not his type. Too all-American. Who gave you this photo, though?"

"I found it online," he lied.

"I thought maybe Aliana gave it to you. You know her, right?"

"I don't think so."

"Short hair. Kind of butch. Really into CrossFit. Anyway, that's her gallery, in the photo. Heinrich. She's been the preparator there for a couple years."

He stood up. "Sarah, you've been incredibly helpful."

"You're not around that often anymore. Why don't you come by and we can talk shop sometime. You're still painting, right?"

He thought of the last productive day in his studio—that had been, what, two weeks ago? Three? "When I have time."

"Between what, basketball and looking for missing girls?"

"Playing ball helps me think."

"And painting doesn't?"

He started to answer but paused, tried to recall the clarity, the polished emptiness that used to follow a long day of painting and drawing.

"You need to work," she continued. "You have to put in the time if you want to get anything out of this."

"I need to talk to Aliana. Could you set something up for me? Tell her that I'm coming?"

"It's almost five. She'll be gone by the time you get there."

"Tomorrow, then."

"I have to work tomorrow morning," she said. "At the bakery."

"Oh, I didn't mean—couldn't you just text her?"

She answered with a coy smile. "I could. But I haven't seen her in ages. Let's do this: I'll make plans with her tomorrow afternoon, right after she gets off work. You can come with me, we'll head up a little early and you two can chat before she and I go out."

He was hesitant to have Sarah around while he asked questions, worried that he might reveal some nuance of his search that repelled her. Trisha's accusation—*stalker*—nagged at him.

It was worth the risk. "Fine. But you know I don't mind going up there on my own. I know you're busy."

"A little less than I was a couple weeks ago, actually. But it's no problem." He cocked his head at her questioningly but she waved it off. "We can get into it later. I'll text you with the details after I hear from Aliana."

"Sarah, you've already been a huge help. I really appreciate this."

She stood up, kissed him on the cheek. "I'll see you tomorrow."

If he wasn't going to see Aliana until late the next day he would need something to work on until then. He went home, to sort through the information Sarah had given him. He made notes on the ride.

A story was coming into focus. Selfish, philandering Franky seduces his friend's fiancée, gets some kick from the cruelty of it. They are at the party together, and she ends up dead. Maybe it was an accident—rough sex taken too far—or maybe all the dark rumors had ripened into something worse.

It wasn't enough to take to Clint, but it gave direction to

his search. He could place Franky at the party if the kids could ID him, but that alone didn't mean much. He needed more about Franky's background—were there warnings, flashes of temper that went beyond Sarah's rumors? And it was critical that he talk to Ju'waun or Tyler—they would know if she left with Franky that night, could prove he was the last person to see her.

That arm, holding the door. That was Franky. It had to be.

When he got off the train he saw that he had missed a text from Trisha.

Tyler says no.

He stopped on the sidewalk to respond, sliding out of the path of the foot traffic spilling from the subway entrance. The sun was down, the temperature plunging recklessly. He fired three texts in succession, first to ask why, then to plead with her to convince Tyler to change his mind. A passing man slipped on the ice, caught himself and winced. Reddick waited for a response for ten or fifteen minutes, until his shivering was an audible constant, like a purr. His phone was silent.

He decided to go see her in the morning to make his case in person.

He went home, warmed up and looked at his notes. The pages were disjointed and cramped, sloppy with parenthetical asides and conjecture. He needed something larger, some way to lay the case out and play with the connections. He needed to see it all at once.

He went into his bedroom, to the wall he had set aside as a work area. There was a small table beside it, with drawers and boxes of materials. He removed the unfinished painting that had been hanging there, untouched, for weeks. He placed it on the floor facing one of the other walls, pried out the nails it had hung from, unpinned the sketches and source photographs and stacked them in a box. Once the wall was clear he unrolled a large piece of white cover stock and pinned it in the center. He wrote Hannah's name, circled it. Next to her he wrote Buckley Seward and Franky Dutton, then Ju'waun and Tyler to the side, all circled, with pencil lines tracing their tentative connections. In the space around them he copied notes from his Moleskine. The party in 3C, the alley, the door—observations and tender conjecture, anything that might spark an insight. He put music on, the sexless indie rock he took so much shit for in high school, the whitest of white boy tunes that confounded his teammates. His foot tapped the rhythm. It was a relief to see it all laid out, at once—there was an alluring clarity to visual arrangements. A map of what was there to reveal what was missing.

When he was nearly done he heard his phone ring. He thought it might be Trisha, and raced to answer. It was Harold.

"Hey listen, my brother. What do you think you are doing?" Harold's voice was faintly slurred, thickened by alcohol.

"What do you mean?"

"So I saw my boy tonight and I asked him for you, about what you wanted. He works for—man, I definitely can't say this name to you but he works for someone who would know, alright. So I asked him and he was not happy."

"What did he say?"

"How do you know Tyler and Ju'waun?"

"I don't. I told you that. That's why I wanted you to ask about them. But listen, I have more information now."

"I don't want nothing to do with your information. And you don't either. You hear me?"

"No, I have a suspect now. This developer who was at the party with her. And I think Tyler or Ju'waun may have seen her with him, could place them together—maybe he left with her. They could really help."

There was a pause. "This suspect. He white?"

"Yeah."

"Man, you are out of your fucking mind. Some rich white girl goes missing from a party in Bed-Stuy, and the last people she was with was a white person and two brothers, and you think anyone is going to believe them when they pin it on the white person? You know how this world works."

"If they help me, we can find evidence. I know this cop."

"Who you think will believe you."

"The cop's black, if that makes a difference."

"Sometimes it does. A lot of times it don't. It's just the way the system is set up."

"I understand that. But I'm trying to find the truth."

"The truth's got nothing to do with it. Look, I'm not even supposed to be talking to you about this shit right now. I told you my boy was mad. He was real *real* mad."

"I don't understand. Mad about what?"

"I'm at Ti-Ti's. I see my man come in, and I move over next to him. We start talking shit a little bit, you know, and I say I have this friend, he has a problem and he wants to know about these two dudes. I say he knows their first names, Tyler and Ju'waun. He immediately gives me this look and I know I should back down, but I can't. I already started and I'm thinking it would look strange if I stopped all of a sudden. So I say that you know some people who saw them with this blonde and he stops me right there. I don't get no further than that. He calls me a drunk piece of shit, like he's actually pissed off at me just for *asking.* I've known this dude a long time and he ain't never been pissed at me like that. He says what happened with that girl is none of my damn business, and none of your damn business, and who are you to her, and all of that."

"What did you say about me?"

"That you were a friend of a friend of this lady, and you were concerned. I mean, that's all I really know. I told him what I know."

"Harold, look, I'm sorry I got you in trouble with your friend."

"I tried to do right by you, man. But you are sticking your head in shit where it does not belong. My man was scared of something, because why else would he act like that?"

"What was he scared of?"

"Maybe I have some idea or maybe I don't, but it doesn't matter one way or the other. You got to stay the fuck away. You hear me? Stay the fuck out of this shit."

Reddick glanced at the new case map on his wall. "I don't know if I can."

"Then that's your ass. But don't ask me to do shit no more. I wanted to help you because you're a nice guy and all that. But I'm done. You hear me? Done."

He hung up and Reddick stared at his phone. Then he got up and wrote Harold's name on the wall, next to Tyler and Ju'waun.

SEVEN

He had to speak with them. Maybe he could bypass Trisha. He spent the rest of the night online, in a fruitless search for information. *Ju'waun Brooklyn, Ju'waun Tyler, Tyler and Ju'waun Bed-Stuy*, across social media, hoping for tags, comments, sifting through pages of hits for some indication of this neighborhood, that party, anything. It wasn't specific enough—there were too many pages to sort through. He wasted hours and moved on to Franky. On a whim he checked the sex offender registry for his name—maybe his bad behavior had caught up with him. Nothing. He went to Franky Dutton Properties, a slick page with details about the company, photographs of their Williamsburg headquarters and lists of projects. It handled development and sales, specialized in working over existing structures rather than ground-up construction. Residential and commercial but nothing large-scale. All in Brooklyn, mostly Bushwick and Williamsburg but a few down here. In a section spotlighting upcoming projects he recognized a townhouse that was barely a block away, across the street from Restoration Heights.

He went to bed, preparing for another early morning at Trisha's grocery store, but could barely sleep. He lay in the dark and rehearsed his approach, role-playing scenarios where she agreed to cooperate, where Tyler tagged Franky as the guy and broke the case open. Go hard or soft, demand or plead. Tap her morals or her self-interest, appeal to solidarity for a victimized sister. Late in the night, two or three, he heard Dean come home, the throaty squeal of the pipes when he turned the shower on. Reddick woke up before his alarm and was dressed and leaving just as the store opened.

She wasn't there.

"She's not in until noon," said the barista.

He ordered a coffee and went home. Dean was asleep. He had four hours to kill. He stared at his wall, at the notations on his map. There were huge swaths of white crossed by soft pencil lines. It seemed fragile, less than a sketch. It could be wiped away or built upon, buried under new facts or abandoned. There was nothing he could add to it now, no move he could make that wouldn't cloud its purpose.

He went back into the living room, stared helplessly at the television, the couch. He only knew one way to pass the time—he put on his coat, grabbed his ball and left. He went to a small park near his apartment—on weekday mornings the Y's courts were claimed by the adjacent Bedford Academy. Reddick played in the park occasionally when the weather was nice—the crowd was mostly teenagers, nearly all of them black. The games at the Y brought out his best play; the rumble of skill beneath the ball-busting jokes, the threat of loss, of being vanquished, revived his dormant focus. Out here was different. He went to the courts in the park to reaffirm his history, to ground himself. Playing outside recalled the idyllic repetition of his adolescent summers, baking in the swamp heat of North Carolina, toting his two indispensable items: a ball and a sketchbook. Sitting courtside between games, sharing Gatorade he and his friends bought with their combined scraped change, filling the pages with his heroes, Magic, Jordan, Wolverine, drops of sweat smudging the graphite, taking suggestions, advice. His work admired for its verve, its accuracy. Then getting up for another game—driving, the thrill of movement and the cessation of loneliness that exists only in shared effort. He was too young to believe there was anything more to it than that, that his passion brushed the live wire of the country's sundering division. Too young to realize that he was an exception. Racial awareness had come in fits and starts, in isolated episodes. Being called a cracker in the third grade—accosted by a crowd of older black girls, teasing him without menace, and he had no idea what it meant, what aspect of him was the subject of the joke, until his mother bit her lip and explained. On the cusp of high school, in a four-week summer program at the School of the Arts, he walked into an all-white class for the first time and had never felt such crushing loneliness, such displacement. In a room of kids who looked like him, scions of a middle class he couldn't comprehend, that seemed descended from another planet. Jokes he didn't know the references for, foods he had never tried, clothes his mother couldn't afford. TV he had never watched. The bully who saw it all as clearly as he did, who whispered *poor boy, poor boy* when the teacher's back was turned until the girl who sat between them snapped and came to his defense, more because she was sick of the litany, the strange onomatopoeia of it, than from compassion. He knew because she never spoke to him again. *You talk like a nigger,* they said. The first time he had heard a white person say it, a transgression that seemed almost biblical, profane. He could draw better than any of them and it didn't matter. He pined for the meritocracy of the courts. He made one friend, who gave him a mixtape of discordant rock that he hated for two years before he learned to adore it, that he still had in some shoebox. He learned that there was more to art than comic books and athletes. And he learned that he was white.

He walked onto the courts in the park, netless hoops and blasted asphalt. They had been shoveled once then ignored, were buried under a layer of filthy ice. A furrow ran diagonally through them, connecting two gates. He could just make out the foul line and he stood over it, took his shot and watched the ball thud off the ice. He picked it up and did it again, aware of how ridiculous it was to be out there but with nowhere else he could think to go. The ball was heavy and tight in his gloved hands, dense as lead. He missed as many as he made. After an hour the blanket of white clouds let go and falling snow blurred the hoop.

He had forced himself to absorb the lessons of his tormenters. He worked on his speech, practiced by-the-book conjugation on his teachers. He looked up movies he had heard them reference, made his mother rent them. He watched their sitcoms until he got the jokes. His friends accused him of changing—he laughed it off, because he was afraid to voice what he had learned, what they already knew, that his white skin was inescapable, his blond hair, and that once he got *out there* again, away from these hermetic blocks, there would be expectations thrust upon him, a way to act, to be, that frightened him. If he wasn't ready he was doomed to see those four alienated weeks of the summer program stretched into a lifetime.

Of course it didn't work. Dean, Beth, the friends he made in art school—on some level he believed they suspected him for a fraud. He was never quite at ease, never natural. The performance drained him; it damaged his ambition. He didn't blame it for his failed art career but he couldn't absolve it either. The minimum requirement for art world success—before talent, before connections, before unbelievable luck, just the starting point, the price of admission—was a fanatical desire to be there. It was an impossible thing to fake; he tried, but found himself searching for opportunities to escape the effort. Basketball was his refuge, waiting for him when he needed it.

He left the court when he couldn't see the backboard anymore—he knew whether his shot went in only by the direction and pace of the ball when it thumped into the powder.

When he got home Dean was gone. He ran hot water over his hands, burned sensation back into his fingers. The remaining hours crawled. He was dressed and back on the sidewalk at a quarter to noon.

The snowfall had improbably gotten worse; the swirling air was white and thick as cream. He pulled the front of his hood down and buried his chin in his collar. He couldn't look up without squinting. He walked west, to the corner of the block where Trisha's store was. Halfway down were two figures, a woman in an ankle-length parka and a tall man in a hooded puffer; the woman's back was to him but he recognized her blazing hair. The man was black. They stood beside the chalkboard sign advertising the store's specials.

Reddick crossed to the opposite side of the street and walked slowly—trying to act natural, to watch them with his eyes and not his head. He adjusted his hood to clear his periphery. Trisha hadn't noticed him. He was unremarkable, one of a dozen hooded shadows in a fog of snow. The couple hugged and as they separated the man leaned in for her cheek while she raised her lips—they smiled playfully at the awkward exchange, the misalignment of intentions. It didn't have to be Tyler. She never admitted that they had hooked up—she could be dating someone else. Except that she was at that party alone. Except that she had seemed so protective.

It occurred to him that she might have changed her mind and not have asked Tyler at all. There were good reasons she might want to protect him. But if Reddick was patient he could bypass her skepticism now and reach him directly. He stopped walking, knelt to untie and retie his boot. Trisha was angled slightly toward the entrance to the store, her back to Reddick. Tyler hadn't noticed him. The couple hugged once more and she went inside. Tyler dug his hands into his coat pockets, turned and walked south. Reddick stood up and followed.

Tyler walked quickly. He seemed anxious to get indoors. Reddick drifted back, pushed the limits of visibility but took care not to lose him. A block later Tyler hooked right and they walked to Clinton Hill. Reddick hoped he was going somewhere public, a coffee shop or restaurant. They were stopped by multiple lights, Reddick always finding some excuse to hang back from the intersection, stopping to adjust his gloves or hat, to check his phone.

He thought of Harold's warning. Were Tyler or Ju'waun involved with Hannah's disappearance? What if he wasn't following a witness, but a suspect—and Franky had nothing to do with it, his malicious history with women just a coincidence? Or maybe Franky did kill her, and Tyler was somehow complicit. In either case Reddick had to be ready for him to play it hard.

Tyler went inside a dentist's office, the entrance tucked beneath the stoop of a brownstone. Reddick stopped outside. It might be a perfect spot to confront him—catch him sitting down, waiting for an appointment. He would need a couple of minutes to check in. Reddick counted to sixty three times and followed him inside.

The lobby was small, maybe a dozen chairs. Two patients waited on opposite walls, both of them staring at their phones. There was an open sliding partition to the left, with no one at the counter behind it. Tyler waited in front of it—Reddick hadn't given him enough time. They made brief eye contact. He was dark-skinned and handsome, Reddick's height and build, his hair twisted into finger coils that danced above heavy eyelashes. Reddick realized that they were wearing identical coats—Tyler didn't look at him long enough to notice. Reddick got in line behind him.

An assistant appeared at the counter, a middle-aged woman holding a manila envelope. She smiled at Reddick and then addressed Tyler.

"Here you go, sweetheart."

He took the envelope, slipped it into his inside pocket and left.

She turned to Reddick. "Can I help you?" He fumbled over a response and stepped forward.

"I just… I just remembered I have to go."

"I'm sorry?"

"I have to go."

He felt her eyes on his back as he hurried from the office. It didn't matter; she didn't matter. He looked both ways on the sidewalk. The snow was finally slowing; he scanned the shuffling pedestrians, looked for someone his own height, wearing his jacket—and realized that it was the jacket that may have started this. Bent over, his face hidden, Hannah had seen the puffer and mistaken him for Tyler that night—it was why she ran up to him so quickly, she was being playful, drunk, trying to startle him. Just a random error, being mistaken for someone else, had drawn him into whatever this was. He wondered how life could turn on something so small.

It also meant Tyler was lying when he told Trisha he didn't know Hannah.

There, across the street, going south. Reddick hurried to catch up, then fell in behind him again.

What had Tyler picked up? Did he work at the dentist's office—was it some kind of paperwork, a paycheck? The assistant called him sweetheart, didn't address him like a colleague. A patient, then—but what would a patient receive in an envelope? Test results, X-rays? It had happened too quickly for that—there was no discussion, no follow-up or checkout.

Tyler crossed the street and went into a bodega. Reddick intentionally missed the light, hovered at the curb where he could see inside. A silver-haired, wiry Latino working the counter passed Tyler an envelope just like the one he got from the dentist's office. He put it in his pocket with the other one and left. The light changed and Reddick followed.

At Fulton there was a large apartment building with a string of commercial spaces at its base—a coffee shop, a yoga studio and a high-end liquor store. When Tyler went into the coffee shop Reddick didn't follow; he walked past him to the corner and waited. After five minutes Tyler came out with a cup, steam tumbling from the lid. He slipped into the yoga studio, reemerged almost immediately and then went inside the liquor store.

Five minutes turned to ten turned to twenty—too long to be shopping. Reddick examined the storefront—Cask, Specialty Liquors and Wines. The midday haze rendered the glass front wall nearly opaque. The cold was sinking into his body, his feet ached and his nose leaked. He eyed the warm interior of the café, the customers on their laptops or phones, their dripping winter layers piled beside them on empty chairs.

There were open seats near the window—he should be able to see Tyler leave from there. He was cold enough to risk it. He went in, kept an eye outside while he bought his coffee and found a stool where he could watch the sidewalk.

There was money in that envelope, there had to be—and in the one he got from the bodega, and another, probably, from the yoga studio, maybe even one from this coffee shop. It was the only thing that made sense. Tyler was a bagman running pickups—but for what? This was Clinton Hill. Maybe a few places still ran numbers but the neighborhood had flipped thirty years ago. Yet what else could it be? And more importantly, whom was he picking it up for?

Harold's warning—*you are sticking your head in shit where it does not belong.*

Thirty minutes later Tyler hadn't come out of the liquor store and Reddick began to wonder if he had missed him while he was in line. The coffee had plunged straight to his bladder but he couldn't risk a trip to the restroom. After another twenty minutes Tyler finally emerged, with a friend, smiling. The other guy was the same age, taller but with the same agile build, his face shrouded by the furred hood of his parka. Reddick turned away when they passed the window, then got up and followed.

The pair retraced Tyler's route, headed back toward Bed-Stuy. The pressure in Reddick's bladder had become so urgent that it stung; if they hadn't been moving closer to his own apartment he would have given up. On the fringes between the two neighborhoods they went into a dry cleaners called Clean City. Reddick waited on the corner and pressed his thighs together. He couldn't wait much longer, began to look desperately for a private corner. He felt betrayed by his body—he might never find Tyler again. He could give them fifteen minutes. No, ten. He lasted almost eight, realized that if he didn't leave now he wouldn't make it, swore and started home.

He banged through his building's entrance and up the stairs, tracked slush and salt into his apartment, was barely unzipped before his bladder released. When it was empty he peeled off his coat and went to the case map. He wrote in the liquor store and the dentist's office, the dry cleaners. The office, the bodega, the yoga studio and possibly the coffee shop were all pickups, but Tyler was in Cask and the cleaners for a while; there was more to both. He underlined them. He needed to get inside, to check them out. He thought about the meeting Sarah had set up with Aliana and glanced at the clock. It was almost two. Sarah had texted to say that she would meet him on the Upper East Side at five, so he had a couple of hours until he had to leave Brooklyn—enough time to do both, if he was quick.

He went to the cleaners first. It was the bottom floor of a two-story building on the corner, butted against a row of tall townhouses. The windows were papered with fliers—music, African dance, hair and nail salons, community meetings in opposition to Restoration Heights. Inside was a worn hardwood counter with racks of plastic-wrapped clothes behind it. More fliers covered the inside of the windows, many of them out of date. A single chair squatted haphazardly near the entrance, beside a toppled stack of magazines. There was no one behind the counter. The air was dense with some industrial cleaner, sweet as cloves and faintly metallic. He stepped forward and tapped the tarnished bell. After a moment a young man shuffled in from a door in the rear, behind the racks. He was black, and young—around the same age as Tyler and his friend. He was neatly dressed and seemed tired; he looked at Reddick like he was the last chore on a long list.

"Can I help you?"

Reddick realized he hadn't thought of what he would say, and stumbled. "Yeah, I was—do you clean coats like this?" He held his arms out, to indicate his puffer.

The guy looked at him blankly. "Yeah. Just fill out a ticket."

"No. I mean. I don't want to leave it now. I just— At the end of the season. In the spring. You know, clean it before I put it away."

"You're an optimistic guy, you know that?"

"I'm sorry?"

"Thinking about spring on a day like this."

"I was just passing by and—you know. I thought this place would be convenient."

"That coat don't have a tag? That you could look at and see if you should dry-clean it, instead of coming all the way over here?"

"Oh. Yeah. It probably does." Reddick backed to the door and opened it. "I'll be back when it warms up."

"Hey, it's whatever, man."

He stopped in the threshold, leaned back in. "While I'm here, though. Do you know a guy named Tyler?"

"Tyler who?"

"I don't know his last name. I met him at a party. We talked about playing ball together but I didn't get his number. I remember he said his friend worked here."

"Nope."

"No, you don't know him?"

"Can't help you, man."

He had already flubbed the encounter—might as well heave something from midcourt and pray. "Then how about a guy named Ju'waun?"

"He at this party, too?"

"Yeah."

"And you guys talked about playing ball?"

"Yeah."

"Never heard of him. And you're letting cold air in."

"Right." He stepped out and let the door close behind him. The kid was Tyler's age, if they were friends it would explain why he had lingered inside. But then why lie about knowing him? Just to put off a nosy stranger? He had hoped Ju'waun's name would pry something loose—for all he knew that was him behind the counter—but the nonreaction didn't have to mean anything. Reddick was a stranger poking into private lives; he had to expect cautious answers.

He hurried south to Cask. Walking inside was like slipping into an empty whiskey barrel—coppery wooden shelves and an aura of sweet malts. The walls teemed with expensive liquor, the wine lined up in two aisles in the center of the store. All of it arranged in narrowing categories of specificity, whiskey-scotch-malt-isle—cataloging the bottles demanded knowledge Reddick wasn't even sure how to acquire.

"How's it going?" The woman behind the counter was at her laptop and didn't look up when she spoke; her thick blond hair hung across one side of her face in a lively cascade. She was in her thirties, still in her knockout prime—thin and busty, in a cable sweater that had slipped down her shoulders to rest on the long slope of her breasts. She had full lips, a hard jaw and soft eyes—she was a collage of American infatuations. But her voice was patient and composed, accustomed to the reaction her looks provoked, willing to tolerate the time it took you to pull it together. "Let me know if I can help you find anything."

She looked up and smiled; her hair fell away and Reddick could see a mottled bruise beneath one eye.

"I will, thanks." He smiled back, not looking at the black eye, not reacting to it. He wandered among the unfamiliar bottles. She returned to her laptop, swayed half-heartedly to the beat of the electronic music thumping through the store. Perhaps Tyler had only lingered to chat her up.

But what about her eye? And the other stops, the envelopes?

He took another lap around the store and approached the counter.

She noticed his empty hands. "Did you need some help?"

Playing timid at Clean City hadn't worked. He drove the lane. "You know Tyler and Ju'waun, right?"

It was a wild shot, but it scored. She looked confused but answered straight. "Yeah."

"I thought I saw Tyler in here earlier."

"Yeah, actually, sure. He and Ju'waun stopped in. How do you know them?'

"From around the neighborhood. Did they just come in to chat?"

"What do you want?" She was getting nervous. She kept glancing under the counter—an alarm button, perhaps, but he wasn't sure what he had said to spook her. If she was already faltering, then maybe he should push.

"Or maybe they have better taste in liquor than I do."

"Why are you here?"

"How did you get that black eye?"

"That is none of your fucking business." It was a harder reaction than he expected, driven by fear. He lined up another improbable shot.

"Did Tyler hit you?"

"I said none of your fucking business, asshole." A miss. Her hand followed her eyes beneath the counter. It might not be an alarm—it might be a weapon.

He was suddenly almost as nervous as she was, and tried to rope the conversation back. "I just want to know what they were doing last Sunday night."

She said a name, asked if this person had sent him, but her voice was shaking and thick with emotion—the name came out garbled.

"Who?" he asked. "Gene? Eugene?"

His confusion gave him away—once she saw he didn't recognize the name her mood changed. She was suddenly confident, became irritated and dismissive. "Get the fuck out of my store."

"I'm trying to figure out what happened last weekend." Vague, still hoping to knock some stray detail loose.

She wasn't having it. She came around the counter and charged him, started shoving him toward the door, a little harder with each sentence. "You creep. You fucking asshole."

"If you're in trouble I could help you."

"You can't help me. You don't know what the fuck you're talking about." They both knew it was true—only she sounded relieved.

He opened the door. "You could tell me."

"Get the fuck out of my store."

EIGHT

It took over an hour to reach the Upper East Side. He rode shoulder to shoulder in the afternoon crowd, the train floor treacherous and filthy with tracked snow, the riders unzipping coats and shedding scarves in the stale body heat. When he finally got above ground the cold air was a relief.

Sarah was waiting inside a coffee shop, where they had agreed to meet. He saw her through the window, in a shin-length camel coat, her ropy braids bunched around its daunting fur collar. She waved and came out, gestured at her massive cup.

"Did you want anything?"

He was still wired from his adventures that morning and said no. The gallery was a few blocks away, and they started walking. "Thanks again for doing this," he said. "I would have been fine on my own."

"I already told you, I wanted to see my friend. You're a convenient excuse."

"I'm flattered."

"Ha ha. I forget how sensitive you are. I'm helping you, remember?" At the intersection they circled wide to avoid an icy pool of filthy water, and paired back up on the opposite sidewalk. "So this is about Buckley's girlfriend?"

"Fiancée. Like I said yesterday, I definitely saw her outside my building the night before she disappeared, and Buckley was such a dick about it that it made me suspicious."

"And based just on that, you're bouncing around the city asking questions?"

"It's weird, I know. At first I just assumed—find whoever she went with, and that would be the end of it."

"And you think that was Franky?"

"It must have been. But I'm not sure that's the whole story anymore." He thought of Tyler's route through Brooklyn, the liquor store woman's unprovoked fear—discoveries too unformed to share. "I thought that if I could come up with something on my own, without the police… I don't know, they would *have* to believe me. And how could the Sewards be upset if I helped them? But if it turns out she left with Buckley's friend…" He shook his head. "I just need more information."

"You want to know what I think?"

"Sure."

"I think you're bored."

It wasn't what he expected. "What?"

"What did you do all morning?"

"Today? I—I went to the park, shot basketball a little bit."

"All day? In the driving snow?"

"Not really, no."

"You worked on this shit, didn't you? I could see it in the way you came into my studio yesterday, like you were finally interested in something. Invested. I'm thinking, he wants to talk about art. I have a studio full of horse dicks, what could be more interesting than that? But no, that wasn't it."

"Sarah, you know I like your work."

"I'm not fishing for a compliment here."

"I know that."

"Although it probably wouldn't hurt to tell me you like my coat, you know."

"Wait. I did notice it."

She cut off his reply with a laugh. "I'm teasing you, Reddick. Let me finish. You know I have a little brother, right? Well, when he was a kid he tried everything—sports, music, all the usual hobbies. I had art, you know, so he thought he should have *something*. He was okay at all of it, but none of it really grabbed him, nothing stuck, and he just kind of shuffled around the house like Lurch or something. You know who Lurch is, right?"

"You're not that much older than me."

"Just checking. Anyway when he was about seventeen or eighteen he started playing that video game, what's it called, *Warcraft. World of Warcraft*. And it was like something just flipped on inside of him. He went to online forums and talked about the game, he had composition books jammed with notes about it, strategies and tactics and, god, I don't even know what all. And at first my parents and I, we're like, he's a good-looking kid, he has friends, why is he spending all his free time at a computer with people he would never know in real life? He would be online with a group of thirty strangers and be the only black kid, you know? It was just so eccentric, and we had never thought of him that way. But it changed him, having a passion. For the better. Gave him a drive and purpose that you could see in the way he carried himself, that grounded him. And in the end it didn't matter if we couldn't understand why he liked it, why he wanted to do it, because we were just happy to see him doing something, happy to see him more than half-awake."

Reddick absorbed this for half a block, then, "Finding out what happened to Hannah isn't a computer game."

"Are you going out of your way to misunderstand my point, here?"

"I think so, yeah." They both smiled and she winged him with her elbow. "Seriously, though," he continued, "if I didn't think this was important, that a life was at stake, I wouldn't be here right now. But I understand what you were trying to say. And thanks."

"You're welcome. This is it, by the way." They stopped in front of a brass-rimmed glass door. "Oh, one thing I forgot to mention yesterday, about Franky and Buckley. There were other rumors, too. That maybe Buckles wanted more out of that relationship than he was getting."

It took Reddick a second. "Are you saying Buckley is in the closet?"

"Not exactly, and if it was just that I wouldn't mention it. What I think—and the reason I'm bringing it up—is that he was crushing on his friend pretty hard, and Franky took advantage of it. Buckles brought out his cruel streak."

"What do you mean?"

"Just that Franky seemed to enjoy having that over his friend's head. He thrived on the one-sidedness of it, the power."

"Buckley really lets Franky walk all over him?"

"At least back then he did. Whether it actually was because he was infatuated with him, I couldn't say. But that was the rumor, and it makes as much sense as anything else."

They took the elevator up to the gallery. Heinrich was a blue-chip franchise with a split identity. One space in Chelsea aimed at the under-forty crowd, highlighting prospects and a handful of older artists who were pacing the trends, and another space here, in an Upper East Side high-rise, catering to safer taste. Contemporary artists inspired by Modernist abstraction, neofiguration. Photographers with one or two images you knew like your own hand.

They asked at the desk for Aliana, who emerged from a set of offices in the rear. She had brown hair and olive eyes, her face prep-school fresh and boyish. She looked familiar, from parties, maybe, or openings, but they had never been introduced. She and Sarah hugged, exchanged pleasantries, before Aliana turned to him.

"You must be Reddick," she said, extending a calloused hand. "Come on, let's get away from the desk and find someplace quiet."

The space was subdivided, maze-like—they went into a smaller gallery in the back. The walls were hung with garish nudes—prurience dressed up as social critique. Sarah wrinkled her nose.

"Looking at these paintings is like being yelled at by a very dull person," she said. Aliana and Reddick laughed. "You know? A shallow idea isn't improved by volume."

Aliana didn't seem to mind the criticism—she was obliged to hang the work, not like it. "There's a photography show in the front gallery I think you might like. We could relocate if you want?"

"You know what? I'll go myself. I'm sure Reddick would prefer to have you to himself anyway. Just come get me when you're done."

"I'm fine either way," he said, but she was already half-gone.

Aliana watched her leave. "It's great to see her. I know breakups suck, but I'm happy she has free time again."

"Breakups?"

"She didn't tell you? Her boyfriend—her ex, I guess—moved back home a couple weeks ago. He hated his job, couldn't get enough freelance writing gigs, was sick of paying his dizzying rent. He had barely been here a year. This town, man—it has a shell, and some people just bounce right off of it."

"I guess you're right." He thought of Gastonia, his old neighborhood—the mill houses cloaked in beaten siding, guarded by chain fences so worn they wobbled like nets. The way life there was reduced to work, getting it, keeping or losing it—status and hope measured in dollars an hour, in cents. Dreams were an indulgence of childhood, to be discarded before puberty. To chase them meant exile. "I don't think I could ever go home."

Aliana seemed to grasp the force behind his declaration, to share it. "I sometimes wonder, maybe some other city? It's not like it's either here or home, you know. There are other places, other progressive towns where I could be happy. But once you've been here awhile, leaving just feels like giving up. I'm too stubborn for that."

"You and me both," he said.

"Anyway, what is this about, again?"

He told her as much as he had told Sarah, in case they compared notes later, then flashed the photo. "Was this taken here?"

She glanced at it and answered immediately. "Oh yeah, totally. That's from the opening of our Richter drawing show in November. Buckley and Hannah."

"Do you know them?"

"Well, Buckley is a Seward. So yeah. His mother knows Jan—Jan Heinrich, the owner—from way back. Jan's father helped Mrs. Seward build part of the family's collection. They don't buy from us a ton, we aren't really in their wheelhouse, but they are around a lot. Jan gives them advice. Sometimes they cut him a check for it. Hannah is missing?"

He hadn't expected her to know the Sewards firsthand. He had to be careful. "It looks that way. But listen, can you not mention that I was here? The company I work for does a lot of business with them."

"Of course, yeah. They're my boss's friends, not mine. If you're cool with Sarah you're cool with me."

"Can you tell me anything about Hannah and Buckley's relationship? Were they jealous, argumentative, anything like that?"

"I didn't spend a ton of time with them or anything. So I'm not the best source for that kind of information? But at our events they seemed great. She was kind of standoffish. But as a couple totally normal."

"Standoffish how?"

"I don't deal with the clients, generally. I make sure the shows get hung, the art gets in and out the door safely, you know, that the gallery functions in the literal—I mean the physical—sense. But I've been here awhile now, so we do have a few clients that I know well, and they're all megarich. Maybe not Seward rich, but still. And their attitudes run the gamut, you know, from being comfortable with the difference between us to being not-so-comfortable."

"And Hannah wasn't comfortable."

"Exactly. She was one of those people who seem to feel like they should maintain some kind of distance, like they have to prove themselves. It's a tough type to work with—it's easier to deal with someone who is certain that they're better than you than it is to deal with someone who feels like they ought to be, but has some doubts. Hannah was a doubter. She could only be so friendly, or else we might find out that she was really one of us, and not one of them. When someone is acting like a jerk it's usually just because they're insecure, you know? So Hannah was like that."

"She seemed fake?"

"Fake is too negative, like she was just shallow. I would say more…like she was acting. Which, considering that family, is understandable. I'm not sure many people are prepared for that life."

"And it was that obvious?"

"When she was in here it was. They aren't perfect, and I'm no great fan of the point-one percent—except that my job basically depends upon them—but one thing they are not is insecure about their status."

"I don't suppose you have any idea how they met?" Reddick asked.

She laughed. "No way. Like I said, it's not like I really know them."

"Yeah. So you wouldn't know what she did for work, then."

"No clue. But I wouldn't be surprised if her only job was Buckley."

"What do you mean? That she was with him for his money?"

"I couldn't say. But just imagine if you were marrying into a family like that. You'd have to love your job to want to keep it." She glanced around the gallery, as if wondering whether her own career would have been worth holding on to. "Anyway. When was she was in your building, again?"

"Sunday night."

"Okay. Because the last time I saw her was maybe…three weeks ago? Just after New Year's, at a holiday gala thrown by another dealer. Jan had a plus-one and took me. Sounds crazy, I know, but that old queen loves me, and everyone else has a family they'd rather spend time with. Anyway I was there, dress and makeup and the whole femme deal, but still feeling really out of place because it was mostly people like the Sewards. Big art world money. And Buckley got into this huge fight with some guy that night."

"Really?"

"It was a formal party, so the whole thing was very hushed and furtive. But Buckley looked pissed. Face was red. I gathered the guy was a friend of his, too."

Reddick did a quick image search of Franky Dutton and showed her the results. "Was this the guy?"

"Yep. Definitely."

"Do you know what they argued about?"

"No idea. But that guy left early. It seemed pretty serious."

"And everyone saw this?"

"I wouldn't say everyone. But a few people, yeah."

"Okay." He extended his hand. "I won't take up any more of your time."

She shook it, but waved away his concern. "It's no big deal. Sarah is one of my all-time favorite people and I'm happy to do her a solid. Plus it's a slow couple of weeks right now before we start ramping up for spring, so I could use the diversion."

He thanked her again and they walked back to the reception desk. Sarah was chatting with the assistant who sat behind it.

"Well," she said when they entered, "did you two crack thc case?"

Reddick felt himself blush. "She was helpful, yeah. Thanks for bringing me here."

"You owe me one, now."

"That sounds ominous," Aliana said.

"Oh he won't like it one bit." She turned back to Reddick. "I'm going to make you come by my studio and talk about art with me. There's still a painter in there somewhere, and I'm going to find him."

He hugged her goodbye, shook Aliana's hand again and left.

He went home and transferred his notes to the map. It had become a nest of names and arrows and notations, his first sketched intuitions reinforced with facts. He made food and brought it back into his room, trying to see what connected the kid at Clean City to the liquor store woman, to Buckley and Franky. He sat with it for half an hour. There was something there.

He changed his clothes and went to the Y.

There was a game beginning to take shape, all familiar faces, familiar teammates and opponents. He slapped five and bumped shoulders. No Derek. He texted him and he replied that he was out for the night, on a date. With a girl, he said, you should try it sometime. They're just like guys but they smell better. Reddick replied with a string of emojis, friendly and noncommittal, his brief afternoon with Sarah lingering.

He played well but his team lost narrowly, a good-natured defeat that didn't contaminate anyone's cheery mood. He hung around afterward, chatting and tossing half-hearted shots—the Knicks and the Nets and their dismal playoff chances, Steph and LeBron, gym gossip, girls. Momentum began to build for another game. Reddick left before anyone began to count on his presence.

He went downstairs and into the weight room; Clint was standing in a circle of other lifters near the bench. Reddick lingered nearby.

"You need me?" Clint asked.

Reddick nodded.

"Alright, hold up a minute." The cop lay down and unracked the bar with a groan. A couple of guys offered sharp encouragement. He lowered the weight to his chest, shadowed by his spotters, and pressed it violently. The crew began to change the weights while Clint stood up and walked over to Reddick.

"Damn, that's impressive."

"I'm coming back from shoulder surgery last year. I'm not where I used to be."

"How much was that?"

"Four twenty-five." He was breathing heavily. "This is about what I think it's about, right?"

Reddick nodded.

"So if you're here, that means you have evidence that a crime has been committed. Evidence." He repeated the word, emphasizing each syllable.

Reddick thought of Hannah's apartment, her closet full of clothes. There was no way to tell the cop what he saw without admitting that he broke in. "Not yet, no. But I need your help."

Clint looked up at the ceiling, exasperated, and walked out of the weight room. Reddick followed.

"Look, I wouldn't be here if I wasn't onto something, alright?" The cop ignored him, went to the water fountain and drank. Reddick waited behind him. When Clint finished he turned around.

"Oh, you're still here? We're done."

"I just need one favor."

"I listened to you the other day. That was your one favor."

"Two favors, then."

"I already told you what you needed to do. If you don't have evidence I can't help you."

"I have a suspect. I don't have evidence yet but I do have a specific person that I am looking at and I know things about him. Things that seem very sketchy. I might have a motive."

"That's not enough."

"I want a background check."

"Didn't I teach you how to use the internet the last time you were in here?"

"I need more than what I can do. I searched the sex offender list. He's not on it. There are these pay sites but I don't know which ones to trust, or if they could even tell me what I need to know. I need a real criminal background check. I went to the State website. I'm not allowed to make a request. I need you for that."

"Do you know why you can't request it? Because you're invading that man's privacy. And you want me to help you."

"I know this guy is shitty, alright? That's not even a question. What I need to know is if that shitty behavior ever crossed the line into something more. Has he ever hurt anyone? Is he a threat? If he's a threat we want him off the streets, right?"

"You said 'the streets.' Oh lord, he just said 'the streets.'"

"Look, he's just some shitbag developer building ugly condos in Brooklyn. He's what's wrong with this neighborhood. He isn't worth protecting."

"Because you don't like what he does, that entitles you to invade his privacy?"

"I don't need to see it. You want to protect this guy's privacy? Fine."

"So you're giving in? I can go? I got a drop set to do."

"*You* look it up. *You* look it over. If it's blank, tell me. But if it isn't, if there is anything violent, specifically violence against women—let me know. You don't have to tell me what it is—keep the details to yourself. Just let me know if this guy has a history. He's got rumors; I need to know if he's got the record to match. I'm looking for confirmation."

For the first time Clint didn't respond, just eyeballed his face, considering.

"Please. I'm looking for help. Just help."

"I'm not doing this out of some bullshit solidarity against The Man, you hear me?"

Reddick nodded.

"The Man signs my paycheck. I work on a task force trying to get drugs out of neighborhoods. That's a real problem. It's drugs and fucking gangs that destroy neighborhoods. Not your landlord. Understand? I fight real problems that hurt real people."

Reddick nodded again.

"Alright. Give me his damn name."

He stopped in the lobby to swap his sneakers for boots. He texted Derek that Clint was going to help, and thanked him for the introduction. While he waited for a reply, Sensei came in, carrying his winter gear. He set his bundle on the seat next to Reddick and began to zip himself in.

"Clinton gonna help you out?"

Reddick nodded. "I think so. Hope I didn't interrupt you guys."

Sensei shrugged. "You heard about Restoration Heights? They're shut down for the winter."

"Yeah. I walked by a few days ago. Boarded up tight."

"We got to take our victories the way we can. I haven't seen you at any rallies lately."

"I've been busy. Work. You know."

"Yeah. Clint told me what you want him to do. You really think this developer took this girl, or are you just lashing out because you don't like what he represents?'

Reddick smiled. "Can't it be both?"

"Usually not."

"He doesn't belong here."

"You don't think so? To a lot of people you probably don't look much different."

"I know how I look. But I moved here instead of Williamsburg or Bushwick because I'm comfortable here."

"How long ago was that?'

"I've been in my building for eight years."

"That's what I'm saying. You were a young man when you moved here, like all these young people you see out there now. And maybe you don't want developers like the one you're after doing their thing down here, but you helped him. Just by being here, with all your friends."

"Derek is my friend and he grew up here."

"Right. What about your other friends, though? At that rally, who did I see you with?"

"My roommate."

"Blond hair. Dresses sharp. That's who developers are looking for. That's who they follow. So by being here you helped it happen. You're already in the negative. You have to actively oppose the situation if you want to get back to zero. Just to be even."

"I wasn't trying to help it happen. That's not why I moved here."

"What you were trying to do isn't important. It's about the effects."

"Fine. But I am opposing it."

"And yet I haven't seen you at a rally in a while. It isn't enough to oppose something in your mind."

"I do what I can. I want to keep things from changing."

"From changing? Look around. How many condos have gone up in the eight years you been here? How many new restaurants and bars have opened? And how many of the old ones have closed? What kind of people do you see on the sidewalks? It's not that shit is changing. Shit has done changed. It already happened."

"But I still love it here. I mean, I complain about the hipsters, and yeah, I know I probably look like one of them to a lot people. But I know the truth about myself, and I know I'm happy here. I like these courts. I like my friends. I like the people I've met. I feel welcome here, in a way I don't in other places. It reminds me of home. Maybe that's specific to me in a way that doesn't translate well to other people, or that isn't easy to explain. But that's why I opposed Restoration Heights. It threatens all of that for me."

"Except it's not about you. You're missing my point. Places evolve. Change is always going to happen. You can't preserve a time, a place, like it's something you can just buy and put on a shelf and look at to make you feel happy. To love a place you got to grow *with* that place. You have to let it move through time with you. We're not fighting Restoration Heights because we want to preserve a moment. That's just another kind of conservatism, another kind of looking backward, and we can't look backward, there is too much ugliness in our history. Too much despair. We're fighting because we want to control our own change. We want to *direct* it. That is how you take a place away from a community. It's not new folks moving in, it's not building certain kinds of buildings. You take a place away from a people by not letting them have a say in the direction it is moving toward. Look at Derek."

"What about him?"

"He knows how money works. He could get the right people together and they could buy that run-down building on the corner out there, and put up another gray condo just like all the other gray condos. And I might not like it. But I would let him do it. You know why?"

Reddick thought before he answered. "His mother?"

"Exactly. See, you do understand. He was raised here. This community belongs to him, and he is entitled to have a say in the direction it goes, even if I disagree with him. He grew up here, he earned that right. All of us did. Now take someone like you. Who comes in, and likes it, and feels at home—I welcome you as an ally. But it isn't your place to lead. You just help us. Support us. You haven't earned the right to point our direction out for us. And that's not a black and a white thing. It's community."

Reddick recoiled at this—he wasn't trying to lead. He just saw something being threatened, something that had welcomed him, and wanted to preserve it.

Clint came into the lobby and caught the last few sentences. "See, that's what happens," he said. "Come in here looking for my help and you end up with a lecture."

"It's not a lecture," Sensei said. "I'm just giving him a little guidance."

Clint's coat was on and his hood was up. "Enough already. Come on before I start sweating."

Reddick watched them leave.

NINE

Hannah was sleeping with Franky and Buckley knew it. They were at the party together—Buckley's refusal to acknowledge that she was in Brooklyn was just cover for his jealous certainty that she was there with his best friend. He knew about Franky's business ties in the borough, maybe about the townhouse nearby, and Franky's habit of taking dates to his properties. The affair had been going on for a while, at least since the new year, because that's when Buckley confronted Franky about it—the blowout Aliana witnessed. This scenario pointed hard at Buckley as a suspect—a spoiled heir lashing out in frustrated rage. Except that his personality didn't fit. The contrast between his lordly voice and gracious, almost timid demeanor made him surprisingly sympathetic. He seemed burdened by his privilege, not entitled; worn down by its persistent demands.

But he wasn't being straight about Hannah's disappearance. So he couldn't be counted out.

On the other side was Franky. His motive was less obvious but his character seemed to fit. A guy whose easy way with women masked his hatred of them—fear, maybe, that the affection they gave so freely, that he depended on for his self-worth, might disappear—a hatred revealed by his habitual sadism. Maybe she tried to call it off and he lost it, imploding from the pressure of her rejection. Or maybe one of his games just went too far.

Reddick was making character judgments about people whose character he was in no position to judge. One of whom he hadn't met. He had to stick with what he knew.

Franky was with her the night she disappeared. So were Ju'waun and Tyler.

Someone didn't like Harold asking questions.

Hannah's presence in Bed-Stuy had rattled Buckley.

Who was that woman in Cask scared of? Gene, Eugene—had he heard the name right?

If Hannah had been killed, where was the body?

Reddick stared at the case map on his wall. After a few minutes he gave up, glanced at the clock. It was almost eleven. He texted the Lelands' house manager and two minutes later his phone rang.

"Do you have information about Ms. Granger?" Thomas asked.

"What I have is a sketch." Reddick glanced at the map. "I'm still trying to fill it in."

"And what do you need from me?"

"First I want to know about her family. Why aren't they involved?"

"They're on the West Coast. Oregon."

"Do you know their names? Have you tracked them down?"

"We had no plans to do anything, other than hire you."

"I thought your boss said she wanted to help."

"We will help by providing you with whatever you need, within reason."

"Then can you find out about her family? Also how she and Buckley met? It seems like she wasn't used to the rarefied air you breathe."

"I will find out what I can."

"Okay. There's something else, too." He gave him a quick outline of what he'd learned. "I need to know more about Franky Dutton."

"Whom you believe Hannah was cheating on Buckley with."

"Yeah. They were old school friends who stayed close. But it seems like they had a falling-out a few weeks ago. At a holiday party attended by your sort of people. I think Hannah might have been the source of this argument."

"You suspect an affair?"

"Yep. Maybe that was the night he found out, and then whatever happened last Sunday was the tipping point."

"And Buckley lost his mind to jealousy and murdered her?"

"Not necessarily. When he heard my story he must have immediately connected the neighborhood to Franky—that's why he reacted the way he did. He was ashamed, maybe even afraid that Franky had hurt her. I'm thinking—what if he had confronted Hannah to try and convince her to stay? After that argument, I mean. Say he finds out about their affair, argues with Franky about it, then gives Hannah an ultimatum: him or me. If the wealth and lifestyle were that new to her, she would probably have stayed—who would give all that up for a piece on the side? But when she goes to break it off with Franky he reacts badly. Just snaps and kills her." He stopped to take a break, to mull it over. "Another possibility is that none of that is true—Franky had a masochistic streak and maybe he finally took it too far. Whatever the details,

I'm still leaning Franky—it's just too hard to imagine Buckley hurting somebody."

"And you think this occurred near your building, where you saw her?"

"Franky's company is remodeling a townhouse nearby. I need to check it out, but it would make for a convenient party spot. Apparently he likes to keep a place to show off to the girls he meets. And it's right across from an enormous construction site, for this new development, Restoration Heights."

"Why does that matter?"

"Construction is shut down for the winter. It would have been a great place to hide her body."

"Somewhere so close?"

"Why risk going farther away? And it might explain some of the other things I've found."

"Like what?"

Reddick hesitated. Maybe Tyler and Ju'waun were dodging Reddick's attempts at reaching out because they were afraid that blame could be shifted to them. Harold called it—a white girl from Manhattan going missing after a night out with two black men in Brooklyn was a scenario that would scrape up the worst dregs of white racial anxiety, that was fodder for the American media machine. The truth would cease to matter; it would vanish in a pit of endless takes as everyone argued about the same failed systems and cycles, the same corroded institutions. The case of two black men railroaded by the cops because a white girl went missing, and all that it says about the country. Devolving into generalizations as one injustice swallowed another, as Hannah disappeared.

But the reaction, the fear it triggered in Harold when he asked about them—that had to mean something.

"There are these two guys she was with the night she disappeared. I think they might be connected somehow." He told him about following Tyler, about the envelopes, and about the pushback Harold received when he asked about their connection to Hannah.

"There's a couple of ways to fit them in," he said. "The easy one is that Tyler's day job has nothing to do with this—he and Ju'waun are just witnesses, and they're worried about being blamed for something they didn't do."

"What's the other way?"

"They or whomever they work for is involved. I don't have any evidence that Franky is crooked, but he would hardly be the first developer to have those kinds of ties. Maybe he's given an envelope or two to Tyler in his time. So—however it went down in that townhouse, now Franky is there with her body, and he needs help. Who is he going to reach out to? Someone close, someone he knows already operates outside of the law."

"You seem convinced that she's dead."

"I don't want it to be true, but at this point—what else? The Sewards haven't heard from her, right?"

"Not to my knowledge."

"So she's just disappeared, and it's not like Franky or Buckley would have any reason to kidnap her. I want you to try and verify if it was really Hannah they were fighting about at the holiday party. I'm sure one of your friends heard something. Do that and find out if anyone knows her family."

"Mrs. Leland may be able to help. I will speak with her and be back in touch tomorrow."

"Perfect. Thanks, Thomas."

He had the cop looking up his record and Thomas getting the society scoop—he needed to meet him. He had to see Franky's face, to read its possibilities.

The next morning he found the address for Franky Dutton Properties, ate breakfast and caught a G up to Williamsburg. Metropolitan Avenue was lively in spite of the desolate weather. The neighborhood's edgy core was years gone but a vibrant fringe clung to its affluent base. Winter shells that were varied and flamboyant, dyed wool and fleece, colorful boots and playful knit hats with poofballs or teddy bear ears. A man in a shin-length wool cape. Reddick threaded his way through them, west underneath the highway, then south on Havermeyer, then west again on S 2nd, to a six-floor concrete office high-rise, an eyesore between two redbrick apartment buildings. He went inside, told the doorman he was going to FDP and was directed to a pair of steel-and-glass elevators in the back. Fifth floor.

There were glass doors across from the elevator, a boxy waiting area inside them and a large reception desk, helmed by a young man with elaborate hair. His teeth were precise as Swiss machinery, so white they stole your attention when he smiled.

"Hello. Can I help you?"

Reddick told him he was there to see Franky Dutton, that he didn't have an appointment. That it was about Hannah Granger. Tell him that. The assistant disappeared and returned.

"If you could just have a seat, he is tied up at the moment but he will try and speak with you soon."

Reddick unzipped his coat and sat on the black leather bench that sprouted from a wall in the waiting area. Ten minutes turned to twenty turned to half an hour. He rose and approached the assistant.

"Is he coming soon?"

The assistant looked at him with surprise, like he was the return of a problem that had already been solved. "He knows you're waiting." Deliberately, as to a child. "He will let me know as soon as he has time."

Reddick took off his coat and hat and thumbed through his case notes to salve his impatience. Another fifteen minutes passed.

The office was an open floor plan, neat clusters of desks split by wide walkways and looming houseplants. One wall was all windows, looking out to the roof of the adjacent apartment building; the rest were red brick, aged to recall downtown chic. Framed prints of past work—sleek, bland building facades. Opposite the windows was a pair of doors, each presumably leading to a private office. The restrooms were in the back. Reddick looked for Franky. He had to be in one of the two offices—he could find him if he got past the assistant. He stood up, hung his coat on a rack by the door and approached the desk for a third time.

"Sorry to bother you again. Do you mind if I use the restroom?"

The assistant directed him toward the back, his smile not quite covering his impatience. Reddick scoped the offices on his way, looking for an indication of which one was Franky's. He didn't see a name on either door, didn't see a face. He turned away to avoid drawing suspicion.

On his other side, through the towering windows, three men shoveled snow from the adjacent roof. They had dug a path across the surface and were working out, radially, their brown noses and cheeks exposed in the clefts of their deep hoods. The heights of the roof and FDP's floor were misaligned and their faces bobbed at the waists of the seated staff. Neither side acknowledged the other.

He went into the bathroom—more corporate gloss. A long stretch of mirror over a stone counter; swan-like, elliptical faucets. Stalls that went from floor to ceiling. Four urinals split by chest-high dividers—all of it gleaming. He realized he should use one of the urinals while he was here. He unzipped, felt the heat of his body release from the layers of winter fabric and tried to work out how to make a play at the office. He heard the door open behind him.

The newcomer left two urinals between them. Reddick glanced at his face. It was Franky. He had one hand on his dick and the other on his phone, reading—Reddick tried to narrow his flow, to drag it out and get the timing right. He still finished ahead of him and made his way slowly to the sink, washed methodically. After a minute Franky joined him, put his phone on the counter and his hands under the faucet. They made eye contact in the mirror, nodded and smiled. His hair was thinner than the images Reddick had found online, his body twenty or thirty pounds heavier, but he was still striking, perhaps more so, his boyish good looks buttressed by the gravitas of manhood. Deeply tanned, blue-eyed and dark-haired, with a wide smile and thin lips. At least two inches taller than Reddick. The hand dryer was between the sink and the door—Reddick got to it while Franky was still rinsing.

"Franky Dutton, right?"

His smile was all smarm. "None other. Who are you working with today?"

"I'm not here as a client."

"Oh?" His face signaled a confusion that didn't seem to touch him, like there were responses—empathy, concern—that had been delegated to his body, to rote action. He took his dripping hands from the sink and nodded at the dryer. Reddick stepped out of his way; the two switched places so that Franky had his back to the door.

"Hannah Granger."

Franky didn't react.

"Buckley Seward's fiancée."

"I know who she is."

"You know she's missing."

"The question here is, how do *you* know she is missing? This is a private matter."

"This is a person's life. It's not some affair that doesn't involve anyone else." Reddick's voice pinched. He watched to see if *affair* stung. Franky remained composed.

"Who are you, exactly?" Hands dry, he folded his arms and leaned back against the door, lethargic with confidence. "What are you doing in my office—my bathroom—grilling me about my friend's girlfriend?"

Reddick reeled himself in. He couldn't repeat the mistake he made in Cask, couldn't push too hard. He had to back up, to change course. He forced a smile.

"You're right—this is awkward. I wasn't trying to come after you. I just came back to use the restroom while I waited."

"This isn't a well-timed ambush?"

"I'm a friend of Hannah's. I'm worried about her."

"Well, I'd love to help you. But I'm not sure why you came to see me. I didn't know her that well. You should really speak with the Sewards."

"What about her family? Has anyone contacted them?"

"Yeah, of course. Both families are working together with a private investigator. Look, it isn't like the police aren't *involved*."

"There's no missing person report."

"You have to understand, for a man like Buckley—this is tabloid fodder. They want to keep it quiet."

"What happens when keeping it quiet gets in the way of finding her?"

Franky reached his arm out, performed sympathy. "That

isn't going to happen. Buckley cares about her. He will do everything he can."

"Except listen to me."

"How did you say you knew her?"

"I'm a friend of hers. We met at a party in Bed-Stuy."

"Bed-Stuy? Really?"

"Near Restoration Heights." He kept his voice even, worked to disguise every jab as mere fact. "You were over there a few nights ago, right? Some friends of mine saw you and Hannah at a party Sunday night."

"I didn't see Hannah Sunday night."

"Really? My friends definitely saw you."

"Look, I'll be straight with you. I go to parties. I bring dates. And, you know, it's not always the same girl." He threw Reddick a look intended to draw him into a philanderer's conspiracy, a we're-both-men-here smile. "So yeah, I was at a party on Sunday. Also a couple of bars. And maybe the girl I was with looked a little like Hannah. I'm not saying a blonde is a blonde, but, you know, somebody else wasn't paying close enough attention."

"You're sure?"

"Of course. It was the night before she went missing. I'm certain."

"So when was the last time you saw her, then?"

"I don't know. I had drinks with them sometime last week."

"With Buckley and Hannah."

"Yes."

"When was the last time you saw her without Buckley?"

"I'm not sure that I ever have." He backed toward the door, half-bored, looking to wind the conversation down.

"Do you want to talk about this in your office?"

"I think we're just about through."

"I'm not judging you. Hannah was—is—attractive. You're

around her a lot, you got to know her and you couldn't help yourself. You and Buckley want to keep it quiet but the truth could help find her."

"What truth? What are you talking about?"

"I know you were seeing each other. I know he knows."

"I listened to you, I answered your questions, and in return you throw unfounded accusations at me. It's time for you to go."

"I know you and Buckley got in a fight at a holiday party, three weeks ago. It was because he found out."

He looked confused—maybe the first emotion that really seemed to reach him.

"Three weeks… How did…? This is disturbing, do you realize that? You're invading my privacy."

"Tell me the truth and we can find out what happened to her."

"The *truth* is that if I see you in here again, or find out you're still prying into my private life, I will call the police. Got it?" He turned and left; the dampers guided the door gently shut behind him, undercut the force of his exit.

Reddick didn't follow. He wasn't sure what he had accomplished, if any of his shots landed. There was a layer of calculation beneath Franky's charm, but he had no sense of its reach, of how large a secret it could hide. He turned to the sink to splash water on his face.

Franky's phone lay beside the faucet.

Without thinking he scooped it up, brought up the password screen. Six digits. He tried Franky's name, then Hannah's, in numeric form. Neither worked. The door opened and he slipped the phone into his back pocket.

It was the assistant. "You have to leave. Now."

Reddick kept his face blank. "I was on my way out."

The assistant propped the door open, his cheeks flushed,

either with anger or the residual heat of a reprimand. He followed Reddick to the front door, stood guard near the coatrack. Reddick waited for him to notice the phone—ordinary, a common model—protruding from his pocket. His own phone was in his coat. He put it on and walked out, expecting to be stopped at the entrance, in the elevator, as he passed the guard in the lobby. He made it outside, turned around at the sidewalk, waited.

No one came out. He crossed the street.

Just look at it and give it back. It isn't stealing if you don't keep it.

At the end of the block he found a low stoop that had been shoveled clean. He sat on the cold cement and took off his gloves. The image on the lock screen was of Franky, years ago, his hair thick, reclining on a boat, his arm strung along the back of a shining white bench. There were taut ropes suspended behind him, and behind that a wide, dark river. He tried another password—the address here, at FDP—the street numbers plus the suite. Nothing. He was reaching too widely; he needed to narrow his focus. He took his own phone out, searched Franky, dug through profiles on social media for hints. On one of them he found his birthday, his high school, his hometown. Details bare to the public, almost indecent. He punched the birthday into the phone, month and day and year. He tried it again, the order reversed. Who else. Did Franky care enough about Hannah to bring her into his life this way, to incorporate some fringe of her into habit? It was doubtful. He looked her up anyway, the same sites he had found Franky on—aggregates of young professionals or collections of distant, attenuated friendships, outlets for mouthy snark. He had tried this with her already, but maybe he missed something the first time. She had one profile, set to private, on one site. A single square photograph available to the public. He brought his pinched fingers to the screen, magnified it. She was looking straight at the camera, skin orange in the bar light, a thicket of blurred bodies behind her. He saw a whole history on her face, a line of successes. Grades, friends, sports, clubs, a private university that you've heard of but can't quite place, New York, an internship, bars, a salary, more bars. Progressive opinions. You pass girls like this every day in this city, by the dozen. The question is why you care about this one.

He put the year Franky graduated college in the phone.

The screen froze, warned him that he was locked out for one minute. He waited until it was active again and entered a variation on the same date. Another warning, five minutes this time. Again, high school graduation—ten minutes, and an alert that once more would lock it permanently. He laid it gently on the step beside him, picked up his own, found a contact and called.

"Derek."

"Am I your mother?"

"What? No."

"Because you call your mother. Your friends you text."

"It's important." He told him what he had done.

"Where are you right now?" Derek's teasing lilt was gone; his voice sounded urgent.

"I'm a block away from his office," Reddick answered. "On a stoop."

"You have to get the phone back."

"I know. I just—I want to know what's inside it. There must be messages, coordinating times. Maybe, I don't know, photos."

"Two things. One, if Franky killed her there is *no way* he left messages or photos or anything like that on his phone. Two, even if he is the world's dumbest criminal and somehow didn't at least try to erase all the evidence, you cannot break into his phone. It can't be done. The goddamned FBI couldn't do it."

"I thought they did, eventually."

"Christ, Reddick, it doesn't matter. *You* can't do it. You have to give it back."

"I've got one chance left. If I could just think of his password."

"What happens when you fail? He sees that his phone is locked and he will know someone tried to break into it. You don't think he'll put it together with your visit? He'll call the police, he'll have you fired or worse."

"I've got it in my hand."

"It might as well be on the moon."

Reddick groaned, blew steam into the air above his face. "I'll take it back."

"Good."

"You're right. He's probably erased anything that would link the two of them."

"Be slick about it. You can't just walk in there and hand it to the front desk."

Reddick hung up and walked back to the building. He nodded at the doorman on his way to the elevator, rode to the fifth floor. The assistant stood up.

"I was perfectly clear with you that you cannot be in here. I will call security."

No mention of the phone. Reddick raised his hands. "I know, I know. But I left my phone in the restroom." He started walking toward it.

The assistant sprang from behind his desk and blocked his path. "Your phone?"

"Yeah. I'll just go back and grab it and you'll never see me again. Okay?"

"I cannot let you do that."

"Look, I'm sorry but I just need my phone."

"What does it look like?"

"I'm sorry?"

"What does your phone look like?"

"It's black. It has a screen. You know, it looks like a phone."

"Wait here. I'll get it." He took two steps then stopped, pivoted. "If you make a dash for Mr. Dutton's offices while I'm gone, I will call the police. Do you understand?"

"I just want my phone."

Reddick watched him march toward the restrooms. He risked a quick glance at the offices, both doors still shut. Once the assistant was in the men's room he placed Franky's phone on the reception desk, near a stack of paperwork. He checked that no one was watching. He placed his own on the floor, beneath the coatrack. After a few short minutes the assistant returned, shaking his head in frustration.

"There is no phone in the bathroom. It's time for you to leave."

"Man, I'm telling you I don't have it."

"Well, it's not in either restroom."

He nodded at Franky's phone, on the desk. "It looks like that."

The assistant picked it up, tapped the screen. "This isn't yours. I'm not sure why he left it out *here*, but it isn't yours so you don't need to worry about it."

"Well, fuck, man, are you telling me I lost my phone?"

"Your phone is not my problem. *You* are my problem."

"Fuuuckk." Reddick walked a lap, inspected the bench where he sat, looked underneath it.

"Sir, is that it?"

Reddick looked up. "Where?"

"There," the assistant pointed, his irritation overwhelming. "Under the coatrack."

"Damn." Reddick walked over, picked it up. "That's it."

"Now will you please leave? Or do I need to call the police?"

"I upset him that much, huh?"

"Go."

"Alright, alright. Like I said. You'll never see me again."

He exhaled in the elevator, alone. He had gained nothing but lost nothing. When the door rolled open he avoided the eyes of the doorman. He yanked his hood up and walked out, hurried past a black sedan that was pulling to a stop in front of the building. He heard doors open behind him. Ducking his head, he cut between two parked cars, crossed the street and risked a look back. Buckley Seward climbed out of the rear of the sedan, the driver holding his door. He appeared regally untouched by the cold, in a black wool coat, a scarf with no hat. He didn't look to either side as he strode into the building. The driver returned to the wheel and Reddick stepped aside to watch the car roll past, the milky exhaust bleeding into the morning's wet air.

TEN

He had provoked Franky into calling him. He wouldn't accept it as a coincidence. The timing was too perfect—by the time Reddick had given up trying to break into the phone and managed to return it, an hour had passed, plenty of time for Buckley to drive out if he had been summoned right away. Something he said to Franky had landed, made him nervous—that he called Buckley, that his friend responded by coming in person, could only mean one thing: they were in it together.

Because why respond by closing ranks unless they had something to hide? It wasn't a case of which one, but of both. Buckley's distress the morning after she disappeared was a performance. Maybe Buckley caught them together, lost it, killed her and convinced his friend that his only route to forgiveness was accessory after the fact. But the friendship Sarah described went mostly one-way—could Franky have killed her, used his hold on Buckley to convince the man to keep quiet about the death of his own fiancée? No, it was impossible. It went down like this:

Buckley has been jealous at least since the gala, but it doesn't stop Hannah and Franky from seeing each other. Maybe they deny it. So Buckley wants proof, has her followed—no—does it himself. After the party last Sunday they need a place to go—she's drunk, he is too, they can't stomach a cab ride so they walk to the townhouse. Maybe they've used it before. Buckley follows and catches them in the act. The ribald shock of it, his soon-to-be wife straddling his old friend—he isn't sure if he wants to be Franky, beneath her, or Hannah, on top of him, but his mind locks up, a spiral of rage, emotions so powerful that they override his timid decency. He kills her. He blames Franky but he doesn't kill him, too—he's betrayed on both sides but he can't lose them both. Instead he convinces him to help. Reddick imagines Buckley's voice, booming like a Shakespearean lead, you betrayed me, you owe me. The flow of power between them shifting, suddenly fluid—Franky weakened by his complicity. We have to get rid of her. *What do we do?* We take her to the construction site, across the street. We take her to Restoration Heights.

He took the train back to Bed-Stuy, walked to the row of brownstones across from the stalled project. There were no signs protesting the development here—the tenants had acquiesced long ago, swallowed objections and strapped their fate to the project. They would drown or soar with it. FDP's townhouse was ringed with a green plywood fence, half as tall as the one across the street, and flimsy. A padlocked chain wrapped the gate. He leaned against the door—there was a foot and a half of give in the chain, whoever used it last was careless. He checked to see if anyone was watching and squeezed inside.

The renovation hadn't touched the exterior. The stoop leaned to one side and brown paint was chipping off the handrail; the door was frail and weathered and several windows were boarded. But the building's heart was intact, the brown bricks sturdy and indomitable. The neighborhood was spotted with houses like this, gutted shells being remade from the inside out. It was a dream project, the allure consistent across decades, for Southern blacks and West Indians in the mid-twentieth century and for white artists and young professionals in the new millennium. Take these strong bones and make them your own, hang your life upon them. This consistency made it easy to market, a symbol so clear that it sold itself. It was an easy repository for hope, the enduring walls thick enough to shelter you from the consequences of your ambition.

Reddick tried the door. It was locked. His head and shoulders were above the line of the fence, visible from the opposite sidewalk or neighboring stoops. He turned and looked for witnesses—the streets were empty, everyone chased indoors by the drudgery of winter. All the first-floor windows were boarded over from the inside, sealed by sheets of blue Tyvek taped around the exterior lining. Getting in would ask more of him than slipping through Hannah's unlocked window, a depth of commitment that would be harder to walk back—but each offense made the next easier. He climbed across the banister and balanced on the edge of the stoop, gripped the rail with one hand and reached to the window with the other. He peeled the plastic back and tested the wood with his fist. There was give at the top—more haphazard work. FDP should have hired better people. He loosened the Tyvek further, to give himself room, and hammered the board repeatedly. A car rolled past and he ducked. He resumed hammering and once there was a gap in the seam he slid his hand in, grabbed and shook, pushing violently. The particleboard howled as the nails slid loose. He clambered onto the sill and slipped inside.

It was dark, the afternoon sun too feeble to follow him into the building. He propped the wood back into place over the window, took out his phone and turned on the flashlight, traced the room with its pallid beam. He was in an open foyer, with a high ceiling and faded floors. A thin layer of ochre dust coated the hardwoods and the windowsills. Construction materials were piled into one corner; a few stray ends of wood, a canvas tarp, two bags of plaster; Reddick tried not to dwell on their morbid potential. He walked into the adjacent room—there was no sound but his footsteps, the dry rustle of his coat. The bottom floor was a single apartment, separated from the stairs by an unpainted wood door. He ran his flashlight across the threshold. The hinges shone like jewels. In the hallway paper cups and bits of trash lay scattered in the dust. There were no appliances in the kitchen, no doors beneath the counters; the knotted bowels of plumbing and gas lines were exposed. He opened the faucet; it wheezed and spat and settled into a smooth flow. He twisted it shut, went into the bathroom. There were two rolls of toilet paper on the floor, one half gone, a bulb in the fixture. He found the switch, flashed it on and off.

Upstairs the floors were finished, the nicked hardwood encased in varnish. The walls were painted in tertiary colors, pale umber and plum. Every surface clean. It was easy to imagine taking someone here, easy to imagine them impressed. But there was no furniture, no place to sit or lie down. The kitchen had no appliances and the bathroom had no mirror. It was warmer than the street but not by much; he could see the soft wisps of his breath in the dark.

He went up to the third floor. It was in the same state

as the second, renovated and empty. He circled toward the front, toward a small room. The door was open, the windows visible from the hallway and through them, across the street, the ragged white plain of the unfinished site. He went inside. When the development was finished the view might be lovely—if the green space came together as promised, the park and the benches and the playground. If you could accept the towering condos as a kind of triumph. But for now it was snow and churned earth, unfinished structures sheathed in plastic, bordered by nests of rebar, metal beams, orange netting and indiscernible components.

He was afraid the flashlight might alert someone on the street; he switched it off and put his phone away. The sun was nearly gone but ambient light leaked in through the windows, refracted and pale as morning. It was the only room with furniture—a sofa, three Eames-like plastic chairs around it. On a table was a pair of ashtrays, a handful of butts inside each one. He thought: DNA, saliva, and sifted through them with a gloved finger, uncovered a roach. He pinched it and held it to his nose—it smelled charred and sweet. There were two more crumpled roaches in the other one. Behind the ashtrays was a Bluetooth speaker, an expensive brand, and beside that a flimsy desk lamp. A wire garbage can stood in the corner beside a thin black space heater.

He looked for bloodstains, on the sofa and floor. He looked for blond hairs. He sat down, bent and smelled the cushions for traces of a recent cleaning. All he caught was old tobacco and marijuana. He did the same for the chairs. The walls were smooth—new drywall, fresh paint—he ran his fingers lightly across their surface, tracing for scars, for imperfections. There were hooked scuffs behind the shoulders of the couch—a few inches to the right. Reddick reached down, slid the sofa over until the shoulders lined up with the scuffs. He looked to the left of the couch. A pair of scabs clung to the newly revealed sliver of wall—spackle, unsanded, unpainted. He couldn't read the circumference of the two holes beneath the sloppy patchwork—maybe a dime, maybe a nickel. He snapped dim photos, not willing to risk the flash, then slid the couch back over to cover the marks. He walked to the window and looked out.

One of the towers was eight floors high, the other taller, at least fifteen. The plastic and the scaffolding gave the illusion of walls, of a lumbering completion. They had removed the towering cranes, to return in the spring like birds. The packed ground frozen and phosphorescent. He imagined Buckley and Franky, arguing over her body: The space heater humming, music piping into the speaker, the air cloudy with weed and spent rage. The smell of the gunshot—what was it called, cordite? And an agreement is made, hammered out. Who owes whom and how much. Which one of them is at fault, which betrayal was the first cause. What must be done to repair the damage. Where can they take her body. And then looking out, on that view, on what must have seemed like the emptiest block in Brooklyn.

Downstairs he hammered the wood back over the window and went out the front door, setting it to lock behind him. It meant leaving the bolt unlatched, but carelessness permeated the site; it would be brushed off. Nothing was taken or broken. Outside he taped the Tyvek down, slipped back out beneath the chain. He crossed the street.

He walked the length of the green wall, past signs that warned of hazards and advised hard hats. Past a list of the companies that made the project possible, past the diamond-shaped windows punched into the wood at regular intervals. Near the end of the block was a door, and behind it a small shed, a guardhouse. The door was chained shut—tightly this time, with barely enough give to pass a hand through. Reddick looked around at the empty sidewalks, at the townhouses across the street. There were lights on, but no faces, none that he could see. The wall was as high as a basketball rim, maybe higher—in the snow, in his boots, he could graze the top with his fingers. He flattened the chain out against the door, wiped it clean. He leaped, planted his toe on the chain—it slipped but held long enough that he got both hands over the edge of the fence. He pulled himself up and slid onto the roof of the guardhouse. Once he was clear he pushed off and he was in.

What would they do with her? Let's say they could have gotten in, somehow—a loose panel maybe—what would they do with her? Would this really have been their instinct—why not put her in a car, drive out to the marshes in north Jersey, take her to the river, where there was a chance she wouldn't be found at all, rather than here, where you only have until spring? Because it was nearby, because they had no imagination. Because they didn't want a body in their cars, the traces it would leave, the remnants. Because they panicked. Because Restoration Heights had a bottomless appetite, the hunger of unfettered commerce—for bribes and backroom deals, for the ambitions of a greedy City Hall, for your history, your family, your community. It craved, finally, a murder, if not hers then yours, anyone, a body to consecrate the ground.

They would have tried to bury her. There were shallow, wide depressions around the site, areas that would eventually be planted with trees or paved into walkways. Maybe in the bottom of one, where the ground was less likely to be disturbed once work began again, where they would be less visible should anyone look inside while they dug. That would have meant cracking through frozen dirt—with shovels they would have had to acquire—hours of hard labor for two men who weren't accustomed to it. Perhaps if there were no other options, or if they had help. Reddick walked to the nearest depression, a wide, sloping crater, like a satellite dish turned on its back, ten or fifteen feet deep. He slid gently to the bottom. He kicked around in the powder, unsure what he was looking for, not surprised when he didn't find it. He shuffled out and a section of snow spilled away from beneath his feet; he went down on his hands and knees. He stood up and swore. The cold was seeping into his body, hardening his sinews, making him clumsy. He should have used the space heater back in the apartment to warm up before coming outside.

He scrambled out and tried another depression. The ground was rough from work, the recent snow too heavy to tell if it had been disturbed. In some places metal sprouted like weeds, ends and fixtures to connect the maze of infrastructure beneath the ground to some future, mysterious function. He climbed out and surveyed the rest of the site. All of the vehicles, the shovels and scoops and claws, were parked against the western wall. There was a row of trailers beside them, stacks of heavy concrete cylinders and large rolls of orange webbing. In the center of the site were the towers, each one wrapped like a Christo.

He walked to the shorter building and found a gap in the plastic. Inside was a forest of beams and pipes. The floor was raw concrete. Bits of snow lay frozen among chalky dust. He stamped his feet, added to it; the sound echoed flatly against the plastic. He went deeper into the building, the darkness shaped by the refracted glow. The sheeting was the color of bone. After a few minutes he saw a dark shape on the floor. He almost spoke her name—instead he moved closer. It was a heavy blanket, forest green and filthy, beside a pile of sopping fabric. Clothes, perhaps. He toed the blanket to make sure there was nothing in it. Torn magazine pages lay beside it. He knelt and prodded them with his pinky, slid one out from the pile. It was stiff from the cold, thin and brittle as veneer, the cover of some gossip magazine. The other pages seemed to belong to it. He stood up and continued searching, drifting through the dusty, improvised passageways until he arrived at the western edge of the building. There was a dark cage outside, scaffolding silhouetted through the milky plastic. He found a gap and slipped through, back out into the snow.

The scaffolding went four stories up, the metal frozen and slick. He grabbed it and shook, testing. There were ladders between the top three levels but the one leading to the ground had been removed. He climbed the side, wedging his boots into the joints of the supports, and slid between the guardrails of the second level to reach the wood platform. From there he took the ladders.

There were recent footprints on the top level, boot prints as large as his own. A collection of empty beer bottles rested in a small drift in one corner. He leaned against the rail. It was colder and darker up here. He was as high as most of the houses around him, the flat roofs spread out like a second, hidden surface, a layer of Brooklyn his life didn't touch, interrupted by the spikes of tenement towers or condos, of church spires. He couldn't see as far as he expected. He was wasting his time. If there was anything to find here he couldn't do it, not alone, not in this weather. Maybe in the spring, once construction began again, someone might stumble over something.

He was shivering constantly now, a sputtering motor that masked the vibration of his phone against his chest. An incoming call. He took off a glove, his fingers red and disobedient, and checked the number. Lane.

It wouldn't have taken Franky long to figure out who he was, not once he talked to Buckley. Maybe he realized his phone had been taken. They must have called Lockstone—Reddick was about to be fired. He prepared himself.

"Reddick, this is Lane calling."

"Yeah. Hey, Lane, how are you." Thinking, *Just be quick. I'm freezing up here.*

"I'm fine, Reddick, thank you. Look, I've got a situation and I think you can help me out, but it might be asking a lot."

"I'm listening."

"This job, with the Sewards, it ran over. They made some changes last minute, we lost a day recrating two paintings we had already hung, we couldn't get the replacements back in time. The thing is they need us out of there before Monday, they're hosting a dinner, but I didn't have anyone scheduled to work this weekend."

Reddick, relieved, thinking, *What day is it?*

"And of course people have plans. I've got three handlers but we need a fourth. I've spoken with the Sewards. They recognize that they created this situation, so they've agreed to let you back on the property *as long as you don't bring up Buckley's fiancée*."

"So this is for, what, Saturday?"

"Yes. Saturday. Tomorrow. I can give you time-and-a-half. But you cannot screw this up. Do you understand? I had to work to save your job after what you did on Monday. This is your chance to prove me right. Show up, work hard, speak only when spoken to. Can you handle that?"

"It's fine, Lane."

"Is that a yes?"

"Yeah, it's a yes. Fine. I'll show up with a piece of packing tape over my mouth and they can peel it back when they need to ask me something."

"This is serious. I'm serious."

"I bet you're smiling a little bit."

"Reddick?"

"Yeah?"

"Thanks for doing this. Be on your best behavior and I'll call us even."

He hung up and replaced his glove. Work meant less time to follow his scant leads—but it also meant being back inside the Sewards' home, which might generate new ones. Access to Buckley's rooms, maybe. His office. He could find time to peel away, to unearth the house's secrets.

He heard something—a wooden clap below him. He looked down, at the empty lot and then along the fence, the construction vehicles, the piles of materials. The door was open on one of the trailers, swinging blithely. A small figure had just walked out of it, layered in dark winter clothes, a black hat. Reddick froze, then started down the ladder. The scaffolding rattled and the figure looked up.

"Hey!" Reddick yelled. "Hey, hold on!"

The person began to run, tripping and sliding in the snow. Reddick hurried to the second level, went to the edge and scrambled down the side. His foot slipped, he reached to catch himself but the end of a bolt snagged his glove, tore fabric and skin. His shin bounced off the scaffolding and his other hand gave out; he plummeted backward into the snow. He landed on his heels and then his ass, thankfully cushioned by a foot of powder before he smacked into the frozen dirt. The figure stopped and watched him, maybe to see if he would get up. It was too dark to see the face. But the person was small, five and a half feet, thin. Girl-sized, he thought.

"Hey!" Reddick sat up. "I just want to talk!"

The figure turned and sprinted east, across the site toward the furthest wall. Reddick clambered to his feet and ran after it, snow inside his clothes now; his bruised shin, his aching tailbone rebelling. He wasn't gaining quickly enough, the soft, clinging terrain mitigated his speed, equalized them. He yelled again. They lurched, high-stepping, stumbling across the open expanse toward another storage area, in the corner—pyramid stacks of cinder blocks and rebar behind a chain-link fence, fifty feet away from the outer wall. The figure grabbed the chain fence, swung one leg over at a time, reached the plywood wall and began to slide a loose panel over. The careful work gave Reddick time to close the distance.

"I don't want to hurt you!"

Reddick reached the chain fence and grabbed it, ready to vault it in stride, but his jeans snagged the exposed wire at the top. He went over almost prone, landed on his back from four feet up—a harder repetition of the fall he had just taken. This time the impact emptied his lungs, rattled everything he had already loosened. He coughed and rolled onto his hands and knees.

"Hey, you alright?" It was a boy's voice, high-pitched and adolescent.

Reddick tried to answer, coughed again, then raised his hand and nodded. He looked up. The boy was peering over the tops of the cinder blocks, standing in a gap he had made by shifting over the loose panel. Reddick hobbled to his feet and the boy backed away.

"I just wanted to talk to you, man." Reddick finally wheezed.

The boy backed out of the site, raised both arms, and extended his middle fingers. "Fuck you, you creepy old cracker." He skipped backward for two steps, reveling in his victory, then turned and sprinted down the slate sidewalk.

ELEVEN

"Did you think it was her?"

"I did. I mean, I didn't stop to consider how irrational it was. Thinking about her body, about where she might be, and then seeing someone."

"A kid. A boy."

"Yeah, but the build was right. The height was right. It's hard to get too specific underneath all this winter gear, you know?"

"Sounds crazy to me." Derek leaned forward in his chair, took another forkful of *ropa vieja*. They were in the Cuban restaurant on Bedford. Once he regained his breath Reddick had realized that he was starving and texted his friend. He hadn't bothered to swing home and change. His clothes dried slowly as they worked through their entrées.

"Did you go back and check out the trailer?"

Reddick nodded. "Yeah. It was just an office. Some file cabinets, a mostly empty desk."

"And you thought, what?"

"I don't know. That she had run away and was hiding. Living there or something."

"But you found a room where you think Franky killed her."

"Or Buckley."

"Whichever. You said there were bullet holes."

"There were holes, made recently enough—since the room was painted. I don't know—if the person I was following turned out not to be her."

"Which it wasn't."

"Right, but I figured, even if it wasn't, whoever it was might have seen something. Like maybe it wasn't their first time breaking into the site."

Derek shrugged. "Maybe. But all of this, this whole case you've built—it's all in your head."

Reddick smashed a *croqueta* in two with his fork, stabbed and ate half of it. "That's not true—there are facts here. Mrs. Leland thought it was suspicious enough to reach out to me. Buckley was so evasive that his own staff noticed. Those are subjective responses, sure—but Buckley and Franky did argue. Those kids in my building did see Franky with Hannah the night she disappeared. His company does own a townhouse nearby, and someone had been hanging out on the top floor. One of the last people she was seen with was picking up envelopes of cash for who knows who. I don't have any idea what I ran into at Cask, but it wasn't normal. And finally, a *fucking girl is missing* while the only people who actually know her aren't doing shit about it. Those things aren't in my head. Those things are real."

Derek held up his hands, conceding—if not to the point then at least to Reddick's passion. "Yesterday you asked Clint to look into this guy's background. A cop. You asked a cop for help. And now you've committed not one, not two, not three—*four* crimes."

"Four?"

"You stole the man's phone, one. And you broke into three different places—an apartment, a house and a construction site. That's two, three, and four."

"I returned the phone. I didn't steal anything."

"Breaking and entering. Not entering and stealing. You broke and you entered."

"Alright, lawyer, damn."

Derek shook his head, laughing. "Not me, man. But you're going to need one if you keep this up."

"I took photos in the townhouse." He removed his phone, showed Derek the images. He cranked the brightness, revealed grainy details.

"I don't know what you think these mean. Those holes could have been made by anything—you said yourself that there was no sign of blood, no recent cleaning. On some level you know how flimsy this is, which is why you thought you were chasing the girl a half hour after you snapped those photos of her supposed murder scene."

He brushed aside Derek's skepticism. All of this formed something; he couldn't see it yet but he could sense it. "Someone had been using that room to hang out in—why not Hannah and Franky? They could have gone there after the party. After we talked in the alley."

"They could have gone anywhere. They could have taken a car back to his place, or to any of a dozen other FDP properties, preferably one that was a little more finished."

"I know. I'm not saying this proves they didn't. I'm just saying that it proves that they didn't *have* to. It could have all taken place right here. In Bed-Stuy."

"Why are you so determined to connect her disappearance to this neighborhood?"

"I don't know—it feels right. It was my first instinct."

"An instinct isn't a fact." Derek shrugged, stabbed a plantain. "Look—the murder, fine. Maybe that happened in the townhouse, even though you have zero evidence to make you think that it did. But there's no way Buckley buries her body on the site of a project he's dumped so much money into."

Reddick put his fork down. "Money? What?"

"It's his first major venture. He wouldn't jeopardize it."

"What are you talking about?"

"You didn't know this?"

"Not at all."

"That Buckley Seward is part of Corren Capital?"

"I thought Corren was that guy from Nevada? The casino guy that's been in the news."

"He's the principal, yeah. He's the face. But there are other stakeholders."

"And Buckley Seward is one of them?"

Derek nodded. "How did you not know this?"

"It didn't come up when I searched his name. I mean, I knew about Corren, from the protests. But if you look up the Sewards, I don't know. I didn't see anything."

"You just don't know where to look. It's common knowledge."

"Common for whom?"

"For me, at least. For the people I work with. For the people who follow this kind of stuff."

"How could you not have mentioned this to me?"

"I thought you knew."

"You just assumed that? You wouldn't, I don't know, check with me just to be certain?"

"I'm supposed to keep track of what you don't know? Look.

What I do, my work, that is serious. All of this other stuff is just fun. Shooting hoops, hanging out with my mom, talking about this shit with you—it's a break for me. An interlude. I didn't give it that much thought, honestly."

"So the work that I'm doing right now, trying to find out what happened to Hannah, that's not serious?"

"We're being straight? Not really. It's another game, out on the fringes—it doesn't affect what matters. This is my home. But I left for a reason. Bed-Stuy isn't a place that things happen *in*, it's a place that things happen *to*. It's the object, not the subject. It gets pushed but can't push back."

Reddick leaned over the table. "That's exactly why this is serious. This is pushing back. Now more than ever. If we connect one of the financial backers of Restoration Heights to a disappearance, a murder."

"Then what? You think that will stop it? You think anything can stop it? You gotta quit hanging out with Sensei. He's contagious with that delusional shit."

"There are the other two sites that haven't broken ground yet. If we connect the project to a murder—the publicity, the scrutiny—maybe we could at least stop those two. Limit the damage."

"A murder that had nothing to do with the development itself. If it even happened. At worst it's a crime from a single backer who everyone else could disavow."

Reddick stopped to think. The server cleared their plates, brought them more water.

"What if it wasn't, though? What if I have everything wrong, if she wasn't killed in a jealous rage? What if her disappearance had something to do with Restoration Heights?"

"Come on. The love triangle thing? At least that kind of fits. I can see it going down that way if I try hard enough. But this is out of nowhere."

"I've thought these two were connected from the beginning. In my gut. Maybe I was just looking for that connection in the wrong place. I was looking at the end, instead of the beginning. The results instead of the cause."

"You want to know why your gut feels that way? I can tell you. You won't like it, but I can tell you." He leaned forward. "It's because you're hung up on this idea that rich people are invading your neighborhood. There's a Seward—excuse me, a future-Seward—at a party in your building, there's a huge development going up down the street. You can't stand it. Is this the only apartment you've had in Brooklyn?"

"I stayed with friends in Bushwick for the first six months after I moved."

"So you know how that went down, how quickly it flipped. But you moved down here where you thought you were safe. You thought Bed-Stuy was too black to change."

"I wasn't thinking that far ahead."

"With you I almost believe that. Almost. You've got people to play ball with, you've got a bodega that spots you the difference when you're short a dollar. The same families on the same stoops in the summer, telling you good morning—you're a simple guy. That's all you need. You have no eye for the future. You see this place in the moment. But you know what I see?"

"Do I want to?"

"I see black capital. There isn't much of it in this country. But it's here. The culture stuff, I leave that for the romantics, for you and Sensei. What I see are little pockets of wealth, of potential wealth. For me it isn't a question of whether or not to sell to a developer, for me it's a question of are you getting a good return, and do you have some other place with the same combination of security and potential growth to put that money into if you sell. All I want from Bed-Stuy is to see the wealth it represents grow and spread among the community, among the people that are already here. The forces that scare you, that piss you off—those are opportunities, man. You know my mom's place, the first one?"

"Yeah."

"She gets phone calls every day. That's not an exaggeration. She gets a phone call every single day from someone who wants her to sell. She usually tells them the same thing, that she's not interested. But occasionally, maybe once every couple years, she plays along, maybe sets up a meeting, goes far enough that they have to put up a real figure. And then she pulls out. She's done it for a decade and a half. She writes the numbers down. You know what it looks like when you put them on a chart?" He held his arm up in a slash aimed at the coffered ceiling. "That includes the crash in 2008. For most situations, in other cities, in the case studies we looked at in school, that kind of steady growth isn't just good. It's fictional. But this is real, the fundamentals are sustainable. Every borough is becoming Manhattan."

"You say that like it isn't horrible."

"It isn't for the people that own property here. You think the Hasids were picketing when it happened to Williamsburg? Once you see the wave coming you can either ride it or be buried by it. The things you and Sensei are worried about are imaginary. You see this food we're eating? You think this is here without gentrification? Black people want good food, too. Remember when that Jamaican spot moved into a larger space? Added a bunch of tables, raised their prices. How do you think they were able to do that? What changes do you think they were responding to? The forces you are opposing—if we play it smart those forces are a gift. What I'm talking about is real economic growth for black people.

True opportunities for upward mobility, the kind that don't come around that often, not on this scale."

"I don't know if it's fair to call them imaginary. Also Franky really is an asshole. Most of those guys really are assholes."

"First, their personalities are irrelevant. And second, you don't even know them. It's all just symbolism for you. This whole thing, the girl, all of it."

"They talk about symbolism in your MBA program?"

"Miami is a good school, bro."

The waitress brought the check.

"Look. You want my advice? You want to make this real, and not just about you trying to strike back against people you resent? Check out those two dudes she was with. Tyler and what's-his-name."

"Ju'waun."

"Exactly. Check out Tyler and Ju'waun. You know that A, they are in some way involved in shady shit, and B, they're connected to Hannah because someone told your man to stop asking about them."

"Don't ask about the blonde."

"Exactly. That is suspicious as *hell*. I know you don't want them to be involved, but you're giving them a pass they haven't earned. White guilt isn't like you, Reddick."

"Well..."

Derek rolled his eyes. "Don't say it."

"It's hard to feel guilty when my grandfather..."

They were both smiling. "Watch who you say that shit to. You're gonna end up a meme on Black Twitter."

Reddick mimed a Howdy Doody pose, squeaked, "But I can dunk," in his best 1950s white-guy parody.

"Looking just like that," Derek said.

They both laughed, counted out cash for their halves of the bill.

"I'm not giving them a pass," Reddick said. "The momentum of the case today, it took me in another direction."

"Then slow down a little bit. I'm starting to think this is interesting. It's strange as hell the way you've gotten into it but I'm with you. I'm at least curious. I just think you're looking in the wrong places. Tomorrow you should follow up on those guys. Go talk to Trisha again. Go to Cask."

"I'm not welcome in Cask."

"Apologize, then. Or provoke her some more, just to see what happens. Dig into that side the way you did Franky."

"Okay. You're right. I have to work tomorrow but after that, I will."

"Work? They taking you back?"

Reddick told him about his phone call with Lane.

"Let me guess. You were hoping to do a little snooping while you were there."

"It wouldn't hurt."

"Nothing I say will stop you. But don't get caught. Don't steal any phones. And keep your mind open."

He took a long shower, as hot as he could stand it, trying to loosen the cold from his marrow. Buckley was invested in Restoration Heights. He wouldn't have buried the body there—Derek was right, he wouldn't have jeopardized his investment. It also gave new context to the unease he showed when Reddick mentioned Bed-Stuy. He didn't want Hannah and the development linked.

Reddick turned off the water and toweled dry, his skin shining and pink from the heat. He could hear voices from the living room—Dean and Beth must have come in while he was in the shower. He wrapped the towel around his waist and slipped into the hallway, traced by steam.

Beth saw him in his towel, catcalled. "Are we gonna get a show?"

"Hello, Beth." He crossed the narrow hall into his room. He heard Dean whistle as he shut the door. He was worn-out from the day—he wanted quiet, sanctuary, the case map. He needed to trace the ramifications of Buckley's investment, to see what connections it formed. He needed to see what it meant for Hannah, how it changed her relationship to the names around her.

He pulled up her photo. For a few minutes, chasing that boy, he had believed she was alive, that she could be helped—a flair of hope, quickly stamped out. His only real chance to save her had come and gone in that alley. He wondered again what he might have done differently. Should he have kissed her? He had barely wanted to—his desire had been shallow, fleeting. If he had done it and it had stopped there, would that have changed anything? Or had he needed to go further? If he had taken her upstairs she would be alive—but the next morning, when she sobered up, could either of them have endured his decision?

He put his phone down, hung the towel from the top of an empty easel and got dressed.

"I was starting to think you weren't coming out," Beth said. She defaulted to flirtation when she had been drinking. Reddick glanced at Dean, who sat dead-eyed, staring at his phone. It was just before ten o'clock.

"Y'all got started early today, didn't you?"

Beth giggled. "'Y'all.'"

Reddick, seeing how much ground he needed to make up, poured himself a shot of bourbon and grabbed a beer before joining them in the living room.

"Hit The Rookery around four," Dean said.

"And you've been drinking ever since?"

"Yep."

"Well, we ate dinner in the middle somewhere," Beth said.

Reddick got the sense that his presence in the apartment had derailed something—or at least postponed it. Beth turned toward him, the radiating glow of six hours' worth of alcohol fixed to him like a spotlight. Dean had yet to look up; he didn't seem annoyed, just lazy, tired. He rubbed his eyes beneath his glasses. They were both drinking water, a kind of surrender.

"You know who was there?" Beth didn't wait for him to answer. "Sarah."

Reddick waited, expectant. "Yeah?"

"I didn't know you went out with her this week."

"I wouldn't say we went out. She was helping me with something."

"She said the same thing but, you know, she's not seeing that guy, what was his name?" She tapped Dean, who shrugged. "Whoever. She's not seeing him anymore, is what I'm saying."

"Yeah, I got that, it's just—you know, I'm busy right now." It was the worst excuse, one even he didn't believe, but he was too acutely sober to talk about his dating life. He upended his beer, emptied a quarter of it.

Beth realized he was brushing her off and rolled her eyes. "Ugh. Look, today was a fun day, and she was there, and you weren't. I'm just saying."

Dean interrupted them, still intent on his phone. "Did Lane call you about working this weekend?" Reddick nodded. "Good. I told him to. I figured you could use the money by now."

"I told him I'd do it. You weren't interested?"

"I've just got too much work to do in my studio. I said if he couldn't get anyone else."

"I'm surprised you answered the phone. I mean, in your condition."

Dean glanced up at him, grinned. "He called early."

"Ha ha. So you guys had a good time? What got you started?"

"We were celebrating," Beth said.

"Really?"

"Well—there's nothing to celebrate *yet*." Dean put his phone down, finally engaged.

"We were celebrating the possibility," Beth said. "The hope."

"Hope?"

"No, that's too vague. I meant… I meant…"

"Potential."

"Yes!"

Reddick downed the shot, hit the beer. "Still vague, you guys."

"I thought we were 'y'all.'"

Reddick waited, silent, hoping the whiskey would rinse away his gathering irritation.

"We had a guest today, in our studios," Dean said.

"Mara Jost."

It took Reddick a moment. "The dealer."

"Yeah." Beth seemed incredulous that he hadn't jumped at the name. "Gorgeous space in Chelsea?"

"I know it, I know it. I saw—some show there last fall."

"Everyone she represents is amazing."

"And?" Reddick asked.

"She liked our work!"

Dean nodded. "She did. Both of us."

"She didn't offer anything yet."

"She didn't *not* offer, though."

"Exactly. She was purposefully ambiguous. But in a good

way. I mean, a way that *felt* good. Just very...positive. Like, positive energy."

"I'm still hungry," Dean said. He got up and walked into the kitchen. "She represents Caleb—on the fifth floor? Who I guess has been talking up my work. She saw some pieces online, came down, and Beth was in there with me."

"So we started talking up *my* work."

"Your jewelry?" Reddick asked, confused.

They looked at him like he was a dense child.

"My *videos*."

He had completely forgotten that she began making videos last year. She had learned the software in college and did freelance editing and production—mostly under the table for friends—when she needed the extra income. Eventually she decided to try making her own stuff—blends of stop-motion animation and performance, layered and twisted as one of her intricate rings.

"And she comes over, watches all three of them."

"So what we're saying is that this has a lot of potential." Dean opened the cabinet, shut it, opened the refrigerator and removed a beer.

"If for no other reason than just forming that relationship."

"Then, congratulations, guys." Reddick smiled and raised his bottle. Dean sat down, raised his own, and they clacked the heels together. Beth caught them both with her glass of water as they were separating.

"To potential."

"So what have you been up to today?" Dean said.

Reddick began slowly. He told them about his confrontation with Franky, the phone, about breaking into the townhouse, his pursuit of the other trespasser at Restoration Heights. Halfway through Dean began to frown. Reddick finished and turned to Beth, hoping for support—but she just looked afraid. They both seemed vastly more sober than when he began.

Reddick got up and opened another beer.

"How many buildings are you going to break into before you're satisfied?" Dean said. "You have to stop."

"I can't believe you did this again."

"It was a different situation entirely. It's not like anyone lives there."

"Yeah, but it's not like you just slipped through an unlocked window, either," Dean said. "I mean, you had to break through the wood."

"I put it back."

"You say things like that as though it makes anything better," Beth said. "What you did, what you're doing—it isn't okay. You don't get to do whatever you want just because you're on some self-appointed mission."

"It's not self-appointed. Mrs. Leland asked me—"

"To ask questions," Dean said. "Not to trespass, not to steal someone's phone. And all for what? Some game?"

"This isn't—I'm not playing a game." All his irritation came flooding back. Franky was obviously a villain, Buckley's behavior was undeniably strange—and a person was missing, probably dead. Add to that what he had just learned from Derek, that Buckley was connected to Restoration Heights, to the deepest cut this wounded neighborhood had sustained—it had to be blown open, all of it. He felt a burning frustration that they couldn't see it.

"He's right, Dean. It's not a game." Beth turned to Reddick. "What you did today was serious."

"It *should* be serious. What I did was appropriate, was the response that this case deserves."

"It's not a case."

"A person is missing."

Beth, almost whispering, "You are going to end up in jail. For harassing that guy, for all of it."

"He deserved it, Beth."

"How do you know that, though?" Dean asked. "You don't know anything for certain."

"I was investigating. I was going where the case told me to go."

"What about those two guys at the party?"

"I'm investigating them, too. This was just one day. I think—to be honest, I think they're all connected somehow."

"Like what, they work for Buckley or something?"

"I don't think it's that straightforward."

"Dean, stop encouraging him. You're going to get him killed."

"I'm not trying to encourage him. It's just—Reddick, I don't think you can trust your instincts. I understand why you're hesitant to put it on the guys at the party, they're black and you're resisting this inherited pressure to view them, I mean people of color, as criminals—but the way you're hounding this developer, it isn't right. It's just resentment or worse, I don't know, bitterness. You see him as an interloper and you want to make him into a villain. You want to pretend that he's motivated by something more sinister than economic self-interest."

"Why does everyone think that? Because I protested Restoration Heights?"

"Who's everyone?"

"Never mind."

"Look, I get that you're passionate about this stuff."

"Passionate? Fuck, man. Because I don't want to watch yet another neighborhood get blasted into a gluten-free, au pair, hip white wasteland?" Mocking now, in a voice that was half Buckley, half Hannah, "This building has so much potential. We'll put a SoulCycle right here on the bottom floor, which will leave just enough room for a juice bar. And on top a lovely restaurant where we take classic American dishes but make them, like, actually good. You know, white trash but artisan." Lapsing back into his own voice, shaking. "Coleslaw, thirty bucks a pound because the cabbage was hand-raised by trust-fund interns and fed nothing but Oregon rainwater. Grass-fed livermush. On the third floor we'll just put some offices, a company headquarters, dog-friendly, where everyone can sit around on vintage couches and talk seriously about pop music. That sounds so amazing. Why do I even fight it? Hold my beer, I'll just go paint the brownstones white and be done with it."

Dean was calm. "You're proving my point, Reddick. Look how angry this makes you. This is why you want him to be a murderer. This is why you are acting so irresponsibly."

"I do want to protect the neighborhood. Obviously. But I'm being objective here, too. Because Hannah matters. What happened to her matters."

Beth's eyes narrowed, her fear and shock beginning to give way to something else. "This is all kind of gross. It's very entitled. It's very…it's just so *white male*, as though this is all your responsibility somehow. Like you're the neighborhood's steward, and if you don't look out for it, no one will."

"What does that have to do with any of this?"

"I didn't see it before but it's true. You're on some Rudyard Kipling shit. The way you think this has anything to do with you, that you have to ride in with, like, a gun or sword or whatever and save everyone."

"Gun or sword?"

"Yeah. Just your presumption. You wouldn't have gotten away with any of this if you weren't white. And you wouldn't care about Hannah if you weren't a man, if you didn't feel this manly responsibility to take care of women. It's very..."

"Don't say problematic."

"It is, though. I'm not joking."

"I'm trying to figure out how all of this makes me racist and sexist."

"That isn't what I'm saying and you know it. You learned this stuff in school same as I did. I'm talking about the social structure we live in. *Systems.*"

"I busted my ass today. Trying to help someone. A person." He held up his finger. "One individual. That's what this is about—a person, not a system. Hannah, and finding out who killed her."

"And how do you even know she's dead? I'm sorry if I just don't buy all this. It doesn't make sense. Everyone wants to help someone, you know? We come across people every day that we could help and don't, not the way we should. Why her? Why choose her, is what I'm saying?"

"Because I was there."

"Come on, Reddick, calm down." Dean cut his eyes at Beth. "She's right. You have to think about how this looks to someone who doesn't share our privileges. There's a kind of, I don't know, moral grandstanding to it."

Reddick lost it, finally overwhelmed by frustration, fueled by a surge of fresh alcohol. "What the fuck are you talking about? Do you know me at all? Privileges? We have nothing in common. You understand that? Nothing."

Beth interjected. "You might come from different backgrounds but you're in the same place right now. You're roommates."

"Beth, where the fuck do your parents live?"

"Don't be an asshole."

"I'm not being an asshole. I'm asking a question. Just tell me where the fuck your parents live."

"Bradenton."

"Doing what, exactly? Hold up, hold up, I know this one. Tenured professors at New College. How about you, Dean?"

"I'm not playing this game, man."

"Some fucking suburb outside of Annapolis. I can't even remember what your dad does but your mom doesn't have a job. She could if she wanted, but who has the time? She has interests."

The two of them leaned back in their chairs, exchanged looks, disarmed by his rage.

"Guess what my dad does. Go ahead." Silence. "I wish you could fucking tell me because it's not like I know. My mom doesn't know, either. She hasn't spoken to him since he quit the mill when I was six months old. I've got photos. I've got a pawpaw that I almost remember and a grandmama that still sends checks to the woman who was never even officially her daughter-in-law. So go ahead and talk to me about privileges. Talk to me about these advantages I have. Tell me again about how we are in the same place."

"Stop taking this personally," Beth said. "We're talking about systemic advantages—"

"You sound like a fucking textbook. This isn't theory, this is real fucking life. This is looking people in the face. Do you think that having these opinions makes you noble? You spend so much time fighting the way the world is, the things that are wrong with it, that you forget to actually connect with the people who live in it. Unplug your computer and go hang out with people, regular people, black, white, whatever—people who don't know who fucking bell hooks is and whose parents couldn't get them into the tiny circle of private schools where you learned your opinions. I mean *hang out*, not be their ally, or march at their rallies, just go have a beer, without an agenda, without patting yourself on the back because you know you've done your duty as a good little white liberal."

"*White* liberal?"

"Give me a break, Beth. You're as white as I am."

"That is the most bullshit racist stereotype—just because Asian people have done well in this country, all of a sudden we're white?"

"Well, you're not fucking black."

"Neither are you." Shouting, her face contorted.

"You know what I am, though, Beth? Fucking poor. You don't know what that's like."

"That doesn't mean you get to erase my heritage."

"What is your heritage? What is it? It's good fucking schools and tutors and after-school programs. It's having a support network. It's great skin and hair and teeth because your parents didn't feed you out of boxes and cans. It's speaking Mandarin and English and passable Spanish that you learned during your semester abroad. It's *success*, Beth. That's your heritage. All your talk about structure and systems, about gender and race—how could any of those things possibly hurt you? What's the worst thing you've ever encountered? You're underrepresented in movies? Somebody speaks to you like you're an idiot because they assume you don't understand the language? I'm so sorry. Sit in your parents' BMW and cry about it. Put on Brahms until you feel better. It's easy to spot all the world's problems from the top floor."

Beth—stunned, hurt—mocking: "I'm Reddick, I grew up with black people and my family was poor so none of your bullshit applies to me." Back to her own voice, angry and firm. "Money doesn't erase everything. It doesn't help when you find out you only got your internship because your boss has an Asian fetish, when he treats you like some sort of sexual treasure. It doesn't make me less afraid to be alone on the subway at night. I don't get to buy my way out of prejudice. You think you're so fucking unique, such an individual, but you're not, no one is."

Reddick stood up and walked into the kitchen. "That's just the problem, though. You know? I *am* an individual, just like you. Just like every single person out there. And you can slice us up by whatever standards you want, by gender or age or ethnicity, by skin color, and you can learn something. You can map trends or uncover injustice or—I don't know, design fucking policy. But every last one of those data points is a person. A real human being. They have history you can't know, fears and hopes and troubles you don't have a category for. Maybe your labels are worth it. Maybe in the end they do more good than harm. But that doesn't mean much to the people you stick them to."

Beth, unbowed, had a reply ready, but Reddick didn't hear it. He went into his room and shut the door.

TWELVE

To the warehouse first, on an empty weekend train. His legs stiff from yesterday's adventures, from lumbering through snow, from being soaked through with this incorrigible winter. Raw from last night's alcohol and spent emotion. He meant everything he said and regretted all of it; it was an argument he tried never to air. It was too embedded in his own past, in his own experiences, for him to expect anyone to understand. He needed an hour or two on the courts to loosen up, which he wasn't going to get. He looked for Harold outside the turnstiles and wasn't surprised when he wasn't there—all of his relationships deteriorating in the wake of his crusade.

After the warehouse—a subdued reunion, his coworkers hesitant to prod the wound of his week off—it was the Sewards'. The house seemed unfamiliar. The limestone exterior, the polished stairways, the rugs and sideboards, the just-so spacing of every arrangement, the abundance of effort that was apparent in every room, every nook—the sense that this was a space maintained by commitment and visual acuity—none of it seemed harmless anymore. It had abandoned the pretense of neutrality, become a testament of character, of motive. It vibrated with meaning.

They weren't planning to be there long—four or five hours, just wrapping up details that the unplanned painting swap had pushed aside. Four paintings in the first floor dining room, a suite of photographs for a hallway upstairs. The dining room was the problem, and had been all week. Dottie had made them rearrange it four times, in each instance unsatisfied with something, the color or the size or some problem with the pattern—too much Leipzig, too clear a historical or conceptual link between whichever four artists were up at the time. Trying to make it work together without seeming like some sort of thesis. Mrs. Seward would have cut off the discussion days ago but she had left the city that morning with her husband, and Dottie's appetite for nitpicking was insatiable.

She pulled Reddick aside when they arrived. "You're only here because there was no one else."

"I already told Lane I won't cause trouble," he said.

"This is none of your business. But I'm going to tell you anyway, in hopes that it will help you keep your word. We have heard from Hannah. She apologized for the way she left. She's gone home to be with her family."

"When did this happen?"

"Shortly after the incident."

"So Tuesday? Wednesday?" Her timeline didn't add up—Franky had admitted that Hannah was still missing yesterday morning.

"What does it matter?" she snapped. "I didn't have to tell you at all. I only did so because I thought it would help you drop it, so please—drop it."

They spent the morning on the dining room, then debated whether to break for lunch or push through and reach their weekend. Reddick voted lunch—it might be his only chance to sneak away. It was an even split—two for and two against—but the tie was broken when Dottie interrupted them again. She pulled them through another walk-through, wondered whether she should send them back to the Sewards' vault at Lockstone to pick up a painting she regretted removing. Finally she decided that it was too late to make major changes, that it would have to stay as it was, but her indecision swallowed enough time that they were all too hungry to keep going.

They split up outside, each to grab their food of choice. Reddick lied about where he was going and doubled back to the house. He buzzed the service entrance, hoped that if Dottie answered she wouldn't bother to ask questions. Other than her initial confrontation she hadn't spoken to him. A housekeeper let him in, a trim Russian woman he hadn't seen before. He started to offer an excuse for his return but she was so obviously uninterested that he let it trail off.

Buckley must have an office or study, but he hadn't seen it. There was a handful of rooms that weren't part of the installation, including a few on the third floor, down the hall from Mrs. Seward's office—he decided to start there. He went up the rear stairs, alert and ready to talk his way out of trouble. Most of the staff was off for the weekend; the empty rooms accepted him with a drowsy disregard. He passed Mrs. Seward's office and peeked inside. The Schnabel glared at him knowingly. The patches of heavy paint read like concrete, spread over the family's secrets. Buckley's parents must have recognized Bed-Stuy as the site of Restoration Heights but had followed their son's lead in keeping it quiet, a level of trust, of loyalty, that he couldn't fathom. He imagined his own mother in their place—she would have bared every detail, her naive faith in the truth unshakable. It wouldn't have occurred to her that his omission was tactical, that he might be hiding something for his own sake. He would have had to explain it all to her first. The Sewards had closed ranks instinctively. He didn't hate them for it; it was more like wonder, like noting an exceptional trait in some other species.

He tried two more doors and found Buckley's office. It shirked the modernist imperative of the rest of the house. Dark wood, low light, Ivy League degrees framed behind a leather-topped desk; it was a room scraping after an outworn masculinity—cigars, brandy, solemnity. It was the only room in the house that was trying too hard. There was a closed laptop on the center of the desk, neat stacks of paperwork around it. Reddick listened. The only thing he heard was the hurried tapping of his own heart. He moved to the desk and opened the laptop.

It was locked. He wasted a few minutes on desperate, Hail Mary lobs at guessing Buckley's password—graduation date, Hannah's name, Franky's name; the options rote after yesterday's failure with the phone. He gave up after the first warning and closed it. He went through the stacks of papers, delicately, like he was handling a sheaf of drawings, laying each sheet facedown to preserve the order. There were three pages with the name Corren Capital in the text. He photographed them and replaced the stack. He wanted evidence for either of his theories—the crime of passion or of finance. He believed it might somehow be both. There were four drawers on either side of the desk and one in the center. He opened the center one first. Inside was a messy assortment of office paraphernalia, clips and pens and a stapler. A jump drive that Reddick almost pocketed. Two small keys on a single loop of wire. He tried the other drawers, working left to right, assiduous and careful. He shot photos of anything related to finance, receipts or bills. He didn't see anything personal, no mentions of Hannah—nothing to indicate a reservoir of jealous rage. It had to leave some trace. A force strong enough to drive someone to kill—it couldn't have been kept entirely quiet. He didn't expect the evidence to be dramatic, a photograph with her face carved out, a journal inscribed with his murderous plot—but something.

If she cheated, how did he know? Did he hire someone to watch her?

The bottom right drawer had been retrofitted with a lock. Reddick tugged vainly once, twice. He opened the center drawer again and removed the pair of wire-bound keys to try them in the lock. The tumbler crackled and the drawer slid open. Inside was a stack of files, a shoebox and a large leather-bound book. He began with the shoebox. It held several sleeves of photographs, from years ago, shot on film and printed commercially. Nearly everyone in the images was white, attractive and well dressed; catalog families captured in redolent happiness. He recognized teenaged Buckley and a younger Mrs. Seward, her beauty less developed, more superficial, her son already affecting a patrician composure. He saw earlier iterations of this house; different art, different furniture, but the same sense of cohesion and care. On the surface their lives were foreign and inaccessible, galvanized by wealth he didn't have the means to understand—a class of people that were only ever portrayed as tropes of wish fulfillment or villainy, as subjects for envy or blame—but in these images, beneath the trim clothes and the polished locations, they seemed blandly relatable. They possessed an intimacy that argued for a shared humanity.

At the bottom of the stack he found a shot of Buckley and Franky, serenely young, posing with another boy in front of what looked like a Gothic manor. Reddick flipped it over, checked the back—"with Franky and Mitchell, freshman year, College Hall," in Buckley's machine-like script. Reddick turned it right-side up, studied the image, three princes framed by a mansion of grassy stone. The third boy, Mitchell, was dark-haired and heavy—a vaguely Asian face with a ruddy American grin. Last night's argument flashed through his mind, Beth's outrage, and Reddick slipped the photo back into the box and replaced the lid. There was nothing in there he could use.

He removed the leather book. It was wider than a notebook but thin. He opened it. Side-tear checks, in columns of three, with stubs for recording the amount and the payee. The dates on the stubs were erratic, no more than one every few months, going back over three years. Thirteen in all. There was no pattern; the payees and amounts were different each time. He wondered if any of them were written to a private investigator. He took photographs of the stubs.

His stomach growled, a reminder that he was working through lunch. He glanced at the time. The rest of the crew would be back soon. He removed the files. Taxes, bank statements—more than he could parse and more than he had time to shoot. He thumbed quickly, looking for Corren Capital, photographing the pages that had its name on them. He didn't understand any of it. Once he was finished he replaced the files and the checkbook and the shoebox, locked the drawer and returned the keys. He went over the room for signs of his presence, like scanning an artwork for damage after you unwrapped it. He opened the middle drawer, shifted the position of the keys and closed it. No oily fingerprints on the laptop, no hairs. Once he was satisfied the room was clean he left.

He padded through the hallway and into the service corridor. He heard the rest of the crew being let in through the main entrance and sped up, tried not to lose traction in his blue booties as he hurried down the stairs. He came out in the kitchen, half jogged through the empty dining room on his way to the foyer. He heard Dottie's voice before he got there.

"You're all back? Where's the other?"

"Here," he called, coming into view from the dining room. Dottie frowned but didn't ask questions.

"Fine," she said, and summoned them all upstairs to finish the job.

He was home by four o'clock. He drank coffee and stared at the case map. It was split in half, a reflection of his uneven efforts. On the left he had the Sewards and Franky Dutton. The white surface around them was scrawled with pencil—arrows connecting names and places, jumbled text, smudges of erasure and reconsideration. On the right there were only names floating in empty spaces, begging for his attention. Ju'waun and Tyler. Cask. The map exposed his bias, the core asymmetry that Derek had called him on, that Beth's prodding had exposed. He had to develop that half, bring it up to the same state as the rest of the map, had to make the two sides speak as equals.

He had looked for answers only in the places he wanted them to be—which was anywhere but Bed-Stuy. Derek was right that what drew him to the neighborhood was uncomplicated—the pace of life, the commitment to simple courtesies. There was something of Gastonia in it, some essential piece of the South, cleansed of the worst of its history, that survived in the weekly rhythms, in the solace of their continuity. He remembered his mother's hands trembling when he told her he was going to Philadelphia, that he would accept U-Arts's offer. She had been as prepared for that moment as he was—the art camp scholarships, the basketball accolades, that year he nearly flunked geometry and she drove him to their second cousin's house in Charlotte every Sunday, an hour each way, for tutoring he paid for with a portrait of the cousin and her terrier, deftly rendered in graphite—all of the work she put him through had been accompanied by admonitions, by advice on what he should do when his talents pulled him away from her, on how things would be. But she was afraid when the moment arrived. He wondered if she had believed it wouldn't happen. It wasn't until he left that he understood what frightened her—that the violence of separation wasn't softened by the desire to go, or to see him gone. That you could miss a place you desperately wanted to leave.

He went home when he could afford the plane tickets but he could never move back. It would destroy his mother, crumble her life's work. Instead he looked for that sense of place in Brooklyn, and found it in Bed-Stuy, in the easy familiarity of strangers, commiserating over headlines while you waited in line at the bodega. Found it in the Caribbean women on folding chairs on the sidewalk, Watchtower pamphlets pressed to their laps, faces serene as glass. In the hyperbolic earnestness of the children's sidewalk games. In the audacity of a block party, the road sectioned off by cars, the streets cleared by repurposed no-parking signs someone had swiped from the last film crew to occupy the photogenic streets. It was there on Sunday mornings, the perfumed women in pretty dresses, somber men in dark suits holding Bibles like shields, hymns seeping from churches onto the sidewalk like fog. It was more than a collection of details, more than specific similarities. It was a feeling, a vibe, a rhythm you picked up in your bones. The underdog's pride of a community always punching up. The qualities of home that he found in Bed-Stuy were mostly things he could not name; they were what he was afraid he would lose. He belonged to them by the randomness of birth, by the accident of biography.

This formed an obligation. Sensei was right. It was why he had opposed Restoration Heights, why he lashed out at Franky and Buckley. But what were the limits of that commitment? Did it protect the names on the right side of his map, quarantine the blank spaces around them? Why was he afraid of implicating them—as though an entire community could be condemned by the actions of one or two of its members.

He picked up his phone and called Harold.

"Hello?"

"Hey, man, it's Reddick."

"My brother. How you doing?" His tone was too warm, compensating for caution, perhaps. Voices rattled in the background.

"Do you know a person named Jeannie?"

"Nah, man. Jeannie? Let me think. Nah. Sorry."

"Gene, then? I'm not sure I heard it right."

"I know a Eugene. In um, uh, wait. Nah, you don't know Eugene."

"Shit, let me think."

"I'm at the bar, young brother. So if you need to think maybe we can just pick this up at another time."

"I'm trying to ask you about someone that might be involved in that girl's disappearance."

A pause. "I know that. I'm not stupid."

"Then you can't help me?'

"I told you, don't ask me about that shit again. I told you that. And you're calling me about that, *here*? Right now? You're putting me at risk."

"What do you mean? Calling you about this where? Where are you?"

"I'm down the street. I'm right in the thick of everything. I'm not saying shit."

He thought about the bars he had heard Harold mention. "Ti-Ti's? Are you at Ti-Ti's?"

"Don't come over here."

"Is someone there with you right now?"

"I ain't talking."

"I'll be there in ten."

He walked in beneath the glowing sign, Ti-Ti's Executive Inn, the letters formed by looping tubes of trembling neon. Harold was alone. The bar was a warm pocket in the frozen afternoon, a narrow basement strung with Christmas lights. There was an old movie on the television, above the jukebox, competing with the Impressions for the attention of a disinterested room. The name alluded to the presidential streets that stepped like the rungs of a ladder south toward Crown Heights—Monroe, Madison, Jefferson—but the only president Reddick saw in the collage of old photos behind the bar was Barack Obama, his dignified and solemn face pasted among a tapestry of civil rights leaders and black intellectuals. Four people sat at the bar, including Harold, all of them black. Two men with their backs to the door and an older woman, lisping through false teeth at the bartender. Harold was on the last stool. Reddick took the empty seat beside him.

"You're not here. Or if you are here, you're not expecting to talk to me about any of that nonsense."

"I'm a friend, having a beer."

"Yeah, alright."

The bartender, a short, cheerful white woman, smiled in his direction. He ordered a beer; after she delivered it she nodded at a sign behind the bar that read "cash only no tabs no exceptions." He laid four crumpled ones on the bar.

"Friends talk to each other about what's on their mind," Reddick said.

"They consider the damage they could cause, too."

"What damage? What are you risking?"

"I have been told, *explicitly*, not to speak with you about this shit. And I have also, *explicitly*, told you that I have been told this. What about this situation don't you get?"

"You said the girl. Don't ask about the girl."

"People was pissed, man. Whoever this girl is, she had got into some shit."

"So don't talk about her. I won't ask about her."

"Those other two cats, too. Ju'waun and um, um."

"Tyler."

"Ju'waun and Tyler. Don't ask about that."

"Okay, fine. No Ju'waun. No Tyler."

"And no blonde. *Explicitly*, those words."

"Fine. No blonde."

"So now we can enjoy our beer."

"Gene. Jeannie. Who is this?"

"Man, you don't quit."

"That name isn't on your list."

Harold looked over both shoulders, eyed the bartender and the other patrons, as though fearing espionage. "That name ain't on my list because that name is the reason I *have* a list. You get me?"

"Jeannie—that's who your friend was so frightened of?"

Harold shook his head and sighed. "You're not talking about a person named Jeannie, man."

"Enough with the runaround."

Harold shook his head. "No, I mean it's not *Jeannie*. It ain't a name. You're talking about *the Genie*."

"The Genie? What is that?"

"It's a who."

"Who the fuck is the Genie?"

"The Genie is a procurer, man. You rub the lamp and the Genie appears and grants you a wish."

"I thought genies give you three wishes?"

"This Genie grants you as many as you can pay for."

"Anything you want?"

Harold shook his head. "The Genie is earthbound, brother. Ain't no fucking magic."

"So what are we talking about? Drugs?"

Harold nodded. "The Genie can get you drugs."

"So what? I know six different corners I can score on."

"Weed, sure. Blow. Molly. But what if you want pills, too? The kind you need a prescription for? Or even the kind you already got a prescription for, only you can't afford to fill it? The Genie can handle all of that. One-stop shopping. But that's not really everything."

"What else?"

"Ass, for starters. What else do people think about when they rub their lamp?" He laughed like he had been savoring the joke for hours, and knocked down the middle third of his beer. Reddick realized just how drunk Harold was.

"So the Genie is a pimp?"

"A *procurer*, I said. When you say 'pimp' I think of some wannabe with a gun he never shot, with about three scared girls he has to hit to keep around. The Genie has a roster, sure, but it's more like a…a family. Don't get me wrong, those girls know who is in charge, but there is some reciprocity there. Some gratitude."

Reddick winced.

"Anyway, it don't stop there, neither. You and me got a problem, right?"

"Do we?"

Harold hit his beer. "I'm saying hypothetically. You and me got a problem, and I can't handle it on my own, either because you got friends, or because there's some politics I can't get caught in, or whatever, I can go to the Genie to take care of it."

"Like, have me killed?"

Harold shook his head. "It don't come to that. Just have some boys come over, have a talk. A rough talk, maybe, but there's no reason to go beyond that. No one wants that kind of trouble."

"So: drugs, sex, violence. Sounds like you do get three wishes."

"That's a good one, brother. But that ain't why they call her the Genie."

"Her?"

"Oh yeah. Women can run shit now."

"Okay. So why do they call her the Genie?"

"Because you don't always get *exactly* what you ask for. You might get some approximate version of it. Like in those old jokes, you know, a married couple is walking on the beach and they find a bottle with a genie in it, and the man wishes that he was married to a younger woman, and poof, the genie makes him twenty years older."

"Oh right. Like the rich guy that's jacked but has a small head."

"I don't know that one."

"Same thing. Guy gets three wishes, he wants to be rich, he wants muscles. Then he can't think of what to use his last wish on, and finally says, *how about a little head*?"

Harold laughed, long enough and loud enough to catch a frown from the lisping woman. "That's pretty funny. I like that one. And that's what I mean. The Genie does shit kind of like that."

"Why? Seems bad for business."

"What you get is always close enough. A friend of mine, a close friend of mine, he's not too great with ladies. So he figures the Genie can help him out. He says, I want a girl with a big ass and freckles. And what shows up at his door? A fat chick with acne."

"And that's okay?"

"He laughed because he knew he had been got, and then he and this girl had a good time, and he was happy. Nothing is perfect. People who go to the Genie understand that. They know you can't get exactly what you want, but as long as you get enough, you know, that's it. It's a compromised world we live in. They might complain later but that's part of the chance you take going to her, is how you encounter her sense of humor. Is knowing she's gonna fuck with you a little bit."

"So where's her lamp?"

"Pardon?"

"Her lamp. Where do I go to summon her? To name my wishes?"

"You can't. She won't help you."

"Because I'm white?"

"How do you know the Genie ain't white?"

Reddick blushed. "Is she?"

"No, brother, but that's beside the point. I'm just saying think about why you assumed. Anyway, she don't choose her customers by skin color. That's not good business. You just aren't the type. You have too much going for you."

"Am I really that much different from you? I work in a warehouse."

"Think about how we met before you ask that question.

I don't hold it against you as a man. But America treats us differently."

"I'm not sure what that has to do with seeing the Genie."

"Look, what the Genie does—you're right, people do it better all over the city. You can find better drugs, better ass, fake IDs, all that shit—you can find people that won't fuck with you when they get it for you, too. But the Genie has been around here forever, from back when this neighborhood was *rough*, and she was there for people. She knew everybody, and could get heat off your back, could keep you alive, get you a fix if you needed it or find you a place to get sober if you needed that. She had a couple buildings that she used for business but if you was in trouble, she might let you stay there for free sometimes. Yeah, she's trying to make money, and yeah, she's got a weird sense of humor, but the people that go to her now, for the most part? They remember when they had no one else. So does that sound like you?"

They drank in silence. Nearly a minute passed.

"Just tell me where people go to talk to her. Even if I can't go myself. I just want to know how it fits together." He thought of Tyler's pickups.

"You aren't going to let this go."

"I can't."

"Remember she hurts people."

"I won't go there myself. I know my limits. I'm just trying to piece it all together."

"You have to swear to me that you will stay away. I am not responsible if you get yourself killed."

"Harold. I swear."

"There's this dry cleaners on Grand Street. Back toward Clinton Hill. Clean City."

Reddick's jaw clenched. "I think I know it."

"But you ain't going."

"I told you I wouldn't."

Harold focused his bleary eyes, taking in Reddick's face. "What am I worried about anyway? If you walked in to Clean City they'd probably just ask you what you wanted cleaned. The Genie is a bunch of things, but she ain't stupid. The way that neighborhood flipped, they'd probably make just as much money cleaning all the white people's clothes."

He laughed again, resigned and anarchic, like a man making peace with misfortune. Reddick waited, held his laughter inside, thinking of the boy telling him to leave his coat, to fill out a ticket—a different sort of joke entirely.

THIRTEEN

Cask was a short walk from Ti-Ti's. It was after five but a haze of mauve sunlight lingered on the brim of the sky, the first sign of lengthening days. He wondered if the snow would stop, at least for a few weeks. For now it lay piled along the boundaries of the street and the sidewalk, charcoal-gray with filth, the romance of it exchanged for nuisance, for hazard.

He saw her through the window as he approached—the same woman, on a stool behind the counter. The glass front and warm lighting made a display of her striking looks. Men outside took long, clinging glances as they passed. She ignored them.

He went in with his hands up, signaling surrender. When she saw who it was her face hardened. She stood.

"You're not welcome in here. This is my store, there's no manager for you to appeal to, if that's what you're thinking."

"I'm not here to buy anything."

She shook her head. The dark ring around her eye had

ripened to yellow. She kept the tumbling mass of her blond hair on that side, masking it in shadow. "I was pretty clear last time."

"And I was an asshole." He lowered his right hand, extended it toward her. "My name is Reddick."

She stared for half a minute before she responded, then shook his hand limply, her skepticism intact. "Mia."

"So do you agree?"

"About what?"

"That I was an asshole."

She rolled her eyes. "Sure, if that's what you want to hear. If it will get you out of my store, then fine. You're an asshole. Happy? Now go."

She had a faint accent, something he couldn't place. Eastern European, he thought—mild enough that he hadn't caught it last time. "That's not why I'm here. I mean, not the only reason. I'm here to listen."

"Why do you think I have something to say to you?"

"Because I know who the Genie is."

She didn't flinch at the name. "So what? I already asked Ju'waun about you. You're nobody."

"Then it shouldn't matter if you answer a couple of questions."

"You haven't asked me a question."

"Fine. How do you know Ju'waun and Tyler?"

"None of your business. Next question."

"Do you work for the Genie?"

"Nope. Next question."

"I was hoping for actual answers."

"We all have hopes. Next question."

"What is your relationship to the Genie?"

"She's my landlord."

"That's it?"

"That's it. You done?"

"Do you know a girl named Hannah Granger?"

She didn't stop to think. "Nope."

"Ju'waun does. So does Tyler."

"They know a lot of people I don't know."

"Why am I being told not to ask about them? About Hannah?"

"I don't see why you'd expect me to know. Or care."

"Because Hannah Granger disappeared Sunday night. And Ju'waun and Tyler were two of the last people to see her."

He thought he saw the last sentence register—she blinked slowly, her mouth tightened. Maybe it was just irritation. She reached for a glass, poured two inches from an open bottle of Malbec on the counter and drank it.

"Who is this girl to you?" she asked.

"Let's say she was a friend of mine."

"What time were they with her?"

"At least until midnight."

"They were with me after that. And there was no girl."

"With you?"

"Look at that. Turns out I could help after all. You should have been nice from the beginning."

"What were they doing with you?"

"Now you're back where you started, and I told you: it's none of your business."

"I'm not trying to pin this on them. Don't think that. I just want to find out what happened to Hannah. Maybe if I could talk to them, if you gave me one of their phone numbers."

"Look. I'm sorry about your friend. I hope you find out what happened. But those two aren't involved. Okay? Go look somewhere else."

She raised her chin to make her point, dipping her hair away from her face. The swollen flesh below her eye called her a liar.

He grabbed a six-pack on the way home. The apartment was his for the night, territory won from his fight with Dean and Beth, the wounds too fresh for a reconciliation. He was grateful for the time; he had work to do.

First: try to fill in the other half of his map, balance his uneven attention. He still didn't have Ju'waun or Tyler's last names but he had more data than the first time he researched them. He went to Facebook, typed in the Genie, got a list of women. Sorted it by city, cross-referenced to friends named Ju'waun, Tyler—every instance of the name, one at a time. Nothing. He went to Instagram, searched hashtags for their names, location tags for Cask. Learned Mia's last name, used it to find a photo of her with other women, clutching each other for a selfie, blowing kisses at the camera, winking. Taken at some club, a lounge on Tompkins. Her friends white, black and Hispanic, the crowd behind them mostly black. Then he searched her page for Ju'waun and found a photo of the two of them. Reddick squirmed in his seat, the thrill of revelation passing like a tremor through his body. She had tagged him in it. He followed the tag to Ju'waun's page and finally got his last name, Ju'waun Stills. He combed through his images, his tags. It was everyday stuff, friends, parties, memes. He saw a cramped room with mattresses carpeting the floor, seam pressing against seam—a window somewhere up high, other towers crowding the view, their redbrick and bland architecture suggesting the projects. Where? More digging and he found it. Lafayette Gardens, on the border of Clinton Hill and Bed-Stuy—not far from Clean City. He went to the location tag, which had a handful of photos and videos from a single user, a community organization. A party, a BBQ—an ad hoc rap battle. A cappella, adults and kids in a circle, clapping time, cheering the dense wordplay, the sharp resolutions. Three videos, thirty seconds a pop, just a few bars, each one featuring a different kid. The last one was Ju'waun, labeled "J-Sword devastating flow." He listened, twice—the enunciation was clear, the delivery polished, even if the rhymes were simple. He went back through his round of searches using J-Sword instead of Ju'waun. There was a second account listed under this nickname, with more photos of Ju'waun and his friends—in Lafayette Gardens, in Fort Greene Park. They were followed by long comment threads—boasts, exhortations, occasional disses. He found Tyler's face, attached to a pseudonym—Remy. He saw two phrases repeated: "Sons of Cash Money" and "Heirs to the Throne," in the comments but also on the profile pages, referring either to a single group with multiple names or a pair of overlapping groups.

"Cash Money, Lafayette Gardens" in his search engine brought him to Cash Money Brothers, a violent gang that ran Lafayette Gardens from the nineties to the middle of the aughts. The leadership had been eradicated in a series of prosecutions lasting nearly a decade—a period that coincided with Clinton Hill's gentrifying ascent. Reddick had walked past the towers a dozen times—they seemed peaceful, green, well kept. From a southbound window you would be able to see Restoration Heights, the two developments mirrored across blocks of shifting territory, their cosmetic similarity a kind of mockery. No one he knew had ever gone inside Lafayette Gardens, the projects rimmed by an invisible wall that radiated the shame of their contrast with the booming neighborhood, the blatant declaration that there were two countries here, their borders inviolable. Clinton Hill's new white arrivals crossed the street, walked on the opposite sidewalk, unable to say what frightened them more—the projects or their own complicity in the forces that sustained them. Their faces dazed with the knowledge of their own cowardice.

Reddick found nothing about Sons of Cash Money or Heirs to the Throne in the news, so he went back to social media, found them both on Twitter. He thumbed through Remy's and J-Sword's timelines—chronicles of their aspiring rap careers, boasts that might have referred to actual crimes or might have been layered metaphors, the slang so thick it bordered on code. The narratives were distinct from those on the account Ju'waun managed under his own name, edgier, more frantic, the kid committed to a double life. Reddick found links to more freestyles, all of the rap stuff tagged *Heirs, Heirs to the Throne, HTBOYZZ, HTNIGGAZ*, a flood of variations on the phrase. He worked backward, carefully reading each post, noting the day. On Monday, the morning after, he found a brief conversation between the two accounts. J-Sword to Remy, "shit popped off last night," Remy's response, "ay she got caught slippin," and J-Sword ending with, "all good find me this afternoon," tagged, "Sons of Cash Money."

It could be nothing. It could be everything. If it was a reference to Hannah it was suicidally reckless. He clicked on the Sons of Cash Money tag. It was littered with a similar disregard. Everyone using the tag—presumably other members of the group—bragged about violence with transparent euphemisms. Settling old beefs, starting new ones, minor robberies or just chest-pounding grabs for status. Sons of Cash Money linked to other crews that used their accounts the same way, as a forum to assert their power, to reach the intended audience of their actions, some of them hiding under pseudonyms but many of them not, enthralled by the swaggering self-assurance of youth or lost to despair, to a genuine indifference to their fate.

He stood up and opened another beer. Voices drifted up from the street, laughter; Saturday night in Brooklyn carried on in spite of the razor cold. He went to the window. Figures on the sidewalk were cloaked and hooded like monks, their identities, their destinations, concealed. Reddick watched until his beer was half-finished and then grabbed his phone.

"Thomas?" He had dismissed Dottie's claim that Hannah went home as an obvious lie, designed to keep the day running smoothly. But it was worth double-checking if he could.

"Did you find her family, in Oregon?" he asked.

"Mrs. Leland never heard anyone mention their first names. But she does recall that they were from Portland."

"Portland. Are you sure?"

"Quite."

"What about the party—what did Buckley and Franky argue about?"

"There was a disagreement. However, no one was willing to discuss the subject. I gathered that it was something personal."

If it was an affair it would explain their reticence. "Any other information? How they met? What she did for work?"

"Mrs. Leland said that Hannah had recently left her job when they met, and that it was in the arts. She recalls her making a joke—something self-deprecating about it being boring work for creative people. She believes she never actually mentioned a name."

"What about how they met?"

"She could offer more details about this—she was there when it happened, at an event at MoMA last summer. Mr. Seward was one of several donors being honored at the event."

"But not Mrs. Leland, I assume?"

"Or course not. Her interests do not intersect with the Modern's. At any rate, she recalls it quite clearly because it was Mr. Seward who met her first. I believe she approached him to discuss some painting he owned, and after they chatted for a few minutes, he introduced her to his son."

"And Buckley was smitten just like that? It didn't take him very long to try and tie her down."

"I don't see why it would have done. She already had the thing he wanted most—his father's approval. The rest was inevitable."

There was nothing in any of that he could verify, but it sounded right. Buckley, eager to please.

"Do you have any further updates?" Thomas asked.

He thought of his trip to FDP, of the revelation that Buckley and Franky were likely colluding, of the townhouse, of Ju'waun and Tyler and their allusions, their association with violence. He thought that there was no way Mrs. Leland didn't know that Buckley was invested in Restoration Heights, and yet she hadn't told him.

"Not yet."

He hung up, pulled up the Oregon white pages. He turned the desk lamp on, put a coaster under his beer. He knew he should eat but couldn't. There were thirty-five Grangers in Portland. In order to access their phone numbers he had to create an account, punch in his credit card. The site held a trove of personal data—email addresses, civil records—all with disclaimers about accuracy, proper use. He paid for a month's access, the minimum. He dialed the first name on the list. The site said she was sixty-nine years old.

"No, I don't know any Hannah Granger. My sister's name is Anne, but she never went by Anna. Annie, for a brief while, Annie Granger, but it didn't take. What is this about?"

He left messages when no one answered, claimed he was an employer trying to forward her last paycheck. Even with the time difference it was late to be calling, plus it was the weekend—he was met with suspicion but pressed until he was satisfied. No one knew any Hannahs, no one had a relative by that name.

Did Dottie know she was lying, or was she repeating what her employers told her? How far had the cover-up spread?

Finally he turned to the photos he had taken of Buckley's documents. He plugged his phone into his laptop and uploaded the images. He sorted them by type first—check stubs, bank notices, letters sent or received. It all seemed banal, trivial—the sloughed skin of financial transactions. He had to try to understand them. Why keep a paper record, was it something particular about these documents or just a general practice? He searched names, memorized jargon, dug through online financial primers and Wikipedia. He realized he would never learn enough to be able to spot an irregularity, so he worked to reach a point where he could at least organize it, get some sense of what he was looking at. After a few hours he had gone as far as he could; he had found nothing to incriminate Buckley. He dropped the files onto a flash drive.

He turned to the check stubs. He searched the name of each recipient. They were all personal names, no businesses. All men. Not every name led to a hit, but the ones that did were like Buckley: New York elite, philanthropy, the arts. The memos suggested loans, personal debts. One just listed "xmas bet," dated in June—a ten-thousand-dollar inside joke. And then there was Franky Dutton. Buckley cut him a check three years ago, in August, for one hundred eighty-seven thousand dollars. The memo had a flat line drawn through it.

Reddick leaned back in his chair. The number was a gut punch—four times what he earned for a year of handling art, with cash to spare, passed between the two men in a single transaction. It penetrated deeper than the blatant signs of the Sewards' wealth—the villas, the massive townhouse, the battalion of household staff—precisely because, by the family's terms, it was so small. It was a number that to Reddick looked like wealth, the payoff for his hard work, his mother's sacrifices. For Buckley it was petty cash between friends, not even worth noting what it was for.

Reddick closed his laptop, stood up and looked at the map. The six-pack was empty, he had progressed to whiskey, the dregs from Beth and Dean's celebration. He hadn't stopped to eat. He wrote in the day's information. The Genie, Mia's claims that Ju'waun and Tyler were with her that night. The pair's association with what looked like a gang, and the messages that seemed to implicate them. The blocks of text made dark, organic shapes on the white page, like Rorschach blots. He focused on the negative spaces, the connective tissue. There was meaning in the contours, the outlines, a unity of shape and intent, facts that could be shimmied into being by proximity, by the tug of two-dimensional gravity. If he could just get the shapes right he could find her. It had been six days. His memory of her was decomposing. In its place he saw the photograph—she was becoming her image. You forget images more easily than you do people because the world is crowded with them—collections of light, data, information. There is more to a person than this. There was more to her. He reached for the person, tried to forget the photograph. He clung to that distinction; he wrote it on the case map: *Find her, not the image of her,* barely understanding what he meant. He lay on the bed and ran the memory on a loop, tried to fix every detail—the colors, the texture, like he was painting it, frame by frame. Tried to delay the claim of death, to see the rise and fall of her chest before he fell asleep.

FOURTEEN

He woke up hungover. His body ached—two days of drinking, of walking, still bruised from his chase through the development. He ate breakfast and sent a text to Derek, asking if he could help him with something.

Derek sent back: *You forget it's Sunday?*

Five-on-five, full-court, every Sunday morning until the fitness classes started up at one—these were the games of record, the contests that all the two-on-twos and three-on-threes during the week were preparation for. They lasted around half an hour, teams gathering off court to cheer and wait their turn. Scores were kept, win-loss records noted, reputations carved gradually, knifed out by consistency and logged hours, by the aggregate trends of weekly peaks and valleys. On Sunday you made your name. Neither Derek nor Reddick had missed one in months.

Let's talk after, he replied. Then he sent a message to Clint, to see if he had found out anything about Franky. They agreed to meet before the games started.

He arrived early and went to the weight room. It was nearly empty, a young couple spotting each other on the bench press, a pale man in glasses reading from a tattered paperback between sets. Two older women with thick Caribbean accents in baseball hats. No Clint. He walked back to the lobby, through the long hall past the cardio room, a forest of treadmills and ellipticals, of bobbing faces at war with tedium. Half a dozen white girls, most under thirty, heralds of change squeezed into lululemon or some other designer gym wear, like the Y was a New York Sports Club or an Equinox. A scattered few of the regular crowd as well, men and women, mostly older, mostly black. All of them, the new faces and the old, united in their dutiful resolve, in their common effort.

In the lobby the sun was beaming, in defiance of the temperature, of the icy streets. The light knifed through his hangover cloud, bored into his eyes. Clint came in alone, his parka open to accommodate his barrel chest, his expression hidden behind aviator sunglasses.

"You can't even let me get settled?" he asked, indicating his gym bag and coat.

"Take your time. I just didn't want to miss you."

"You know what? It's better we get this over with." He nodded for Reddick to follow him. They went to the top of the stairs, where the hallway overlooked the lower level. It was quiet; patrons passed but didn't linger. The cop set his bag on the floor.

"Why are you asking about the Genie?" he said.

"What? I asked you about Franky Dutton." For a moment he worried that he had misspoken, somehow given Clint the wrong name. "I didn't even know who the Genie was when I talked to you."

"You still don't know. All you know is what you've been

told which means you don't know jack shit. Did I tell you what I do for a living?"

"That's why I'm here."

"I mean *specifically*. Have I told you what I do *specifically* for the police force? I have a memory of saying it but I want to clarify. I want to give you the benefit of the doubt."

"Drugs. You said drugs."

"Very good. Drugs. So don't you think that if you start asking questions about *the fucking Genie* that it's going to get back to me? Or did you think you could trust that drunk Harold to keep his mouth shut?"

Reddick's world was shrinking. "Harold? You know Harold?"

"Yeah, I know fucking Harold."

"From…through the neighborhood?"

"Because all black people know each other."

"That's not what I meant."

"I'm fucking with you. I know Harold because he's a snitch, because he loves to talk and he'll do it with anyone. See, Harold knows people that I actually do give a shit about, the kind of people that work for the Genie. Because that's how my business works. It's my job to know people that know people. And to make sure those people run their mouths."

"That's what Harold does? Runs his mouth?"

"Imagine my reaction last night when he unloads all of this on me, after I had already looked into that developer for you. I was riding high on it, my good deed for the week, and I think to check in on good old Harold—sitting right where you left him at Ti-Ti's—and he starts in on how he's scared for some naive white kid, and he shouldn't have said anything but he wanted to help. I'm thinking—it's impossible that you and Harold know each other, but there is no way in hell anyone else is asking about that same missing white girl so maybe it's not so impossible. And sure enough."

"I swiped him into the subway a few times. Then we ran into each other and just started talking."

"So you swiped him in, huh?"

"It's not a big deal. I mean, I already have the MetroCard."

"You know why he asks, right?"

"I never brought it up. Everybody faces hard times."

"You know he has a job, a house that was paid for when his mother passed?"

"Yeah, he told me."

"So you could probably deduce that it isn't a money thing?"

"I mean..." Reddick shrugged, submitting to the cop's momentum.

"He thinks there are tracking devices in the cards."

"What?"

"He thinks Giuliani and Bush did it. After 9/11 they teamed up, got all of the cities off of tokens and onto cards in order to track people. Especially black people. He says it wasn't enough to round up the homeless into vans, to put street cameras on every block. They needed a way to monitor people's movements."

He felt embarrassed for Harold. "Why are you telling me this?"

"Because you don't know how little you know. Because you have been talking to a paranoid functioning alcoholic about a career criminal, and worse, you kept talking even after you saw how scared it made him. The Genie is not that dude in your dorm who sold you kush while he played Phish records, alright? She has her hand in more things than you could ever know. I don't know what nonsense Harold tried to feed you about how she used to help people, but if that was ever true it's in the dead past. She hasn't cared about anything but her bottom line for a very, very long time. This is a world you want nothing to do with. It will grind your skinny ass to dust."

Three girls brushed past them, headed downstairs. Clint leaned over the rail, eyed their swaying hips.

"I learned some things," Reddick said. "It may have to do with the Genie, I don't know."

"Did you not just hear me?"

"I believe you. I don't want anything to do with this, believe me. I was just trying to find these guys that went to that party with Hannah, and I stumbled into all of this. If I ask you, if I hear it from *you*, I don't have to ask anyone else. I won't have any reason to dig into the Genie's business. If you really want to keep me safe just answer my questions."

Clint looked skeptical. "And what if you take what I say and go charging into even deeper shit?"

"I'm not stupid. I'm just determined."

"We'll have to agree to disagree about that."

"What is Sons of Cash Money?"

"Harold tell you about that, too?"

Reddick told him about his investigation, the tags, the crew names, the pseudonyms, the allusions to violence. Clint listened, stone-faced, and sighed when he finished.

"You're right about one thing."

"What's that?"

"If I don't tell you, then you're going to get yourself killed trying to find out." Clint removed his aviators and leaned against the rail. "These guys have no real connection to the Cash Money Brothers—somebody's uncle ran a corner for them back in the day or something. This always happens, nobodies trying to leach some cred off the real hard-asses. Sons of Cash Money is one of a few crews that rose up in the empty space left by Cash Money Brothers' takedown. Tyler is one of the older members. Spent eighteen months upstate. Pretty sure he was the shooter on a homicide in East New York a few months after he got out—this was maybe four years ago—but they couldn't get him for it. He's been quiet since—on my radar because he's still in the game, but no guns, no assaults. Guys like that are usually doing a second bid by now, but he's stayed out. He's a good-looking kid—you saw him, right?—and smart, well spoken. Gets around the bar scene in the neighborhood, plays down his gangsta side, chases hipster girls."

"What about Ju'waun?"

"Never heard of him. That doesn't mean much, there's a thousand of those guys we don't know, and they don't matter unless they connect to whatever larger case we're building. But that split identity thing? That's unusual. These kids are all in—that's the only way they do it, because they have nothing else. And they don't tolerate frauds. If I had to guess? I'd say maybe he didn't come up in this shit, that he and Tyler met somewhere else and his friend is vouching for him while he plays at being a thug. Could be a cousin or something."

"They're pretty open online about what they do."

"You should have seen it before we started popping some of them with their tweets." Clint laughed. "We use social media to know who is with who, when, where. We build whole cases off of this shit."

"Jesus."

"They post photos of themselves flashing the stolen property, bragging about hits. It's honor culture stuff—why do it if you aren't going to advertise it, get a little status from it, make your rivals think twice."

"So the Genie—is she Sons of Cash Money?"

"Fuck no. I told you that woman is the real deal. People like the Genie use gangs like SOCM to move some product for them, but that's as far as it goes. The kids like the violence, the guns, the gangster posing—that's their whole lives. It's how they become somebody. But older heads like the Genie, they've been in the business for a while, they stay clear of that stuff. It gets in the way of making a profit."

Sensei came in, nodded at Clint and took a long look at Reddick before smiling and walking toward the back.

"All that iron back there isn't going to lift itself," Clint said.

"Sorry. We haven't gotten to Franky yet."

"Before we leave this subject—you got any more questions about these guys, the Genie, any of this street shit—you ask me, okay? Not Harold or anybody else. And if you come across any hint that these people are involved with that missing girl, even a suspicion—I'll let you talk to a detective, and they can follow up if it's worth it."

"So you believe me, that she's missing?"

"If I really believed you I would already have called that detective."

"So what do you have on Franky?"

"This will make your day." He looked resigned, like it hurt to say it. "Drunk and disorderly. Possession. An assault charge."

"I knew it."

"Don't gloat. Every one of the charges got dropped eventually. Amazing how hard it is to get things to stick to that white skin. It's like you're coated with something."

"What's the assault?"

"A woman in a bar. He tries to pick her up, she says no. She says he got angry and grabbed her wrist. Gave her a bracelet of bruises. He says he just caught her hand when she tried to slap him, that his opening line must have been a little too straightforward. As I mentioned, she eventually dropped the charges."

"So he gets violent when women say no."

"There's more. I saw that his name was mentioned in connection with a gun case in Bushwick."

"He has a gun?"

"Hold on, let me finish. Two officers respond to a call about some hophead with a gun, loitering in front of a building in Bushwick. When they get there the guy is sitting on his stoop, practically nodding off. He lives there. He has a piece tucked into the back of his waistband. Now they know right away something is wrong. The call was anonymous, the caller didn't give any specifics, didn't say how he knew the guy had a gun in the first place. The junkie was too fucked-up to flash it. And this isn't the kind of guy they find guns on; this guy is just some addict. He's like fifty. Getting guns off the street, this is priority number one for this squad, this is what they do, so they know how it goes down. They have instincts for this sort of thing. Of course once the guy sobers up he has no recollection of having it on him, he seems like he's telling the truth, and they don't feel right about busting him for it."

"What does this have to do with Franky?"

"They ask around, turns out the building is being sold, the new owners want everyone out so they can gut it and turn it around, but there are holdouts, people that have been there long enough that they're protected to some degree—they'll be pushed out eventually but it will be a long process, and expensive."

"People usually just take buyouts."

"Some do, some don't. Old-timers like this guy, no way. He gets his check, first and the fifteenth, blows it on dope, panhandles a little bit when he's short. His dealer works out of the Chinese takeout up the street. He's not relocating, that block is his entire world."

"So what are you saying?"

"Turns out there have been a bunch of calls on the tenants in this building. All anonymous. Various minor crimes, possession, whatever. All of them happening after the building was sold."

"To Franky's company, FDP."

"Took you long enough. Framing the tenants to get them out. Franky is questioned, did you or any of your employees plant the gun, did you or any of your employees make the phone calls. Of course nothing came of it. I tracked down the officers that chatted with him and they said they would have loved to wipe the smirk off his face but they had no evidence. They knew, he knew they knew, but it just wasn't the kind of case anyone was interested in building. ADA would rather go after someone more dangerous, Feds would rather go after someone with more clout."

"Fuck."

"And again, no evidence. So this guy is a real asshole after all. Feel vindicated?"

Reddick was silent for half a minute, absorbing it. "Hannah could have said no. I had been thinking jealousy, collusion. But maybe it was just Franky. He can't handle not getting his way."

"There's a long road between entitlement and murder. And you have to pave it with proof."

Reddick shook his head. "That can't be it anyway—there's too much it leaves unexplained. Like why Buckley is refusing to cooperate."

"What about this girl's family?" Clint asked. "Her friends?"

"I don't know any friends. She only had one social media account and it's private. It's like she barely existed. The Sewards are claiming she went home to her family but no one with her last name in her hometown claimed her."

"Maybe they're unlisted."

"I guess. But the timing, the matter-of-fact way the Sewards' house manager told me about it—it's too convenient. It's damage control, trying to get me to leave it alone."

"This girl has to know other people. Her fiancé's family can't hide it from them forever."

"I'd love to talk to a family member, talk to a friend, just to find out what lie the Sewards are feeding them."

Clint leaned forward. "That's not what you need to know. It doesn't matter what the lie is. What matters is *why* they are lying. What do they have to gain by delaying the inevitable?"

"You seem almost interested."

"Don't get cocky. I'm just making conversation."

"We'll see." A child raced by, giggling, her haggard mother yelling for her to be careful on the stairs. "Maybe that's how Restoration Heights fits in. The delay. Buckley has a chunk of money tied up in the project, I don't know, maybe there is some deadline or something. A milestone to reach, after which a scandal would be less damaging."

"Do I want to know how you found that out?"

"Derek told me."

Clint laughed. "You con the whole damn YMCA into helping you?"

"I guess people like me."

Two men came up the stairs. Reddick recognized one of the faces but didn't immediately place it—young, pocked skin, sharp braids. He caught Reddick's gaze.

"Oh shit, it's Skinny Tom Hardy," he said, laughing. "You here to ball, Skinny Tom?"

Reddick kept his face flat, affected an arrogant calm. "I'll be up there."

"You owe me. Alright? You owe me." He and his friend walked toward the rear stairwell that led up to the courts.

"Who was that?"

Reddick winced. The sound of the guy's voice had reinvigorated his hangover. "He got hot because I dunked on him. It happens."

If Clint was impressed or surprised he didn't show it. "You don't look shit like Tom Hardy. You know that, right?"

"Don't we all look alike?"

"Oh, you got jokes now?"

Reddick shrugged and Clint shook his head, as though this final provocation had exhausted his patience.

"Tom Hardy," he muttered. "That's an insult to a fine actor. Did that guy even look at your face?"

"It's not *that* far off."

"See, that's the problem with people. They don't really *look* at each other. They just see some approximation that more-or-less conforms to whatever vague ideas they already have in their head. For us, for cops? We have to learn to nix that shit real fast. All the details that the approximation leaves out are the details that will break your case. You really want my help? This is the best thing I can do for you, is tell you this: see things for how they are, and not for how you think they are."

Reddick offered his hand, Clint took it. "Thanks. I'll try."

"And stay the fuck away from the Genie."

He was the last guy to walk in. The other players had drifted into teams, arcing warm-up shots beneath opposing baskets. Braids was on the opposite end from Derek. Reddick joined his friend and managed a few layups to loosen up before the game started.

See things for how they are, and not for how you think they are. He thought he had been building this case objectively, using facts like stones, setting one on top of another. But it was still his decisions, his hunches, that determined which stones he used—and he couldn't cleanse that process of his biases.

On the first possession he came off a pick with a long look at an open jumper—not his shot but it was there, waiting; he had to take it. It hit the inside of the rim, caromed and spilled out.

Of course he went after the guy he was hardwired to hate—a stereotype of an irresponsible developer. Franky was an entitled bully, Buckley one of his crony enablers, twin incarnations of indifferent affluence. You can't help but resent guys like that, unless you're one of them. They invoke all your petty, bitter envies.

He went three straight possessions without touching the ball. After the next rebound he clapped his hands in the backcourt, received a pass, beat his man off the line but another defender closed hard and he had to kick it out, restart the play. Derek chided him for not waiting for a screen.

But the image he hung on them was accurate. He knew that Franky mistreated women—that wasn't projection. And now he knew that he pushed people out of his properties, displaced lives without regard to how his decision affected anything other than his own profit. Those were facts, not stereotypes. He didn't suspect Franky because he was entitled—he suspected him because he was cruel and unscrupulous.

Braids switched off his man to Reddick.

"Your eyes are all red, Skinny Tom. This game just started and you already look like you want to cry."

Reddick went right at him, hard—which was what Braids wanted, but he underestimated Reddick's first step and caught an elbow to his gut as the art handler darted by. Another defender crashed the paint and Reddick dropped an easy floater over the top.

"There you go," a teammate yelled.

When they lined back up Braids was smiling.

Applying the same question to Ju'waun and Tyler—how true was the image he had pieced together of the two of them? Dean was of course right—there was an abiding pressure to view all young black men as criminals. But he and the rest of Reddick's Bushwick friends absolved themselves by pushing the source of the idea elsewhere—Hollywood, the media, flyover states—yet would stare at their own feet if they passed Ju'waun and Tyler on the sidewalk at night, hearts racing, minds firing excuses. They would sooner be skinned than admit to it. Of the crowd Reddick grew up with, in his old neighborhood, two of them never graduated high school. They were both black. They were both in prison. There were consequences to the uneven toll of the war on drugs, to the wreckage that mass incarceration laid on certain communities while passing others by, and if you couldn't admit that it created a criminal class out of undereducated black youths you couldn't begin to fix it. Pretending the problem wasn't there, that it was all media bias and stigma, helped no one. Reddick saw Ju'waun and Tyler as reminders of his own near-misses, of his undeserved luck—there but for the grace of god, for the grace of my white skin. Dragging them into the murder of a white girl felt like harassing victims of a virus he was born immune to.

ay she got caught slippin.

The other team missed a pull-up jumper off the break, Derek and Reddick were still at half-court but their man was there for the rebound—he fired the ball out to Derek. Reddick was already two steps past the defense and Derek's pass was quarterback-precise; Reddick laid it up uncontested. He didn't look but knew from the awkward way it left his fingers, from his teammates' reactions, that it rolled out.

"You alright?" Derek asked.

Reddick waved him off.

The next time Braids touched the ball he drained a three over Reddick's raised hand.

There were only so many ways the pieces fit together; perhaps only one way. It was about the points of contact. Franky was connected to Buckley by their history. Buckley was invested in Restoration Heights, which was in the Genie's territory—where Franky also had a property. Considering his illicit history Franky might have tapped one of the Genie's services in the past—maybe she sold him the gun he planted on that poor hophead. She arranged things. Harold had said no murder, but the fear her name invoked suggested he was underselling her capacity for violence.

Reddick was pressing. He saw a teammate backpedaling to the three-point line, away from his defender, knew he should kick it out but couldn't, not with Braids daring him to come forward. He shot and missed, again. His open teammate shook his head, admonished him. They were down four points.

So: Franky hires the Genie to kill Hannah. She sends Ju'waun and Tyler to do the job. Either by themselves or to lure her to someone else—the honey in the flytrap. It's Ju'waun that Hannah latches onto, and he's happy about it, he's eager to prove that he's hard, that he deserves to be in the crew. Mia, the clerk from Cask, is their alibi, the black eye her encouragement. And why? Because Hannah had finally said no—cut Franky off, decided to be a faithful wife even if she hadn't been a faithful girlfriend. Buckley had blown up at the gala, forced her to decide, and she chose her future husband. So Franky reacts like he had with the girl in the bar—violent rage. He does it near Restoration Heights on purpose, perhaps to hide the body there, perhaps just to link her to it, because Buckley is too gutless to follow her trail if it leads there, too afraid of jeopardizing his investment. Franky counts on Buckley's infatuation with him to keep him in line. Their meeting after Reddick's visit to FDP was more damage control, Franky checking in to make sure Buckley's suspicions were still hemmed in by avarice and fear.

The thing was, Braids could shoot. A mouth is a jab; it works fine alone but it's better when it prods your opponent into eating a right hook, when you can capitalize on the reactions it provokes. Reddick was tired of being stuck by it—he wanted to make a play, to shut him up. He bit so hard on a crossover that he fell to one knee and Braids buried a silky jumper over his exposed back. The spectators moaned, one of them whistled.

"I still owe you, Tom. That ain't it. That ain't even close to it."

The narrative flouted Clint's warning about generalities. All the actors were in their most obvious roles. Vindictive, scheming, rich white men. Black killers, thugs for hire. A young, pretty, white female victim. It was a collection of biases, of preconceptions, of the worst stereotypes—some he shared and some he abhorred—but he had built all this on facts, observations. It fit the events. The truth does not care about your sensibilities.

He saw a gap, planted his foot, rubbed Braids off his hip with an off-ball screen, raised his hand and caught a crisp bounce pass. But he took the wrong angle off the pick, was too eager and cut too sharply toward the hoop, which put him right back into Braids's face—only he decided it didn't matter, it was time to end this, put it right down his fucking throat. You know you can outjump that son of a bitch, just do it, up, up, up, up.

Braids slapped the ball with his open palm, firing it into the pads behind the basket.

The groans of both teams exploded in the cavernous gym. Braids caught his hand, too, maybe before the ball, maybe after, and followed through like he was winging a baseball. The motion spun Reddick in the air, he flailed to get a foot beneath him, came down on the outside edge of his toes—not nearly enough to stay up. He spilled onto the hardwood like a stack of plates. The ball bounced past his face. When he opened his eyes Braids was standing over him.

"We even now."

"Foul!" Derek yelled. "That's a fucking foul, man!"

"Come on." The other team protested.

"He threw him onto the fucking ground."

"I ain't throw that man. He fell."

"I fucking saw you, asshole."

"Derek, brother. Calm down, man," his teammates trying to settle him. "Calm down."

"I watched you."

"Yo, Skinny Tom, tell your boy I ain't push you, man."

Reddick got up, slowly, hurting. "Let's just keep going."

"You don't have to do this, bro." Derek said. "He fucking shoved you."

"It's fine."

"Did I shove you or not?"

"I said it's fucking fine."

Braids sneered. "That ain't no answer."

"Who the fuck are you anyway?" Derek got in his face. "We're here like every Sunday and I've never seen you."

"*Here every Sunday*, like I'm supposed to be impressed. Y'all niggas strut like you at the Gersh when you at the damn YMCA."

"If we aren't shit how come you can't even cover my boy without fouling?"

Braids rolled his eyes. "Defend him all you want, you still gonna wake up black as me tomorrow morning."

"What did you say to me? What did you just say?"

"Listen to how you talk, *bro*."

"Everybody just calm the fuck down." One of the regulars edged between them. "Derek, your man already said it's okay. And you," turning to Braids, "you got to learn when enough is enough. Alright?"

Braids grinned.

To Derek. "Alright?"

Derek sucked his teeth, shrugged.

"Now, can we finish this game?"

They limped through the final point, both teams playing loose D, mostly silent, relieved when the final shot went in. Reddick's team lost. They lined up to shake hands, except for Braids and Derek. A few of them patted Reddick on the shoulder in gestures of consolation. On his way out Braids slapped the threshold, a firecracker pop in the quiet gymnasium. He went down the stairs three at a time. A few of the older guys shook their heads.

"You sure you're alright?" Derek asked when they were alone.

"Thanks for having my back."

"That dude is an asshole."

"It was my own fault."

"He suckered you into playing his game. It happens." Derek squirmed into his hoodie. He seemed calmer now, Braids's insults forgotten. "So what did you want my help with?"

Reddick told him about breaking into Buckley's desk, and taking photos of the financial documents.

"What about the guys she was with that night?"

"I'm getting somewhere with them, too. I think I have an idea for how it all fits together."

"You come up with this idea just now?" He nodded at the court. "Out there?"

Reddick winced, the memory still sore. "Some of it, yeah."

"Don't ever try to walk and chew gum at the same time."

"The thing is, I need to figure out some of this financial stuff first. Maybe it's worthless but I want to check all the boxes." He pulled the flash drive from his pocket, thankfully undamaged from his fall. "I put all the photos I took on here. Do you think you could take a look for me? Just glance over them to make sure there isn't some obvious fraud or something?"

Derek hesitated. "Yeah. Okay. I doubt you have anything. I'll deny ever having looked if anyone asks me."

"I'd never mention you. I really appreciate this."

"You're either in *over* your head, or you're entirely *inside* your head. I'll let you know when I figure out which."

FIFTEEN

He walked home on thawing sidewalks, along the edge of Restoration Heights. Melting ice collected in filthy estuaries along the curb. He stopped to look through one of the windows in the plywood barrier—the site was still blanketed in white. Whatever secrets it covered were safe.

Perhaps Buckley was blameless, a victim of his own weakness, but it didn't taste right. He had the resources of his entire family behind him; he could shield himself from suspicion and still make an effort to find out what happened.

So how did Restoration Heights fit? Reddick's eyes drifted along the fence, past the warnings and endorsements, past the promises of sustainability, to the list of investors, Corren Capital at the top. Who were the others? He walked closer to the list. There were at least twenty names, mostly corporate—in it for the money but also for this, for the chance to stamp their name on a project that would shape the neighborhood, that ten years from now might define it. Ambition of this scale was never merely about profit—it was about legacy, reputation. He thought of Sons of Cash Money and its members' online swagger—this was no different; why do it unless everyone knows that you've done it, unless it could serve as warning and boast. There was only one game, played in different arenas. He didn't recognize any of the names. He took a photo of the list.

Arcs of pain pulsed his hip—Braids had dumped him on the bruise he took chasing that kid in Restoration Heights. He was grateful that Derek stepped in. There had been a moment of doubt that anyone was on his side—his old fear that the skills that had opened friendships also bred resentment. Derek's help meant more to Reddick than he had expected.

He went home—Dean still out, giving him space—and sat at his computer. He started on the investors list and found his way to an opposition blog. It was hackish, frantic—the pages an acrid yellow, the text jarring blue, peppered with images of white men in suits, hyperlinked to evidence of corruption and insider dispensation. It was a blend of conspiratorial mania and shrewd investigation. There were photos of black leaders, city council reps, church elders and lists of what it took to buy them off—appointments, seats, endowments. It veered at times into hysteria— anti-Semitism, rants about neoliberal overlords. There was a blog roll on the side, links to community sites that had posted about the project, however briefly. He followed it, tried to corroborate the accusations, pin down facts. The other sites were less wild-eyed than the first, with posts that ranged from chronicles of the various protests—he recognized the one he had met Sensei at—to hard-nosed looks at the blows the community around the project had already suffered. He read complaints from landlords who were bought out early, before the plans were announced, and watched helplessly as their properties were flipped for double the amount that, just weeks prior, they had been thrilled to accept. Testimonies of displaced families that were bullied into selling homes they had lived in for generations, taking buyouts because they could see the scope of the pressure arrayed against them, the will of a system that seemed constructed for no purpose other than to take what they had, a teleology of plunder. When they can no longer profit from your body they will profit from your history—the soul of a place is just another consumer good.

He looked for connections to Hannah. She didn't appear on any of the blogs. He changed tacks. Maybe she worked for one of the investors. He went to the New York State website, where LLCs were registered. He found filing addresses, occasionally a name. He searched the addresses—sometimes they pointed to development offices, sometimes to some other business entirely. Looking for context, he found that individuals and companies often created a separate LLC for their real estate holdings, to quarantine the risk. Returning to the list, he followed each connection as far as he could take it.

After an hour he went out for a sandwich, came back and kept working. Another hour in and he was halfway through the list—nothing that connected to Hannah. It didn't help that he knew so little about her, that he was reduced to looking for references to Portland or to her name. He picked up his ball, spun it, dribbled into the living room and back. He settled down again. A little over an hour later he was finished, with no hits.

But there were two ends to any transaction, buyers and sellers—maybe she and the Sewards were on opposite sides. He went back to the blogs, compiled a second list, of the landlords and homeowners who sold. Depending on the blogger the sellers were alternately treated as turncoats or as victims. He grabbed many of the names from a threadbare watchdog site. It was haphazardly maintained, with calls to rallies that had already passed and notes on rulings that had already been superseded. There were dead links to petitions. The list of landlords was compiled before many of them had sold, in the hopes of encouraging their continued resistance.

He went back to the State website. He repeated his system with the sellers, working through the list methodically, pulling the addresses they were filed under. He was so worn down from the monotony of entering the information, the fruitlessness of it, that he nearly missed it.

Tompkins Mac LLC, registered to 229 South 2nd Street, Fifth Floor, Brooklyn.

That was the address for Franky Dutton Properties.

He went back to the watchdog site. The Tompkins Mac property had already sold when the writer compiled her list. Looking at the time frame of the other posts, it appeared that the LLC was one of the first to cash out of the area—how did that affect his bottom line? Should he have held out for a better offer, did Buckley pressure him into selling quickly? Tompkins Mac wasn't mentioned on any other blogs or sites—it was out of the game before most protestors started cataloging victims and traitors. And he didn't see FDP listed at all—Franky had been using Tompkins Mac to protect his personal holdings, keeping his company separate.

Did Buckley fuck his friend over on the Restoration Heights deal? And was Hannah a pawn for revenge? How would *that* have played with Franky if she then rejected him—her desires frustrating his retribution? It might have compounded his rage, perhaps been what finally pushed him all the way to murder—a way to pay them both back while sating his anger.

It amplified the motive but it wasn't evidence. It wasn't anything he could take to Clint, not yet—but it was worth more digging.

He called Derek.

"This is what we do now? Talk on the phone like it's 1993?"

"It's about Franky."

"It's only been a few hours, man. I haven't had time to look at that flash drive."

"Not that." He told him about Franky's other LLC, and that he owned property that was swallowed by Restoration Heights. "From what I can tell he sold pretty early. I was thinking Buckley might have pressured him or something—maybe he missed out on a big payday?"

"I doubt it. These deals usually go down the other way, the friends and insiders make out like bandits."

"Well, is there any way to check one way or the other?"

"I could do that. Pretty easily, actually. There are public records for those transactions."

"Just tell me where to look."

"It will be easier if I do it." He sighed as though it was a burden, but Reddick heard enthusiasm beneath it. "It might take me a bit to get to it."

"I really appreciate the help. And not just about this."

"You mean this morning? I told you it's all good."

"I know. I just— It was nice having some backup."

"Bro, that guy is an asshole. I did it for everybody."

"Thanks all the same, though." His phone buzzed. "Hey, I got another call coming in. Talk to you later."

"Be safe."

Reddick hung up and switched to the incoming call.

"Reddick?" It was Lane.

"Hey, Lane, what's up? Did you need me to come in this week?"

"I'm afraid not." His voice was nervous and firm.

"Okay. What's going on, then?" Reddick was buzzing with

optimism, with the rush of new information. Whatever was bothering Lane couldn't possibly touch him.

"I'm calling to hear your side."

"My side of what?"

"Why you wandered around the Sewards' house while everyone was at lunch. Why you ignored the one thing I asked you to do. How you could be so selfish as to put this ridiculous agenda of yours ahead of Lockstone's relationship with our most valuable client."

"Agenda?"

"I don't know what else to call it. Obsession? I mean, what is wrong with you?"

Reddick's confidence was upended. He scrambled to recover it. "Lane, I—"

"Just stop."

"I thought you wanted to hear my side."

"I've changed my mind."

"I was just late coming back from the bathroom."

"I'll need a better story than that if you want me to save your job. Dottie emailed Mrs. Kruger." The Krugers owned Lockstone. They followed the progress of their company from their Westchester village, rarely getting involved in the day-to-day. "I have a call with them tomorrow morning. Do you even care what I tell them?"

"I mean. I need a job. I need money."

"Yeah. Well, don't get your hopes up. You're a nice guy, you work hard, but you're an art handler. You wouldn't be that hard to replace."

"Insult to injury, Lane?"

"You're the one who is so interested in the truth."

There was nothing to do but wait—on Derek, on Lane. It was nearly six and dark as midnight, the bright afternoon wasted on his laptop. He was out of leads but restless. He put on his coat and boots and left.

He went to his usual spot on Tompkins, a narrow coffee shop that had been in the neighborhood as long as he had. His restlessness was manifesting as nervous energy; he made small talk with the barista, played along when she answered with bored flirtation. He took his coffee with him and left.

Someone was waiting on his corner, tall, a dark parka zipped tight around his thin frame. Reddick couldn't see his face but felt him staring, noticed his aggressive, focused posture. His first thought was Braids—somehow finding out where he lived and coming back to talk more shit. But this guy was too tall, and as Reddick got closer he could see him clearly.

"Ju'waun." He seemed younger in person, and even better looking than his friend. Large feminine eyes, cheekbones like cliffs, hair stacked high over a crisp fade. His pulchritude undercut his attempt at menace.

"You're Reddick, right?" he said. "The man with all the questions."

Reddick kept his face composed, forced his muscles to relax. He felt himself sliding into his body the way he often managed to during a game, the way he had failed to do this morning; both hyperconscious and distant.

"I'm trying to find out what happened to Hannah."

"See, that's what I'm talking about."

"You were the last person with her. Tyler went home with Trisha."

"I'm not here to help you man," Ju'waun shoved him to make his point. Reddick held his coffee away from his body to keep the steaming liquid from slopping onto his clothes. "I'm here to tell you to lay the fuck off."

His voice was soft and laid-back in a way that made Reddick think of the beach. Despite it, and despite his romantic face, he seemed convinced of his ability to inspire fear. But there was nothing hard about him—he seemed exactly what Clint said he would be, a poseur. He pushed Reddick again, who barely moved. He had taken rougher shots on uncalled fouls.

No way this kid killed someone.

"First you get a warning." He cocked his head to the side. "Keep poking your nose where it don't belong and I'll come back."

"Why?"

"Fuck do you mean, *why*?"

"I mean, why just a warning? You came all the way over here for that?"

"So you understand that I know where you live."

"If you want to make a point, just make it. Why leave and then come back? Save yourself the trouble and do this right now."

"Fuck is wrong with you, dude? I'm trying to let you off easy."

To his credit, he wasn't backing down. He looked surprised but unafraid. Reddick hadn't been in a fistfight since junior high. He wondered whether he should ball up his fist.

"Do you need help?" Neither of them had seen the woman approach. She was middle-aged, her pale face shining concern between her cable-knit hat and high collar. She stood in front of a double stroller, both bins sealed against winter, holding coffee in a cup that matched Reddick's. "Do you need me to call the police?"

"On which one of us?" Reddick said.

Ju'waun looked at him. "You serious?"

"I'm fine," Reddick said to her. "That was a joke. I'm okay."

"He pushed you. I saw him."

"We're friends. Aren't we, Ju'waun?"

Ju'waun turned and smiled at the woman. "Old friends, ma'am."

She looked at both of them for a moment, shook her head, turned and pushed her stroller away.

"That's racist," Ju'waun said.

The interruption had leached the air of violence, left Reddick feeling buoyant, playful. "You *were* threatening me," he said. "Maybe she's not racist, maybe she's perceptive."

"Come on, man. She wanted to call the cops to help you, not me. Maybe that push was self-defense. Dead ass, that's racist."

"Can pushing someone count as self-defense?"

They were both almost smiling now, the stolen tension replaced by a kind of boyish giddiness. "Maybe," Ju'waun said. "How is that lady in a position to know?"

"At least tell me you see the irony in what you're saying."

"It's not irony, it's—this isn't a joke." Ju'waun seemed to suddenly recall his purpose. He tried to put his scowl back on but it didn't take.

"Why are you here?" Reddick asked. "Really?"

"I fucking told you." Ju'waun was trying to amp himself back up. "Lay off the questions."

Reddick saw how off balance he was, and pressed. "Did Mia tell you about me? Was I close to something?"

"You aren't close to shit."

"Did you give her that black eye?"

"Man, come on."

"Then who? The Genie? Who did she piss off?"

He looked away, half mumbled. "What do you know about any of this shit?"

"I know the Genie provides things. Drugs, guns. I know you and Tyler and maybe the rest of Sons of Cash Money work for her sometimes, running pickups back to Clean City. I know you're not from Lafayette Gardens like the rest of them, and I thought you might have taken Hannah out to prove yourself to them, but now I know there's no way that's what happened, because if you were hard enough for that you would have popped me in the fucking mouth by now, no matter how many white ladies walk by with strollers."

For half a beat it seemed as though he would—the encounter had slipped outside of anything he might have rehearsed, and Reddick could see him searching for a way to retake control.

"But if you weren't involved, why did someone tell my friend Harold not to ask about Hannah? And why did you tweet at Tyler that she 'got caught slippin''?"

Ju'waun stopped. The moment was as still as the cold air—until he blew it up with laughter.

"What the fuck," he said between gasps, bent at the belly, staggering away with the force of it. Now it was Reddick who was off balance, suddenly humiliated, their positions reversed.

"Oh man," Ju'waun said, wiping his eyes. "What do they say about a little bit of knowledge or whatever?"

Reddick waited, with no option but to let Ju'waun enjoy his victory.

"We was worried, is why it's so funny. About nothing. About bullshit."

"Tell me already."

"*Mia*, man. We was talking about fucking Mia. We've been seeing each other for weeks now. You got your boy asking about some blonde chick and bringing up my name with her, what the fuck else is people going to think?"

"I told him her name was Hannah."

"You think that drunk Harold remembered that shit?" He shifted into an unfriendly impression of Harold. "'Uh,

I was wondering about Ju'waun and this white chick, uh, um. Mia? Yeah, that sounds about right. Ju'waun and Mia, what's up with them?' And on top of that you said Sunday night. Crazy man."

"What happened Sunday night?"

"Mia got fucking robbed, man. 'Caught slippin' means she got jacked, how white are you? That's what happened to her face."

Finally Reddick began to catch up. "The drop. Somebody stole the money she owed the Genie, that's why she was so worried."

"Not money she owed her. That's the Genie's money. Money leaves the dry cleaners dirty and comes back clean—how about *you* appreciate *that* irony."

"She launders money in a boutique liquor store? A dentist's office?"

Ju'waun shrugged. "That's the neighborhood now. The Genie is adaptable. That dentist is working off debts, man. And Mia—well, her and Mia go way back. That's how it is."

"The Genie would be that upset? She couldn't just go to her and tell her what happened?"

"Yo, this clearly has nothing to do with that Hannah chick, so can we just drop it? It's cold out here."

"Just tell me so I know what not to look for. So I don't waste more time."

Ju'waun considered his logic, then shrugged. "Me and my cousin were at Black Swan, that spot on Bedford."

"Your cousin? Tyler?"

"You want to hear this shit or what? That girl you're talking about, Hannah? We met her at the bar. Tyler is trying to talk to her, you know. She says she's gotta bounce for this party, so we go with her. Halfway through the night it doesn't matter because Tyler is on this other chick, and he's making pretty good time with her. But here's what's up. I was supposed to get Mia's drop earlier that day, only I didn't because I knew I was going to see her that night, after she closed the store, at like ten. But Tyler's not trying to leave at no ten o'clock, you know? He's about to hit. So I text Mia, I tell her to take the drop home with her, and I'll come over after we leave the party."

"What was Hannah doing? Who was she talking to?"

"I don't know. I stopped paying attention. It was a party. That's not what this story is about."

"Because Mia got jacked on her way home."

"Now you get it. Two dudes came up behind her, one punched her in the eye, the other grabbed her bag and took off."

"Was it a hit? Did they know she had the money?"

"Nah, man. Not around here, not if they knew she was with Sons of Cash Money. More like it was a couple of punk-ass kids trying to cop a cell phone and a wallet and they ended up with the Genie's cash."

"But the Genie holds you responsible."

"Both of us, to be honest. We lost the money—plus, you know, she has a strict no fraternizing policy, right? I'm mixing business with pleasure; she wouldn't like it. She'd say it might cause complications—man, it did cause complications. And we'd have to own up to seeing each other to explain it right."

"So Mia was freaking out."

"Yeah, and that's why my boy pushed back at Harold when he asked about me—he didn't want what happened with her to get around."

"How do you know Harold anyway—he didn't know your name when I brought you up."

"He don't know me. I know him but he don't know me. He's always hanging around, talking about how things used to be, dropping every hard name from back in the day like he was one of them." He saw Reddick's sympathetic look, and softened his tone. "I'm not trying to diss the man, he just can't get out the past. That world is gone. Anyway, it doesn't matter. We're all good with the Genie now."

"You picked up the money on Thursday."

"That's just creepy, dude, that you know all this stuff. But yeah, Thursday. Mia paid it out of the money her store brings in—she knows Tyler and me are gonna find the dudes that jacked her and pay her back. So we're all set, except for your nosy ass stirring shit up, causing problems, not knowing what the fuck you're even talking about."

Reddick backed away, so far that Ju'waun nearly followed, and looked down his street, where he first saw Hannah, with the half-finished colossus of Restoration Heights rising behind her.

"Was she still at the party?" he asked. "When you and Tyler finally left, was she still there?"

Ju'waun shrugged again, untethered by the distance between them, nearly adrift. "I think so. Yeah. Yeah she was there."

"What time was that?" Reddick's defeated voice barely reached him.

"About midnight, I guess." Reddick turned and started to walk home, but Ju'waun interrupted him. "Hey, yo, Reddick."

"Yeah?"

"Keep your head up, man. It's not as bad as you think. I promise you that. It's not at all like you think it is."

SIXTEEN

In the space occupied by his adrenaline—once he was home, once he had accepted Ju'waun's revelations—there was an encompassing fatigue, and the remnants of a resurfaced hangover. He finished his tepid coffee. First he verified Ju'waun's story, looked up a neighborhood crime report—a woman mugged Sunday night on the edge of Fort Greene, no name given but the details fit. He wrote it all down on the case map—the two halves pulled even now, but disconnected, a pair of circles whose edges barely crossed. All the connections were severed. He rummaged in his drawing table until he found an X-Acto knife, unscrewed the knurled grip and slipped in a fresh blade. He returned to the map, placed a metal straight-edge against it and cut the paper in half. On the left he had Bed-Stuy and the Genie, Ju'waun and Tyler—all of them now free from Franky and Buckley, from Mrs. Leland and her son and their grasping wealth. He gave Hannah to her fiancé and her lover. He split Restoration Heights in half—conceived by one side, endured by the other. He wished he could have carved it out.

The operation left him with almost nothing. In Bed-Stuy he had a story that didn't need him, that he had no claim to. On the other side was a class of people who cared about him only insofar as he might be used—rearrange the furniture, hang the walls, run errands. None of what he had learned was of any use to him, and worse, none of it was of any use to Hannah. She was fading—she existed a little less by the minute. He couldn't stop it.

His phone buzzed—Sarah.

hey what are you up to tonight.

trying to put an end to a very long day.

She sent back a frowning emoji, and after a few minutes:

this might cheer you up. you still interested in Franky Dutton? because I'm at a party with his ex-girlfriend.

It was a shotgun apartment, first floor; the press of bodies generating so much heat that someone had propped open one of the wooden windows, spilling music and conversation onto the sidewalk. Reddick came in through the kitchen, went to the rear bedroom and added his coat to the pile on the bed, then went looking for Sarah.

He sorted through the thicket of mostly white faces—the crowd almost entirely under thirty, young enough to neglect their ambitions without guilt, untroubled by the prospect of a late Sunday night. The men with thick mustaches or square beards, the women in clinging dresses or high-waisted jeans. He found Sarah in a crowd near the window, the oldest person here by nearly a decade but untroubled by it, like a guru or revered elder, a forerunner. She wore a slick dress, a 1950s cut, and had combed out her braids.

She hugged him. "I can't believe you came out. You *never* come out."

"I needed some good news."

"Was your day that bad?"

"We can talk about it some other time."

"Are you trying to make a date?"

"I'm sorry?"

"This is like our third time seeing each other in a week, I thought you might want to keep the momentum going. You used to come by all the time. It's almost like you're not interested in horse pornography."

"It's not that, it's—"

"I'm *joking.* Come on, let's get you a beer."

She took his hand and led him into the kitchen. He had drunk a second cup of coffee on his way over, trying to revive his lost focus, but it had only ramped up his anxiety. He wanted to learn what he could from Franky's ex and go home, sleep it off.

She handed him an open bottle of beer; they toasted and drank.

"So where is she?" he asked.

"Guess."

"Guess?"

"We can see her from where we are standing. You've been playing detective for a week now, right? Let's see what you've learned." She laughed. "Find the ex-girlfriend."

"I don't think I've learned anything, is the problem."

"How do you know unless you try?"

"Sarah."

She grabbed his biceps, shook and didn't let go. "Humor me."

He sipped his beer and relented. "Fine. We can see her right now?"

"Clear as day."

"Alright, so there are…twelve girls. At least half of them we can eliminate right away, for obvious reasons."

"You're so shallow."

"Not me. Franky. He went out with her more than once, right? He's too insecure to spend that much time with a woman who isn't an obvious looker. So that leaves…five. Now, when you saw the photo of Hannah you said she was too all-American, so that's two more gone."

"Which two?"

He pointed out two white girls, a blonde and brunette, sorority types whose classic looks had nonetheless drawn a crowd of hip young suitors.

"Alright."

"How am I doing so far?"

"It's too easy." She still hadn't let go of his arm.

"So we have three candidates. They all have style. They all have the traditional attributes you might expect Franky to be drawn to."

"Tits and ass, you mean."

"Also nice smiles, pretty eyes."

"This is what it's like on the other side of the male gaze? I feel dumber already."

One of the girls felt them staring, turned toward them. Sarah smiled and waved. The girl didn't react, returned to her conversation.

"That's one more suspect eliminated," Reddick said.

"Are you always this lucky?"

He looked at the other two, a tall Latina and a pale white girl, both with petite faces and an avalanche of thick black hair.

"Her," he said, pointing at the white girl, who was standing in the den, near the speakers.

"Okay, but why? Because guesses don't count."

"See that tattoo on her forearm? *Je est un autre.*"

"I am an other."

"That's Rimbaud."

"So?"

"So anyone who dated that asshole knows how to appreciate a season in hell."

She laughed. "Come on, I'll introduce you. But I don't think that counts."

Her name was Marie, and she was French. She had dark eyes rimmed with shadow and an ankh tattooed behind her earlobe. They pried her from her conversation, tried to move away from the thumping speakers.

"This is the guy I told you about, who wanted to know about Franky."

"Oh right. What do you think he did again? Kidnapped your girlfriend or something?"

"No, I— It's complicated."

"You know what? Don't tell me. I don't actually give a shit. Ha ha. What do you want to know?"

"How long did you two date?"

"We still kind of do, really."

"You told me that he was your ex?" Sarah said.

"Ex is maybe accurate? In the beginning we saw each other a lot, but now it's more off and on." She caught concern in Reddick's expression. "I'm not going to tell Franky about this, unless you want me to. It's not like that. There are no emotions. It was mostly last spring but also a few times since then. I saw him…two?…yeah, two weeks ago."

"Two *weeks*? Do you know this girl?" He showed her the photo of Hannah. The caffeine was making him jumpy, slightly manic. He tried not to appear crazed. "Were you friends with her?"

"Oh, that's Hannah. No, I only met her a couple of times. She wasn't around when Franky and I started. She's your friend? Not to be a cunt but I didn't like her. She's one of those girls who doesn't want other girls around—she was needy? She wanted all the attention, from all the men. Even having a lapdog for a boyfriend wasn't enough."

"Buckley?"

She sneered. "He was wrapped around her finger—but he seemed like that kind of man, like it would be easy. The kind who wants to follow but feels as though he is supposed to lead—so she just treated him like a lion and then he would do whatever she wanted. This is basically how Franky deals with him, too. A little flattery and he abases himself for you. Some men have a cheat code. Hannah knew his, and she didn't like having me around to watch her work."

"Do you think Franky was sleeping with her?"

"I wouldn't be surprised. He is cruel that way—it's one of the things I find sexy about him. But it's also one of the reasons why there are no emotions. Buckley brought it out of him especially. There is history between those two, and Franky envies Buckley's family, his position—also of course his money. I think this was why he tormented him, to alleviate that jealousy. He told me— I shouldn't say this."

"Really?" Sarah said. "After everything you've said already?"

"You're right. Fuck it, I don't care." She took another drink from her Solo cup. "Franky told me that Buckley sucked his dick in college. That they were drunk, and he asked him to, said if he loved him he would do it. Mostly just to torture him, not thinking he would go through with it, but then he did. And they don't speak of it. But it's not like they have to, it's still another knife Franky can twist."

"Really?" Sarah rolled her eyes. "I thought the only people who cared about a little cock-sucking anymore were Republican politicians."

"You haven't hung out with these old money types," Marie

said. "They reserve separate morals for themselves. They want gay artists, gay friends, but not gay *sons*. There is a legacy to preserve."

"And Franky used his family's bigotry to control him," Reddick said.

"Toy with him, more like. Don't look at me like I'm horrible. Like I said, that kind of disregard—it can be very sexy. It's like pounding your fists against a wall. It's frustrating and painful but the strength of it, the implacability..." She smiled and finished her drink. "It doesn't even matter that he's broke."

"Franky is broke?"

"Yes. Look, I need another whiskey."

They followed Marie into the kitchen. The liquor was on the table, the ice bowl empty. She poured three Jamesons neat while Sarah and Reddick went to the refrigerator. Their beers were opened before they realized what she had done.

"No, it's perfect," Marie said. "Get me a beer, too, and we'll all go two-fisted."

The crowd had swelled while they talked, leaking into the rear bedroom. They went in and sat on the bed, among the coats. Marie raised her cup.

"To lousy men with good dicks," she said.

Sarah laughed and lifted her drink. A group of girls standing nearby whooped. Reddick shook his head.

"You brought him up," Marie said.

He raised his cup. "To hard truths."

They emptied their whiskies and chased them with beer. Reddick felt instantly better, buoyed by the liquor and the rush of information. "So Franky is broke? What about his company? His properties?"

"I don't know the details. He never copped to it exactly, but you can tell. The circular way he talks about money, the excuses. He tries to find ways to impress you without actually paying for anything."

"Like taking girls to buildings his company owns?"

"He did that with me. Because the company is doing fine. It's just that he doesn't have any cash—he's always borrowing money without paying it back. I found out pretty early on. We were at a bar once, maybe our second date, and this guy came up to him, yelling about some deal, and having to pay somebody right away. Franky got pretty upset."

"Did you catch his name?"

"Yeah. Mitchell something. Yang? Mitchell Yang. He looked a little of some kind of Asian, but he talked just like Franky and Buckley, you know, that Ivy League like..." she pinched her fingers together. "Very precise. No accent."

Reddick's thoughts felt soft, furry—it made them difficult to retrieve. "Mitchell?" he asked, slowly.

"Yeah. Kind of a husky guy, thick dark hair," Marie said. "You know him, too?"

He caught up, finally. Mitchell Yang—the photo from Buckley's desk. "He's another friend of theirs," Reddick said. "From school."

Sarah frowned. "At Penn? I don't think I ever met him. How do you know him?"

"I don't. I saw a photo in—never mind where."

Sarah frowned again, unhappy with his secrets, and he slid his hand to hers and squeezed, to reassure her. The bones in her fingers felt thin and fragile, the skin around them rough from years of dexterous work. She squeezed back.

Marie continued. "Mitchell wasn't the only one, though—I guess he and Buckley got into it also."

"Franky and Buckley argued about money?"

"Franky told me about it the last time we went out—they got into a huge fight at some holiday gala."

"That was about *money*?"

"You knew about this?" Sarah asked.

"The fight, sure. But I thought it was about Hannah. I just assumed."

"No way," Marie said. "Buckley doesn't have the backbone to make a scene about a woman, not with Franky. He told me it was business, he tried to be vague—but it definitely had something to do with some money that Buckley had given him."

Reddick thought about the check stub that he found, from three years ago. If Franky was broke, could he have been bleeding his friend for cash?

A man entered, whiskey bottle thrust aloft like a trophy, and was greeted by cheers. He circled the room, splashed a few ounces into everyone's cups and then joined the group of girls.

"So we're done?" Marie said. "I don't want to spend the whole night in the coatroom."

Sarah looked at Reddick. "I'm good," he said to Marie. "Can I get your number in case I think of anything else?"

She punched it into his phone, kissed them both on the cheek and left.

"If I didn't have a conscience," Sarah said, "that girl and I might end up best friends."

"Could happen anyway."

She wrinkled her nose. "I'm a libertine, not a libertarian. I don't see how anyone could tolerate someone as selfish as Franky."

"She was pretty clear about why *she* does it."

"There are plenty of good dicks out there that aren't attached to assholes."

"Anatomically speaking."

"You've seen my paintings. I'll put them wherever I want."

They shot their whiskey, and Reddick waited while she fetched two more beers. Half an hour later the guy with the whiskey bottle poured them another shot as he and the girls left the room, leaving the two of them alone. Half an hour after that they were kissing.

He wondered why they hadn't done it sooner. It was easy, almost rehearsed, her mouth wily and pliant. He felt rubbery from the liquor, numb; they pressed harder to override it. It went on. He put his arm around her. The kisses carried into her body, her shoulders arcing like wings, her spine undulating like ribbon. She nipped at his ear, his neck; he mirrored her, like playing Horse—match the shot, raise the stakes. Touch my thigh and I'll touch yours.

Finally they stopped to catch their breath. "Which one of these is yours?" she said.

"I'm sorry?"

"Your coat. Which one of these is your coat?"

He found his puffer near the pillows, under a stack of wool overcoats. She got hers and they walked through the dissolving party toward the door.

"I'm not that close," she said. "Do you want to take a car?"

Her phone was already in her hand, the car already summoned, before he could answer. "I don't have any cash for my half."

She pulled him into another kiss. "Buy me coffee tomorrow."

She lived in a fourth-floor walk-up in Greenpoint, small and airless as a casket. Her roommate was asleep, or gone, she said. She filled two glasses with water from the tap. They drank and refilled them.

"Do you want a smoke?"

He was spinning. "I'm good."

She opened a window by the couch. The brick wall of

the neighboring building was almost close enough to touch. There was a glass bowl on a nearby table, already packed. She picked it up and lit it.

Reddick had his head out the window. "How do you even get back here? If you dropped something it would just be gone."

"There's a building," she said. "That way, the gray brick? It has a back door. Also you can drop from the first-floor windows but it's a bitch to get back in."

"I love this kind of shit. All the weird spaces that happened as the neighborhood grew. This is what developers are killing."

"As far as losses go, I'm not sure dirty inaccessible alleyways rank that highly. Come back in, goofy. I opened that to let the smoke out."

"Sorry."

She moved up to the arm of the couch and he sat on the cushion beside her. The blazing radiator overwhelmed the cold air pouring in from the window. She ran her fingers through his hair. "So you want to tell me about this long day, or keep it buried?"

"Maybe buried."

"Did Beth reach out to you?"

He reclined against her hip. "No. Why?"

"She was pretty upset about your fight."

"Yeah? She wasn't the only one."

"I heard. That's part of what got her upset. I think you scared her."

"Scared her? That's ridiculous."

"To you it's ridiculous because you know you wouldn't hurt her—on some level maybe she knows that, too, or believes it, but when a man is angry, it can be frightening. It's like a little alarm goes off, reminding women of all the impolite truths we have to repress."

"Like what?"

"Like if there was a fistfight we would almost always lose. And no matter how much progress we make, that imbalance won't go away, which is bullshit and not fair, and being reminded of it makes you feel like whatever power you have managed to take for yourself is just flushed away."

"Then what am I supposed to do? Never be angry?"

"Don't ask me—I'm a cynic. I don't think any of this stuff gets better. You just find a way to live with it. I'm only describing it to you for the sake of accuracy."

"Maybe I will have some of that," he said. She passed him the bowl.

"She's not entirely wrong, either," she said.

"To be afraid of me?"

"No, I mean about her argument."

He exhaled. "I know. It's just that woke hipster shit, it's irritating. They quote theory like scripture—or worse, tell you to go read it."

"The 'it's not my job to educate you' line."

"Exactly. It's so smug, when most of those kids went to all-white high schools. They read as a substitute for living. That's all I was trying to say to her." He passed the bowl back.

"I get it. But most of those books have black authors. People like Beth and—your roommate—"

"Dean."

"Beth and Dean can't change how they were raised. But they can listen when they have the opportunity. That's part of what those books are for, to expose people to a point of view they might not otherwise be able to get. Yeah, it can be annoying—a bunch of twenty-two-year-olds who just discovered systemic racism and now they won't stop pointing it out everywhere they see it, like a toddler who just learned a new word—but their intentions are good."

"Sure, but when you don't parrot all of it back at them, then they assume your intentions *aren't* good. Like there's no other way to be right."

"Maybe, but that's just in-group out-group shit. That's human nature, which I've already told you is something we just have to accept. Yeah, they're smug, and insular, and in some ways remarkably closed-minded. But at least they're trying."

A burst of cold air whipped across her lap, biting his whiskey fog away. He pressed his shoulder into her thigh, felt the give of her flesh. He sighed. "She wants me to stop this."

"She's being your friend. She told me some of what you did—she's afraid you're going to get yourself arrested, or hurt."

"What about you? You're helping me."

"I'm not afraid of the world," she said. "That's one of the perks of getting older—you realize just how little there is to be afraid of. How open it all is. I'm helping you because I think you can succeed, and even if your motives are messy it seems like a good thing, a worthwhile thing." She brushed his face with her fingers. "It doesn't hurt that I think you're cute."

"I wish you'd tell Beth that." She raised her eyebrows. "I mean that it's worthwhile," he said.

"For what it's worth, I did."

"I owe her an apology, I know that." He stood up and faced her. Her knees pressed against the point of his hips.

"She thinks you caught some of that white rage that's going around."

"It's not that. She just hit a sore spot. I hate that feeling that you're being judged based on the category you belong to, because I feel like those categories are drawn so carelessly."

"Of course you do. White boy from a black neighborhood, like that makes you different." She was smiling.

"We're all different."

"In a black girl's apartment at three a.m. Working out whatever issues you got to work out."

She was teasing, playful, but there was a brittle edge. It was too late for this; they'd drunk too much, smoked too much, to be this nimble. They were skirting disaster.

"It's not like that," he said.

"There are—what…two…of us with studios in that building?"

"Two what?"

"Black girls."

"So what are you saying?"

"It's a big building, with a lot of girls. All those other chicks, white, Asian, Hispanic, whose apartment you could be in right now."

"I'm flattered but you are *seriously* overestimating my appeal."

"New York is a tough market for ladies. The numbers are in your favor. But who do you go out for drinks with, what—the first week your roommate moves in? One of the two of us in the whole place. And who are you out partying with now? The same."

"It isn't like that. I'm not here working out some issues, or trying to pretend to be something I'm not. I just liked you when we met. I enjoy your company. And tonight—I don't know—didn't you kiss me?"

She looked at his face and sighed. "I guess I believe you." She slid off the couch and went to the refrigerator. "I have exactly one beer. Split it?"

"Sure."

She opened it and came back. "You know who else went to an all-white high school?" She pointed at her chest. "So you'd think I would have a radar for this sort of thing—white boys who only talk to me because of my black mother, for their bucket list or to make some half-assed political point. Proof of their purity, of how different they are from all the other white boys trying to do the same thing—like fucking a black chick gets them a pass for life. You'd think I would have developed an instinct for seeing that nonsense coming—but I never did. Instead I'm just paranoid about it." She fixed him with an unreadable stare, her playfulness evaporated. "Mostly I try and stay away from you."

"Sarah. I'm here because of you, not because you're black."

"That's the thing. You can't separate those two."

She sat down, took the beer from him, drank and gave it back. They sat in dumb silence for several minutes, then, "I waited tables in college."

"Yeah?"

"I'm going somewhere with this, okay? It was a couple shifts a week—spending money. It was a nice place, fine dining, on the water. Don't forget I'm older than you are, this was—god, too long ago. I remember it as a naive time but it was probably just me that was naive. Anyway, black people don't tip. That's what we believed—me, too. I mean, I believed it. I had evidence, we all did—we had data on our side. Shifts upon shifts of fieldwork—and this place wasn't small, maybe a hundred covers a night, a pretty good sample size. The rest of the staff was white. We were all friends, went out after work, that sort of thing—and we talked about who tipped well and who didn't, you know, me included. The hostess tells you that you've been sat and you look in your section and there's a black couple there, and you think, *great. Here comes ten percent.* And because waiting tables is a really shitty job—I mean just hard on your soul—have you ever done it?"

He shook his head.

"Well, it wears on you, and because it does you develop a bitter humor, to tolerate it. You and the rest of the staff, trying to outdo each other to see who can be more caustic, more jaded. I don't know, maybe it's not like that anymore. So one night I've got a four-top, black businessmen. Really nice suits. You wouldn't know this, but men in suits? That's who you want. Not couples, not families. Just a table full of rich men, that's your best bet to get the most money per table—which is all you're trying to do. You absolutely cannot think about the politics of it. You only get so many tables a night so you have to squeeze as much money from each one as possible. So four men in suits—great—but four black men? That's a crapshoot. It's like, which stereotype will carry the day? I say 'stereotype' but remember—this is what we actually see. This is based on lived experience, so maybe it's more like which trend, which tendency. Anyway these brothers are ordering expensive wine, appetizers, medium-rare steaks. And they love that I'm waiting on them. It's all *sista, can you please*, and *sista, thank you*, and I have this feeling like we're in it together—like we've made it together. Like we are together in our blackness but still excelling in a white world, like we've gotten everything without giving anything up. They're asking me about school, telling me how they can't wait to see my paintings in New York, all of that. *Sista, can I have the check.*"

"Sarah, you don't—"

"I do, though. And you have to listen. Twenty dollars on

a three-hundred-and-fifty-dollar total. It takes me a minute to process the numbers. I have to go back to the computer and close out the tab. I have to enter that tip amount, see it on the screen in front me, and I'm so humiliated that I'm fighting back tears, and this other waiter, she's standing behind me, and she sees the amount on the screen, sees the table number, and kind of snorts, and says, *Saw that coming.* Then she walks away. This girl was my friend."

She took the beer and didn't return it.

"In her mind she didn't do anything wrong—this was something we had probably joked about before, 'Oh I love my brothers and sisters but I wish they would tip, ha ha ha,' but the joke was always on me. I just never realized it until that moment. Because to everyone else who worked in the restaurant, that's *me* at that table. A white person stiffs you because of some character flaw, because they are cheap, or selfish—but when a black person stiffs you the only flaw is their blackness. They're stiffing you on behalf of their entire race. So at the same time that I'm receiving the shitty tip I'm also giving it, at the same time that I'm enforcing these bullshit norms about how much more money you're supposed to pay on top of what the actual bill already says—some arbitrary figure that who knows what white person came up with anyway—at the same time that I'm enforcing this norm I'm violating it. I'm implicated on both sides. I'm selling out and not getting paid for it. Because I wanted to make some beer money."

"Sarah, I'm so sorry."

"I didn't tell you that story because I wanted sympathy." She got up and disappeared into her bedroom. When she came back she was holding a sheet and a pillow. Her eyes were damp. "I told you so that you know what I'm talking about when I say there's no separating the two. So that you know what it costs me to say that there's nothing to do but live with it."

She handed him the pillow and sheet. "It's very, very late. Get some sleep."

SEVENTEEN

He woke up first, after dreaming of water. A basketball court on a ship, skyscraper waves that never washed him away. His shots missed the rim, the backboard, by feet.

In his sleep he had heard someone—the roommate, home after all—swear, rummage through the kitchen and leave. Sometime after that he got up, poured himself a glass of water and peeked down the hall. Sarah's door was closed, her lights off. He sat down with his phone and placed a pillow over his hard-on. He had slept in his boxers but had only hazy memories of getting undressed. It was after eleven.

The calls he was waiting on—Derek, Lane—hadn't come in yet. Needing to kill time, he wondered if he should reach out to Thomas, ask him why Mrs. Leland hadn't brought up Buckley's investment in Restoration Heights. There was an off chance she hadn't recognized the neighborhood when they spoke the first time—though she seemed too canny for that—but Reddick had referred to the project by name to Thomas, and the house manager hadn't said a word. Maybe she had asked him to stay quiet about it—but why? The omission thickened the wall around her motives. There was something he couldn't see, something that informed her contradictory behavior—why she hired Reddick but gave him so little help. It was time to find out what it was. He had been too indulgent of her secrets.

He picked up his phone and opened a search window, typed in the family's name, saw the same results as the first time he tried this—a solid page about her son before any discussion of the family as a whole. He had already skimmed the pages about Anthony Leland—now he dug deeper. A Rockefeller Republican, the state senator was halfway through his second term; the *Times* said he was a shoo-in for a third. He dressed like an extension of his mother's house—stately, immune to trends. He had no bad press. There were photos of him shaking hands with President Bush, of his wife and the current First Lady in a Bronx elementary school. His online presence was as tailored and pressed as his suits.

Reddick heard a door shut down the hall. The shower came on. He adjusted the pillow. He should have gotten dressed but he wasn't sure where his clothes were.

He added Restoration Heights to the search field, saw that Anthony Leland was a vocal supporter of the project. The position made political sense—Restoration Heights had the mayor's endorsement, the backing of the state senator's campaign donors. There he was at a dinner three years ago, with the head of Corren Capital, after the development was announced. He was seated beside Buckley. There they were again, much later, Buckley and Anthony Leland on a porch in the Hamptons. The image embedded in a Tumblr page, a series of posts focused on exposing the money behind Restoration Heights—insinuations of collusion, images of the mayor with the principals of Corren, of various investors with various landlords. It was nothing new, in theme or content—allegations without proof. There were six shots of Buckley, and Anthony Leland was in five of them—a variety of places, in the city and out. He searched their names together, found a short post on a lifestyle blog about their friendship, how Anthony was taking Buckley under his wing, possibly grooming him for politics.

Reddick struggled to make this fit. Mrs. Leland had claimed to know the Sewards well—he had imagined galas, foundation boards, charity dinners, anything but some partnership between Buckley and her son. The relationship opened up new possibilities, evoked the threat of conspiracy.

He flashed a text to Thomas, told him he needed to talk. He tapped his fingers on his bare knee, stared out the window at the shabby brick of the neighboring building. He wished he had his map.

"You hungry?"

He jumped—he hadn't heard Sarah coming. "I could eat the world."

He turned around. She wore sweatpants that hung low on her rangy hips, a tank top with straps thin as twine. Her hair was dry, and bobbed in caramel rings around her face. Her swollen eyes were lined with dark from their late night, her lips pale but full. Her freckles were a celebration—a dash across the bridge of her nose and a cascade down her bare shoulders.

"What are you looking at?" She sat down and he slid over, the pillow pressed into his lap.

"I'm wondering how I managed to bungle last night so badly."

"Oh yeah?" He saw relief on her face, a glimpse that her confidence was as contingent as his; an improvisation. It surprised him.

"And trying to figure out how I might hit the reset button."

"Life doesn't have resets."

"So it would be a terrible thing to try and pick up where we left off?"

"It wouldn't be terrible. But I've got a better idea." She reached beneath the couch, pulled his jeans out by the belt loop. "Put these on and cook some breakfast with me. Then, later this week, come see me at my studio and we can talk about art, have a drink and see where it goes."

He wasn't sure whether to feel let down or not. He leaned forward and kissed her. Her body went soft—her resolve wavering. While their eyes were shut he took his pants from her hand. "Deal," he said when they separated.

He got dressed, freshened up in her bathroom. When he came out she was in the kitchen, laying out dishes and ingredients.

"Thanks again for calling," he said.

"This wasn't why I called."

"Ha ha. I mean about Marie, about this case." He joined her and they started cracking eggs, chopping vegetables. "I need all the help I can get."

"What a scumbag Franky is. I knew he wasn't a nice guy at Penn. But I assumed he had mostly grown out of it. I mean, everyone is some kind of asshole in their twenties—but he's just gotten worse."

He told her about Franky's arrest record, and planting the gun to force tenants out. "I think he killed her. I really do."

"That is too awful to think about. A murderer? It's not like I was close to the guy, but I could never have imagined."

Reddick's phone began to vibrate. He flipped it over, saw Thomas's name, then eyed the half-prepared food strewn across Sarah's counter. He sent it to voice mail.

He grabbed a tomato. "How small do you like these? Diced?"

"That wasn't important?"

"No, it— I can deal with it later."

"I don't mind if you want to call the person back. You can use my room. You're entitled to privacy."

"The way you say that makes me wonder."

"You were a little cagey last night—with how you knew about that classmate of Buckley's."

"Mitchell Yang."

"Not that it's strange I didn't know him. The only Wharton guys I met were the ones prowling the Morgan Building with their dick in their hands. But the fact that you did—I know you've done a lot of work on this thing. I told you, Beth filled me in."

He started to explain and she cut him off.

"I'm not going to judge you—or, I've already judged you, and you came out alright."

"I'm not the only one looking for Hannah. I was, well— hired by someone. Another Upper East Side family." He told her about his meeting with Mrs. Leland the day after Hannah disappeared.

"And you didn't think this was strange?"

"Completely strange. I just didn't care."

"But her motives."

"They made no sense. But as long as we wanted the same thing—I thought she could help me. That she could help Hannah."

"Only now you're beginning to doubt?"

"I should have doubted from the beginning. I was too eager." He showed her the article about Buckley and Anthony, the photos of the two men together. "I don't know what the connection is between the two families. But I'm not sure that she ever cared about finding Hannah."

Sarah thumbed through the search results. "It could be completely benign—maybe the fact that they're friends is why she was interested in the first place."

"Honestly?" He flicked the tomato between his hands in a precise rhythm, left to right and back, a metronome for his unspooling thoughts. "I'm beginning to think she only asked me because I was already nosing around in her business."

"You need to at least hear what she has to say." She jabbed her knife at his phone. "Go ahead. I'll take it from here."

He sent the tomato arcing toward Sarah and she caught it nimbly at her waist. He dialed the number, paced into the hallway while it rang. Thomas answered.

Reddick brushed off his greeting. "Talk to me about Restoration Heights."

The house manager answered slowly, his reserve intact. "What about it?"

"The main site is a block away from where Hannah disappeared. You didn't think it was worth telling me that Buckley was a principal investor?"

"I assumed if it were noteworthy you would find out on your own."

"What about her son? He's been cheerleading the project. A state senator—who knows what strings he pulled."

"I'm not sure what Mrs. Leland would like me to say on that topic."

"Then how about you put her on and she can tell me herself."

"Her schedule is quite full. I will pass on your concern about her son's relationship to Restoration Heights, and she will discuss the matter with you at the appropriate time."

"What about her son's relationship with Buckley Seward?

The two of them seem pretty chummy. When does she want to discuss that?'

There was a pause on the line, then, "Wait one moment."

Mrs. Leland picked up the phone almost immediately. "Reddick. I understand you would like to discuss the case."

"I thought we were on the same side."

"I believe we share a common goal, yes."

"Then why have you been so slow to help me? Why did I find out about Buckley and Restoration Heights from someone else? Why did I have to go online to learn that Buckley looks up to your son as some sort of mentor? Why haven't I heard all of this from you?"

"I informed you that I had dealings with the Sewards on the day that I hired you. The two are friends. This is no secret."

"But that's just it. Why hire *me*? If you wanted to find out what happened to Hannah, why not get a professional? I assumed you had some play in mind, only I didn't care what it was—I figured as long as we're on the same side, what did it matter? But now I see it exactly. You thought Buckley might have been involved in Hannah's disappearance—his suspicious behavior worried you as much as it did me, maybe more so because you also had to consider whether or not he would have involved your son. Maybe you even wondered if your son did it—if she found out something she shouldn't have, some collusion between the two that went beyond the usual greased palms. So you needed to know what to expect, how much damage to plan for—was it only his reputation at stake, his proximity to a scandal, or worse, something criminal? Maybe Buckley wouldn't even be a suspect. Maybe he wasn't involved, or if he was, maybe his cover-up would work. I was the only one pushing back at it, so you pulled me in, partly to keep an eye on me, to learn what I learned, and partly to control me. A private investigator would have dug too deep, found out more than you wanted and come back with blackmail or worse, the press. But me? I was just some dope."

Dead air—so long he thought she had hung up. Then, "Suppose for a minute that those were my motivations. What does any of it have to do with Hannah?"

"Because she's still gone. Because she went to a party with Franky Dutton and was never heard from again. And because I might have found out what happened by now if you hadn't been keeping things from me this whole time."

"That's all I'll be needing from you."

"What does that mean?"

"In four generations the Lelands have gone from house servants to the state senate. My son is the result of decades of hard work. His legacy is not his responsibility alone. Yes, he has been a vocal supporter of Restoration Heights, of the revitalization that such a project offers for that benighted neighborhood. And yes, he and Buckley are close. Anthony sees promise in the young man, and only wants to offer a positive influence that, frankly, no one else in that decadent household is capable of providing. So naturally I was concerned that Hannah's disappearance might result in a scandal. I will not allow scandals. Fortunately this one will not reach my family. It has become increasingly clear that Buckley's fiancée simply decided to leave him, which makes it no concern of mine, and certainly no concern of yours. You have performed adequately, and my mind is at ease. I see no need for you to investigate further."

"So what do you expect me to do now? Keep quiet? They murdered this girl."

"I don't think they did anything of the sort. You said it yourself, she went home to Oregon."

"There's no Hannah Granger in Portland. They just said that because it's about as far from New York as you can get, because I can't look for her there."

"You overestimate your significance. Hannah herself told me that she was from Portland, when I met her months ago."

"It doesn't mean she's there now."

"Well, it certainly doesn't mean she isn't. You have no evidence of violence. To the contrary, you have several people telling you that she has left, that she is safe and that this is a private matter. What about that story doesn't fit the facts at hand?"

"That's not how it looks. That's not what actually happened."

"Tell me, Reddick, do art students read Wittgenstein?"

"I don't know." The question flustered him. "Yeah. We did. A little."

"There's a story about a conversation he had that I like to believe is true. He asked a colleague why most people said that it was natural that people once assumed that the sun went around the earth rather than that the earth was rotating. His friend replied that, obviously, it was because it just looked like the sun is going around the earth. To which Wittgenstein replied, 'Well, what would it have looked like if it had looked as if the Earth was rotating?'"

"What does that have to do with anything?"

"How a thing looks, how it seems to be, isn't a straightforward question. Whether or not your interpretation of an event aligns with your intuition depends upon your ideas about that intuition."

"We don't make our own truth, Mrs. Leland."

"You've missed the point entirely. I never said otherwise. The truth exists, but your ability to perceive it depends upon the assumptions you begin with. Go outside and watch the sun. This is how a rotating earth looks."

"Okay. I don't need you to believe me. If you want to be done, fine." His phone buzzed—another call coming in. He checked the ID. Lane.

"We're both done," he heard her say.

He brought his phone back up to his ear. "Not me. I'm onto something. I'm going to keep digging."

"As I said, you have performed adequately. I am greatly reassured on this matter and it is only fair that you be compensated. I will write you a check. How about, say, three months to make your art full-time. Simply tell me what figure is required to make that happen."

His phone vibrated—Lane left a voice mail. "Are you trying to buy me off?"

"It isn't a moral failing to accept payment for your work. This is an opportunity that most in your situation would envy. No one has been murdered, in spite of what you believe, and if you keep at this you will bring unnecessary embarrassment to everyone involved."

"You mean you, right? If I tell the police what I've learned? Or the press?"

"Insinuations of this sort never fully disappear, not once they are in the news."

"No."

"Six months."

"No."

"I have other options. This one is the most gentle, the only one where you stand to gain. I will not allow you to go to the police, or the press."

"I owe her more than that. More than selling out."

"You poor man. Do you know who worries about selling out? People without ambition. I will give you until the end of the week to make up your mind. Do not speak to anyone before then. It won't end well for you."

She hung up. Sarah was staring at him, the omelets cooling on their plates.

"I heard your half of that."

"Fuck." He told her what Mrs. Leland said.

"How much is she offering?"

"Six months."

"Six months of what?"

"Six months of whatever I want. She says she'll write a check, cover my living expenses, rent, whatever. I could probably tell her sixty grand and she would pay it."

Sarah put her hand over her mouth. "Oh my god."

"I can't take it."

"What if she's right? Maybe Hannah just left?"

"Then what is she scared of? Why try to buy me off if there's nothing there?"

"It's like she said—insinuations. Remember that congressman whose intern was killed? To this day people think he did it. I probably think he did it, and I don't remember one thing about the case, one piece of evidence. Once you connect a person to something publically it doesn't matter if it's true or not, all anyone will remember is the accusation."

"But if she believes Hannah is safe."

"This guy is a politician. The damage might be done before anyone finds out that Hannah just ran home to her parents. And anyway there is still the possibility of corruption."

"It's more than a possibility—there is nothing about Restoration Heights that isn't corrupt."

"You say that, but no one has found anything to prove it yet. The opposition was hungry enough, searched hard enough, and they never found anything that stuck, anything that could slow it down. Maybe there is something, and maybe it has to do with Anthony Leland."

"I don't know. It feels thin to me. And giving up on Hannah—how could I consider that now? I've been so sure this whole time, but once there's money in my face I start doubting? How could I live with myself?"

"You could quit your job."

"Shit. My job." He picked up his phone. "Lane called while I was talking." He played the voice mail on speaker.

"This is Lane. I just got off a call with the Krugers. I couldn't save your job this time, and honestly, I didn't try that hard. We already talked about this so I'll keep it short. Best of luck, and—I mean this—I hope you get yourself straightened out. I'll mail your last paycheck."

"Reddick, I'm so sorry."

"I just got fired twice on one phone call." That he expected Lane's answer didn't dampen the impact—he wasn't sure how long his barren savings would last. He wondered briefly about the timing, if it could somehow be connected, Mrs. Leland cranking up the pressure. But Lane's call came in before she made her threats. It was just bad luck—his rash decisions bearing their inevitable fruit.

"Are you even still interested in breakfast?"

"What? Yeah. No, let's eat."

He ate slowly, his appetite strangled by nerves. When they were finished she made tea and they moved to her couch.

"You want to tell me the rest?" she said. "Lay it out for me. The whole case."

He struggled with where to begin. "This might be easier—do you have a sketchbook around here? Would you mind if I used it?"

"Of course. Let me get it." She disappeared down the hall toward her bedroom.

"And a pencil."

When she returned he opened the book to a clean page and took her through it, reproducing his case map as he went, step by step. Some of it she already knew but he included everything. Hannah's abandoned apartment. How he had spoken with the kids in his building who threw the party, how Hannah had been with Franky that night but had arrived with two other guys, Ju'waun and Tyler, how he had followed Tyler and inadvertently discovered that he was a bagman for someone named the Genie. How someone had warned Harold not to ask about the blonde. His confrontation with Mia. Franky and FDP, his phone and his townhouse. Hannah's name was in the center, Ju'waun and Tyler to the right of her, and beside them Mia and the Genie. He wrote Restoration Heights below Hannah's name, told Sarah about his misadventure there, the discovery that Buckley was an investor, that Franky might have used Buckley's infatuation to take advantage of him on the property deal. He wrote Buckley's name to the left, the Lelands above him, Franky below, hitched all three names to Restoration Heights with emphatic lines. He told her how he plundered Buckley's office for financial records, enlisting Derek to decipher them. His belief that the Genie was involved, that she used Sons of Cash Money to run a hit on behalf of Franky, an arced line across the top of the page that was the only real connection between the two halves—and then the sundering of that belief by Ju'waun's revelation that Hannah wasn't the right blonde, that Harold had bungled the job and the warning was about some other incident entirely. The news report of a mugging that verified it. He didn't bother to erase the connection, just reached down and tore the page in two, a reenactment of the moment he severed his case map.

"Everything else you've been here for."

She fingered the torn page. "So this entire half, on the right—all of it is unrelated?"

Looking at it, he recalled the futility he felt right before Sarah texted him. Days of work he was forced to cast aside. "I think so. She was at a party with them, but they could have just met her at a bar, like Ju'waun said."

She turned that half of the map facedown. "So we're left with the relationship between Franky and Buckley, which is plenty fucked-up enough to make me sympathize with Hannah."

"According to Marie she fit right in," he said.

"I don't know. She might have had Buckley wrapped, but that doesn't mean she knew how deep it went between those two."

"So maybe she underestimated Franky, thought she could control him the way she did Buckley." He ran his fingers over the names. He strained against the sensation that there was nothing remarkable here, nothing sinister. "Maybe I'm not clear on the motives yet. But there was a love triangle, and now someone's missing. Isn't that enough?"

"Look. I'm telling you this as a friend—she might just have left him."

"You can't believe that."

"Mrs. Leland is kind of right. I didn't hear anything that can't be explained just as easily by her leaving. Buckley's reaction, that first set you off? That was jealousy because he knew that Franky had a townhouse down there. The two of them meeting up after you went to FDP? That could have been a coincidence."

"Coincidence?"

She raised her hand. "Don't get upset, just hear me out. Coincidence *or* Franky was warning Buckley, like you said—but not about someone catching on to her *murder.* Look how terrified of scandal they all are—if Hannah had left him because of an affair, then of course they wouldn't want that information getting out. I know Franky is an asshole, and he takes advantage of Buckley, but they are friends, at least they were when I knew them, and if Buckley was facing some threat—like the possibility that you might inadvertently put his name in the papers—then I don't see anything alarming or out of character about Franky warning him. And as far as the financial stuff between the two of them and Restoration Heights, you haven't found anything that connects her to that." As she spoke she pointed at each name on the page, dismissing them in turn. "We've already talked about Mrs. Leland. You can be pretty convincing when you manage to get worked up about something, so maybe she did believe you for a little bit, but that's more a credit to you, and to whatever preexisting tension she had with the Sewards, than to there actually being any evidence that someone killed her. You've done a lot of work—it's honestly kind of amazing how much—and you haven't turned up anything that points to Hannah being murdered. Don't you think that speaks for itself?"

Reddick felt stabbed, his conviction eviscerated. "But she just disappeared."

"Maybe that was by design. There are still private people out there." She saw his face hardening. "I'm not against you. I just think you should consider it."

"What is it, like, two o'clock?"

"Reddick."

"I've got to go." He stood up, began to put on his boots and coat.

"Don't be like this. You wanted my help, I'm helping."

"Yeah."

"If all you wanted was someone to agree with you, you asked the wrong person."

“I’m not upset.”

“I didn’t ask if you were.”

He zipped his coat, pulled his beanie over his ears. “I’ll think about what you said. I promise.”

EIGHTEEN

The money was an avalanche caving in his objectivity. He had returned to his case map but no longer trusted what he saw. He used the X-Acto knife to carve Hannah away from Franky and Buckley, a careful line around her name and the notes beneath it. He stepped back, holding her, and looked at what was left. Nothing was damaged by her absence. Sarah was right, Mrs. Leland was right: his case had produced a pair of self-contained narratives, viable by their own logic—but did he think this only because it was the required first step to accepting the money?

He got a text from Sarah saying she hoped he would still come by this week.

He put his coat on and left. The afternoon was already darkening, the day spent before he could use it. The sky and the hardened snow were an identical humming lavender, the townhouse windows seeped orange like cracks in the shell of winter. He cut up to Madison and walked west to Franklin. He hadn't noticed the mosque on the corner last time; a man in a ragged coat was salting the sidewalk in front of it, his movements stiff and deliberate. Reddick tried to make eye contact, to nod hello, but the man didn't look up. Finally he gave up and crossed the street, toward the neon flicker that had called him out here, and went downstairs into Ti-Ti's.

The bartender was leaning on her elbows in front of the only patron, a black woman in her sixties; they both looked up when he entered but only the bartender smiled. Reddick went to the battered ATM, then walked past them and took a stool in the back. The bartender remembered him.

"You were in here with Harold the other day, weren't you?"

"Yeah."

"He's such a sweetheart."

"You think he might stop by?"

"That depends. Does the day end with the letter *Y*?" She winked. "What can I get you, sweetie?"

She brought him a bourbon and left him to drink in silence. People arrived, separately and in couples. He had a second whiskey, felt himself sliding into another drunk evening, curdling with guilt at blowing money he was going to need until he found another job. Probably going to need. He kept one eye on the dwindling liquid in his glass, one eye on the door.

When Harold walked in, Reddick studied him for symptoms of Clint's diagnosis. A twitch or tic, some betrayal of the paranoia that had cleaved his mind. Were there other plots he feared, were they clustered around the same themes—a panoptic government, his targeted race—or was his dread vague and diffuse, shaping all of his habits? Reddick imagined sheets of wrinkled foil draped like curtains across his windows, imagined him ducking under awnings when helicopters buzzed the city. Imagined bouts of terrified rage at personalized advertisements. But he looked the same—his beliefs, irrational or otherwise, invisible inside the meaty, exhausted shell of his body. Heavy-footed, almost shuffling, his wide wingspan made him seem like a man who was all back, who was burdened by a near limitless capacity for physical work, even as his face, his demeanor, sagged from fatigue. A man punished by his own endurance. He saw Reddick. His eyes slipped over the narrow room, as though looking for another seat, weighing his options for escape—then back to Reddick's face. He smiled.

"You thinking of becoming a regular, young brother?" He took the stool next to him, laid his nicked hard hat on the bar.

"I like it here."

"Uh-huh. Okay."

"I didn't come to talk about the Genie, if that's what you're worried about."

"Then why are you even saying her name?" He placed a stack of small bills beside his hat. The bartender approached with an open beer. He smiled at her as she set it down, watched her pluck two ones from the stack. "Thank you, Natalie."

She nodded and walked away, and Harold turned back to Reddick. "People got ears." He cut his eyes toward Natalie.

"She was here the other day. It didn't stop you from talking then."

"I wasn't necessarily in my right state of mind—to be honest I feel like you took advantage."

"I didn't realize how much you had had to drink, not right away."

"Didn't realize or didn't care?"

"What do you want me to say? I was chasing something."

"*Was?* So you aren't anymore? Then why are you here?"

"I was thirsty." Reddick sipped his whiskey, as if his claim required evidence.

"Passed a lot of bars to get to this one."

Reddick wasn't sure what he hoped to accomplish. Harold was the first person he had told about Hannah, the first to offer help. Now that he was here he found he wanted to talk about anything else. He let Harold's insinuations fade into the clink and murmur of the sparse happy-hour crowd. They drank with quiet resolution.

"So I stayed at this girl's house last night," Reddick said, finally. It was an attempt to reset the conversation, to talk as friends.

Harold chuckled, eyed Reddick's sullen face. "That usually puts me in a better mood."

"Well, nothing happened, really—actually, things were happening, but it got complicated."

"Complicated? Why did you let it get complicated?"

"We stayed up too late, talked too much."

Harold mulled this over. "So this was a onetime thing or you gonna see her again?"

Reddick thought about her invitation, imagined himself in her studio—Leland money in his pocket, talking about her paintings, maybe preparing some new series of his own. A swell of happiness accompanied the image. All he had to do was lay off a search no one else believed was going to lead anywhere. He knew it wasn't fair to link these things together. Sarah had made it clear that she would see him again no matter what he decided to do about Mrs. Leland's offer—but he couldn't stop himself from building these contingencies. They gave his options clarity.

"See her again, I'm hoping."

The sound of girls laughing interrupted them. Three white kids spilled through the open door, hounded by a gust of winter air. They claimed seats at the top of the bar, devil's perch, the two girls continuing to giggle while the boy went to the jukebox. They barely seemed old enough to drink.

Harold grinned wryly. "There goes the neighborhood." He was on his fourth beer, Natalie removing and replacing each bottle in silence, subtracting the appropriate bills from the dwindling pile of his cash. The process was machine-like, determined. Its effects were beginning to show—his suspicion had evaporated, the throbbing impact of his fatigue had been dampened. He had a lucidity, a calm, that Reddick associated with their morning conversations, before the demands of the workday had taken their toll. A final peak before the inevitable slide into boozy sleep.

"So you really did come here just to have a drink?" Harold said. "That's the truth?"

The white kid's song hit on the jukebox—some track from *West Side Story* that opened with a lengthy skit, that seemingly no one in the bar knew was in the machine. The kid and his friends were hysterical as the actors' lines, nonsensical without context, permeated the room, their faces red and crying. The attitudes of the other patrons ranged from bemusement to annoyance. Natalie reached behind the bar, to the dial for the speakers, and turned the volume down. The kids were laughing too hard to notice.

Harold frowned, and Reddick stared at his glass, feeling suddenly out of place, silenced by what felt like a trespasser's shame.

"The truth?" he said. "I wasn't just thirsty. The truth is I came here to think."

Harold looked at the laughing white kids, and back to him. "This used to be a good place for it."

"You're putting me in with them?"

"Do you feel different? I mean, I see you trying—some

ways you're trying too hard and some ways not hard enough. But those differences you feel—you can't see any of that from the outside. You look a little older than them. A little sadder. That's what Brooklyn is now, though. A place where white kids go to become old and sad. You and those three, brother? You just look like different points of the same life."

Reddick absorbed it, chased it with bourbon. "You know I was wrong."

"About which part?"

"All of it. Tyler and Ju'waun. The Ge—the woman they work for sometimes. It was the wrong blonde entirely."

"Wrong blonde?"

"That someone warned you about. I guess you never said her name, the message got confused—it doesn't matter. None of it has anything to do with the girl I was looking for."

Harold furrowed his brow. "I said Ju'waun. I said Tyler. I know that. How many blonde white girls do those cats know?"

"At least two, apparently."

"Huh. Damn."

"It doesn't matter. The girl I was actually looking for—Hannah—I can't even figure out if she's actually missing."

"It was a good story, what you told me. I liked the details, the way you framed it, with the snow all around you, and the rows of garbage. Romantic, but corrupt. Question is, brother, how did you think it was going to end? I mean for you—what did you think was going to happen? You rescue her and she's so grateful that she becomes your girl?"

"I thought she was dead."

"Then what? You just wanted the tragedy of it?"

"I only wanted to find out what happened."

"Nuh-uh. That I don't buy. That's way too clean. Man, listen. I could see how all this got to you, so I offered to help.

At a certain point, though—what did you find? I mean, ask that question honestly. Because if you had found something you wouldn't be sitting here. And if there really was anything to this, why hasn't anyone else backed you up?"

"There was one person who believed me. Or at least, she acted like she did—she offered to help, to exchange information. Except that I found out she only did it to make sure there wasn't a scandal that might affect her family—her son is a politician. Now that she's satisfied there isn't one—unless I make it—she wants me to stop looking. She will pay me to stop."

"What's wrong with that?"

"The fact that she's willing to pay me makes me think there is more there."

"True. That could be." He frowned, his head cocked in thought. "Or, could be she's doing it because she knows nothing has happened to her."

"That's too simple—it lets me off easy."

"Sometimes the truth is simple. And simple can look easy, but it ain't. It's just simple. You got to find a way to accept that."

"I'm trying."

"But look—you got a way to profit from this shit now. That lady is offering you money. I know you got some other shit that you do—this is New York. Everybody has a screenplay or a blog or some shit."

Reddick was sure he had told him about his art—hadn't he? Or had it not even seemed important enough to bring up?

"I make paintings."

"Then go do that shit. Stop asking about this missing white girl that—for real?—sounds like she ain't even missing."

He grabbed Chinese on his way home and ate, in silence, on the couch. It was nearly nine o'clock. Harold had left once his stack of cash was gone—a self-imposed limit, he said, to avoid future indiscretion—while Reddick stayed for another. The alcohol had only made him more muddled.

After a few minutes he heard the rattle of Dean's keys in the door.

"Hey man, I was hoping you'd be around." He was with Beth. Reddick apologized first; Beth and Dean followed suit, each of them careful to acknowledge the legitimacy of the other's feelings without wholly conceding their point. Beth cracked a joke. They opened beers while Reddick finished eating.

He told them about his conversation with Mrs. Leland.

"What do you make of it?" Beth asked, cautiously, as though the subject might explode their fragile détente.

"I have no idea what to think. I can't trust my own judgment. I talked to Sarah about it."

"Sarah?" Beth smiled coyly. "Do go on."

"It's nothing. I mean, maybe it is, but that's another story." He felt himself blushing. "What I want to say is that she saw what Mrs. Leland saw. And this is why I can't trust myself, because if I resist their versions, am I just doing it to make a point about how the money can't sway me? But then if I accept it, am I letting myself be swayed?"

Dean nodded. "I see your point. Your judgment is undermined."

"Dean."

"It's okay, Beth," Reddick said. "It *is* undermined. That's my point."

"He could have thought of a nicer way to put it."

"Sorry." Dean said. "I'm just— This happens to me in my studio. I get attached to some little bit of a sculpture, some element that maybe I've spent a ton of time on, and when the piece isn't working, I can't make a decision about that element because I'm too invested in it."

"Of course," Beth said. "This happens all the time."

"Right. And when it does, I get other people to look, because even if they aren't totally objective, they're fairer than I am."

"I already did that, with Sarah."

"Only you don't trust what she's telling you."

"I want to. But I don't know how I can."

"You need more perspectives," Beth said. "How about fill us in, and we can give it a shot?"

He considered it. "Maybe I should just show you."

They followed him into the bedroom. He turned the light on and let them look, silently, without direction. Beth realized what it was first, while Dean was still tracing pencil lines, measuring the relationships of shapes to which he hadn't yet bothered to attach meaning. She went right for the names.

"You've mapped it all out. Your theories, everything."

"It isn't a drawing at all," Dean said.

"In movies they have photographs, and pushpins, but I just had a pencil and eraser. It made more sense than a notebook. It's closer to the way I think." He tried to see it the way they were, as strangers—crisscrossed lines, circled names and scrawled notations, the dragged tones of hasty erasure. He had that sense of public nakedness that came with showing someone his artwork, stronger than he had ever had with his paintings—as though the case map revealed him more completely.

"Is it weird that I get it now?" Beth said.

"What do you mean?"

"Well. That there was this activity generated by it. Once I think about it like that, it makes sense to me. You've been making art this whole time."

"I've been trying to find someone. A person."

"Sure. But what does that *mean*? And more specifically, what does it entail? You have this goal, this obsession—it doesn't just sit idly in your mind. You respond to it. And that's what I see on your wall. It's art, Reddick."

Dean jumped in. "It's not just that, though. It's more like two parallel activities. I see probing, you know? There are elements here, gestures, that go beyond merely recording other movements, that are movements in and of themselves."

"Don't talk about it like that. That isn't what I'm doing at all. I'm not making art."

"But you are."

"I thought you were going to help me."

"We're just responding to what we see," Beth said.

"Then you aren't looking at it the right way. You're treating this like an end to itself, when it isn't. This is just to help me find her."

"You could flip that, though," Dean said. "Why does your search have to be the end? Maybe it's the starting point, to get your studio practice going again."

"You're talking about using someone else's misfortune."

"He isn't, though. What he means, what I see here, is your own fascination. That's very different."

"We've been friends for a decade. We've seen each other do good work and shitty work. I think this is probably the most interesting your studio has ever been."

"Same." Beth's expression was solemn.

"I mean, it's just potential right now. Don't get me wrong. But I see things here that I haven't seen from you in a long, long time. I see passion, I see personal investment. You shouldn't squander that."

"I don't want this to be art. That's not why I care."

"That's just it, though," Beth said. "When you're an artist

that's the only way you know how to care about something. Anything that is important goes into your work. That's what your work is, what it's for. It's literally the way you care. When something grabs you it *has* to go into the work, I mean by definition—or else it hasn't really grabbed you. Because that's all the work is, is fascination manifesting itself."

"There is so much of you in this."

"All the racial stuff is potent. It's everything you got so worked up about the other night." She smiled. "Look at this, the way you've literally cut all the black people away, just disempowered them completely. Their neighborhood is being taken away from them. And the format evokes a police investigation, which implies that a crime has been committed, which summons the whole history of racial injustice at the hands of the police. I mean that *is* this moment, you know?"

"Clint is the only cop involved so far. And he's black, and lives here, so it really isn't that simple."

"Right, right. That complexity is a nice layer, though. Systemic injustice pitted against personal ties. Some of these elements you would have to clarify, take a position. It is just a beginning. But it's *so* promising."

"And look, this is a pretty remarkable coincidence," Dean said. "To get this offer from this woman now? You could quit Lockstone." Reddick almost interrupted to tell him about being fired, but thought better of it. Dean continued. "The timing is unbelievable. You'll be able to devote full attention to your work at the precise moment when you have some work that deserves your full attention."

"Right. Which, her offer—I wanted to get both of your opinions."

Dean cut him off. "My opinion is you have to go with this. Let Hannah go, man."

"Opportunities like this don't come around all that often," Beth said.

"Six months? Opportunities like this *never* come around."

"Speaking of opportunities..." Beth cut her eyes at Dean.

"Oh, right," he said. "We should get another beer first."

"I need one, too." Reddick followed them into the kitchen, dazed that the night had spun out of his hands so quickly. What they said couldn't possibly be true—he had never thought about the case as art—but their confidence caught him flat-footed. He needed to peel away, to go for a walk or play ball and work through their reactions.

Instead he opened a beer.

"Remember Mara Jost?" Dean leaned against a counter.

It took him a moment. "That dealer that came to your studio?"

"That's the one."

"He got an email from her today."

Dean nodded. "She wants to put me in a two-person show next year. In her main space, in Chelsea. If it goes well..."

"Which of course it will."

"If it goes well she's interested in adding me to her stable. Permanently."

Reddick paused, absorbing it. He turned to Beth. "And you...?"

She shook her head. "She didn't mention me, which is fine. You know, fine. I'm just so excited for Dean right now." She grabbed his hand and squeezed to make her point.

Reddick paused, then hugged him. He felt no envy—which surprised him—only a kind of stupefied joy that Dean had thwarted the impossible odds, had skirted the gatekeepers of professional success. It had the thrill of an athletic feat.

"That is fucking fantastic, man. Seriously. That is really,

really great. You've worked so hard for this." He let go. "So what's next? How ready are you?"

"Well." Dean went to the couch and sat down, Beth beside him. Reddick followed. "That's kind of the other side of this. You know how long these pieces take to assemble. I need to finish two more by the show, and at my current pace that isn't going to happen. So I'm leaving Lockstone."

Beth scooped his hand back up, beaming. As proud of his success as if it were her own.

"It's a huge gamble, I know. But I have some savings, I talked with my parents already and they think it's a great idea. This chance will only come once. I have to go all in."

"Definitely. You have to go for it." Reddick paused. "Did you tell Lane yet?"

"I'll call him tomorrow. I'll offer two weeks but he probably won't take it. I'm sure there's a line of guys he could plug in."

Reddick winced. "Yeah. I got that impression as well."

"What do you mean?"

Reddick told him about getting fired. "Holy shit," Dean said, "now you *have* to take Mrs. Leland's offer."

"I wouldn't say I have to—I'm not completely broke. I could maybe make it a month. Don't worry, I'll be able to cover my half of the rent regardless."

Now it was Dean who winced. "The thing is—that's where I was going with this—leaving Lockstone puts me on a pretty tight budget. An I-can't-afford-two-rents tight budget."

"Oh."

"I'm going to move out."

"Right."

"It's what I need to do. I'll give you a month—over a month, until March first—to find someone to take the room.

You know it won't be hard, with the demand for this neighborhood."

"No, right. Sure."

"I'm sorry, man. But you can see it's the right decision for me."

"What will you do?'

"I'm just going to sleep in the studio."

"Well, if you need a place to shower."

"One of the guys down the hall actually put a shower in his studio. He has this weird corner space with his own sink, so he just rigged something up."

"He's, like, an actual certified plumber," Beth said. "I mean, that's what he does for money."

"So it's pretty nice," Dean continued. "We've been using it the past couple days. He's offered it to the entire floor."

"You've got it all figured out, then." Reddick leaned back into his chair. The sense of shared joy was already dissipating. Dean was taking his success with him, and with Beth. Reddick had seen it coming, but he had expected it to fold into their current lives, to offer surface upgrades—reform, not revolution. This was something larger; it was dividing their futures. Their relationship already straining against the momentum of separate trajectories.

Maybe one day, in some house—not thc Sewards' but one just like it—he'll install one of Dean's sculptures.

There were still beers to float the optimism, to aid the natural buoyancy of good news. They talked their way through a pair of six-packs. The conversation darted occasionally back to Mrs. Leland's offer. Dean and Beth doubled down on their position—he couldn't let an opportunity like this go.

"You've never lacked talent," Dean said. "Just a subject. Just something that you were truly passionate about."

Which was how the night ended. After a final round of congratulations for his friend's improbable break, Reddick stumbled into his room thinking of passion, thinking of how he had made a mistake—he was not wrong to be consumed by the case. He was wrong to try to contain it.

NINETEEN

In his dream he watched Hannah's body dissolve beneath an avalanche of water, bits of flesh carried away by swirling eddies. He woke up without a hangover—his body adapted to the increased frequency of heavy drinking, accepting the nightly abuse as routine. Beth had slept in Dean's room instead of on the couch. He made coffee and took it to the window. It had rained overnight; the snow and the sidewalks were soaked, the sky gray as ash. His macabre dream lingered, begged him to read into its details—Hannah washing away, a girl's body surrendered to water, Coney Island all over again. His case had seemed as concrete as that one, the crime as obvious, but now all he saw was his own conjecture, his ineffectual desire to make this into something, to make it fit what he wanted it to be.

Dean and Beth got up and the three of them ate breakfast. They found a somber iteration of last night's good mood and clung to it. Beth left first, Dean a half hour later, his work ethic undiminished by success. He credited his long hours in the studio for getting him this far. It was only a partial truth. A driving capacity for hard work was just your price of entry. It bought the lottery ticket but didn't determine which number was called. That was left to vaguer forces, to the alchemy of an inscrutable system—to motivations too subjective and innumerable to prepare for. Take fifteen years of your life, encase them in lead and drop them in a fire. Perhaps they will turn to gold.

But it had happened for Dean. Or was in the process of happening, and Reddick might have been too pessimistic about what it could mean for him. Perhaps there would be some spillover. Perhaps if he had the right subject. Harold's advice came to his mind, its hard-nosed clarity. *Then go do that shit.*

He thought of her hands disintegrating, the B movie details. What did it hurt to try? It could just be a way to stop thinking about the way she looked in his dream.

He went into the studio.

He imagined an installation, a collection of objects that could function individually but worked together. Start with a pencil because it was easy. Quick sketches—a natural extension of the map. The construction site, augmenting his memory with photographs, working loosely, playfully, not bound by naturalism. It came back so easily. A tactile reflex stored in the fibers of his hands, independent of the mind. Drawing *felt* fantastic. The sensation of it was the facet that no one talked about enough, the physical pleasure of the movements. Restoration Heights, a Brooklyn street—did he have a photo of Sensei? Search, search—there, on a blog documenting the last protest. Wait, no, that wasn't him. The kufi threw him off. But it didn't matter, what he needed was the suggestion of a man. For now. The hard facts of individuality could come later.

He drew the alley and Hannah at the end of it. He tacked the page on the wall and found a tube of black acrylic and filled in the space around her, punched up the lines around her face, the drama and the composition nodding back to his days copying Frank Miller—wait, no—Eddie Campbell. Much better. He didn't think about it, didn't think about anything. He ran on instinct for an hour and a half, stopped to wet his throat. He came back and looked at Franky and Buckley.

What about those two? Maybe he should build something for them. A physical structure to embody two men making a career out of the erection of physical structures. *Erection* sparked a phallic chain that he quickly disregarded—too ham-fisted. He recalled a professor saying that you should start obvious or you risk not making your point, but no, not now. He had to build something ramshackle, disheveled, something that aspired to grandiosity but was tainted by an obvious, inherent corruption. Ambition as a moral flaw. Only he didn't have materials to build with. He could make a list, go shopping, but he couldn't leave now, couldn't break his surging rhythm. He decided to sketch the structures out—as they came together he realized the sketches might work on their own. Maybe. What kind of building was Buckley, what kind was Franky? Did they rot in different ways? These were decisions that seemed right on the page.

He felt the beginning of hunger but ignored it. His confidence grew. Some of this stuff looked really good. Better than anything he had done in a few years, for sure. Dean and Beth had a way of burying what they meant in jargon but they were perceptive. He ought to trust them more—what had Sarah said about the messenger not affecting the truth of the message? Sarah. It was too soon to text her but she would be thrilled, he knew it. In the glow of the work anything seemed possible—pieces of his life coalesced into something he could bear. Like in games when the hoop swelled to twice its diameter, the size of a garbage can—he couldn't miss. Yeah, it was only a start—just a few hours in to what would have to be hundreds, and he knew bad days would come, but this was everything he needed. It felt like he had been asleep for months, years.

He was empty after four hours, raw and tender and calm, moving with a sort of slow-motion clarity, without the possibility of frustration or disappointment. He stepped back to look at what he had done. It was all fledgling ideas and first steps, but it was rich with promise.

He needed air. He left, headed up to his coffee shop. The rain had stopped, the afternoon warm—ten degrees above freezing—and humid. The streets seemed less like roads and more like a series of interlocking waterways, navigable channels through islands of slate and brick, cars splashing across their surface, hinting at illusory depths. Sopping drifts disintegrated, feeding puddles that ran the length of the block. The barista was outside smoking.

"Hey," she said, "are you coming in?"

"Yeah, but take your time. In fact?" he nodded at the pack in her hand. "Maybe I could bum one and join you?"

It was a habit he toyed with in college—reset your mind with nicotine after a few hours' work, then head back in and evaluate. Eventually he had gotten tired of the smoke sapping his stamina and quit. This was his first cigarette in half a decade—it tasted like seared garbage, but it let him chat with the barista, pass the time. They went in, she poured his coffee and he tossed a few extra dollars into the jar, for the cigarette, and walked to the tables in the back.

"You serious?" Clint was seated with his back to the rear

wall, his bulk dwarfing the tiny table. He was reading his phone, ignoring the Walter Mosley paperback in front of him, the folded *Daily News* beneath it. His aviators rested near the apex of his shaved head, unneeded in this soppy weather, but ready. He had removed the lid from his towering coffee; the milky liquid inside looked tepid, nacreous. He put his phone down, leaned back and folded his hands over the crest of his hard belly. "Is there anywhere I can go to get away from you? I got dinner plans with my wife tomorrow night, you going to show up at the next table?"

"Only if you think they won't have room for all three of us to sit together."

Clint kicked the chair out from beneath the table next to his, catty-corner to his own, and nodded at it.

"I don't need to bug you right now," Reddick said.

"Man, sit down already."

Reddick didn't want to stay, he felt too airy, too aloft, to have this conversation. He wanted to sustain his buzz, to amplify it. His studio full of fresh artwork called to him. Clint was a reminder of commitments, of failures, that he suddenly wanted to wiggle free from.

But the cop didn't know any of that. "You think about what I said? That you need to look carefully? Pay attention to specifics?"

"I did. I made some progress, actually."

"That's good—because there are facts, if you can get to them. That's what I was trying to say to you, about what good police do. We got eyewitnesses we can't always believe, evidence we can't fully trust—plus you got your own self-interest distorting the tiny bit of solid information you do manage to dig up. It's not a question of whether or not you're getting something wrong, only how much. But listen to me. That doesn't mean there isn't a truth behind it all. There is a fact of the matter—always—even if you can't see it. What you have to do is keep sorting through all the bullshit to get as close to it as possible."

Reddick twitched, nervous to reveal what he had learned to Clint—that all of the cop's favors and support had come to nothing. "I'm starting to worry the whole thing has been a waste of time."

"You said you made progress?"

"I did. That guy Ju'waun found me."

Clint looked concerned. "You alright? He threaten you?"

"He tried, at first. It was like you said, though, his heart wasn't in it. We ended up just talking." He told him about Ju'waun's revelations, how the connections Reddick had imagined between the two sides of the case were almost all a misunderstanding. "I'm starting to feel like you were right, what you said to me the first time I came to you. Maybe she just left him, and there was never anything to this at all."

"So you believe him?"

"I checked it out. There was a mugging that night. And his reaction—he wasn't acting."

"That sounds like some shit Harold would do." Clint frowned. "What about the party, though? She was definitely there with those two."

"If she was about to leave her fiancé, I don't know, picking up a guy at a bar makes sense, doesn't it? I remember she said to me, about being so wasted, that she had earned it. That sounds exactly like what someone would say if they were leaving an unhappy relationship, right? She had earned a night out, earned a random hookup. If she decided, despite the money, she wasn't happy with Buckley—it couldn't have been easy to leave, and she was doing it. She had found the strength, she was celebrating. I didn't think about it before. I didn't want to. It all seemed like too much of a coincidence. But the harder I look, the less mystery is actually there."

"You know who you sound like? Me, a week ago."

Reddick glanced across the table, expecting smug satisfaction, but all he saw was disappointment. "I thought you'd enjoy saying that a little more. I'm sorry I wasted your time."

"You kidding? Most of what I do is a waste of time. That's the job, crossing off all the things that don't matter until you're left with something that does." He looked down at his phone, his book. "So that's it, then?"

"I haven't made up my mind yet. But I think it might be."

"What are you going to do now?"

Reddick thought about Mrs. Leland, the money. The possibility of following Dean's lead, grinding in the studio, of having more days like this one, when the work becomes a catalyst for a beatific calm. He thought of Sarah, and that his world was somehow blooming with promise.

"You know I'll be in the Y."

"I know. You should try the weight room sometime, though. Adding a little muscle to your scrawny ass would probably help your game."

Reddick stood up, reached across the table and shook Clint's hand. "Anything's possible."

The afternoon stretched in front of him. He had to make a decision, to call Mrs. Leland and either swallow his pride or sacrifice the money to his principles, but why do it today, why ruin this. He went home, decided to take one more look at the work, to restart the high that Clint had interrupted. The drawing of Hannah was tacked between the two halves of the original map. New paper was collaged around it, riffs on his original, probing notations. He had been thinking of texture, the faint shine of the graphite and the hairy softness of the paper.

That drawing of Sensei was pretty wonky. He removed it. He shifted another page to fill the gap but now the left side was off. Alright, fine, just tweak a few things—what else did he have to do with his time. He went to unpin another one but realized it wasn't so much the arrangement. It was the drawings themselves that weren't quite right. They lacked backbone. He had aimed for a kind of carefree invocation of mood—instead they seemed frivolous. The few areas that he had knuckled into looked overworked, verging on academic. He went to Hannah, the nexus. Okay, she was still fine. The composition was nice. But her face was kind of fucked-up. How had he not noticed? There was a weird mark that he had intended as cheekbone but instead looked like some piece of misplaced ear. He could make it read as cheek if he squinted, but only if he worked at it. The cigarette had left a lump of ash in his gut that the coffee was propelling to his limbs, his head. He picked up the sketched plans for the constructions. There was something fresh about them—a gestural inquisitiveness that called back to the map—but they couldn't stand on their own, not really. Perhaps they would be fine concepts to plan structures from but he didn't have the skills to refine them into workable blueprints, much less to build them.

He stepped back from the work, to view all of it together. He felt hollow. The room wasn't bad—simply lackluster. Nothing looked as good as it had felt to make. The discrepancy gutted him—that such thrilling activity could produce these middling results. He was hot with shame. How had he ever thought he could he bet his life on this?

He gathered the loose drawings into a stack, left the map in disarray and went into the living room. Maybe this was an opportunity, but it didn't matter if he hadn't put in the time to be ready—or worse, flat didn't have the talent. He couldn't remember when he had traded painting for basketball. There had been no conscious decision—it was an emergent choice, an ever-expanding sequence of tiny failures of will. He couldn't reverse it on a whim, on a mercantile impulse. Some decisions you can't come back from. Perhaps the world accepts such opportunism but the work flatly rejects it. Inauthenticity was smeared on every drawing in that room, page after page calling him a liar. The work will tell you, even if no one else will.

Fuck art, fuck Hannah and—why not—fuck the money. He had to find a job—worse, he had to find a career. Past thirty and listless, he had made only one bet but hedged it to irrelevance. Actually, don't fuck the money—maybe take it to use for something else, leave art alone—he wondered if he could bargain Mrs. Leland for enough to make a down payment on an apartment in the neighborhood. Root himself here. Derek could help with the financing, the searching. The idea echoed in the space left by that morning's enthusiasm—he needed something there, to fill it. Even if it was something he didn't really believe in.

It would be terrifically stupid not to take the money.

He grabbed his ball and went to the courts up the street. The ice was gone. Puddles guarded the paint like stone-footed defenders. After several minutes two kids wandered over and the three of them improvised a wordless, scoreless game of Horse. It started tentatively but they raised the stakes with a succession of increasingly elaborate shots, until they were all tossing no-looks and spins, Euro steps to off-handed hooks, half showing off and half just testing the limits of dumb luck. All three of them giggling; Reddick's threadbare joy spun delicately over his anguish. The kids were genuinely good but so young that it was impossible to say if their talent might come to anything. There was too much time for their bodies to betray them, to pick some height under six-three and stop there, no matter how much they ate or prayed. Time for their proportions to go awry, legs too short, hands too small, time to become slower, clumsier. What would Reddick have done if he were two inches taller—those Division II schools might have asked him to come in and score, play his natural position, rather than offering to make him the token try-hard, a smart system guy who set picks and played effort defense. Two inches taller and a little faster, a little more explosive—one more dollop of genetic luck might have gotten him there, possibly even into Division I, into televised games. Never mind that that would have been years gone by now—he would at least have those memories to sustain him.

The kids left. He went home. He ate and showered without looking at the remains of his map, then, when he was ready, braced himself and went into his bedroom. He sat down on the edge of his bed and stared—some part of him had hoped for a rebound, for it to look better with fresh expectations. Instead he felt embarrassed by the disarray, the days of careful work obliterated by a few hours of frantic activity. He was ashamed that the money had exposed him so thoroughly—that what he thought was moral courage had instead been self-deception, a commitment to ignoring his own colossal failure. He stood up and went into the other room.

TWENTY

He slept for ten hours after his first sober night in a week. The temperature had fallen again; the morning was cold and white as a corpse. He made coffee and breakfast and wondered where Dean was.

He hadn't decided whether he would take the money but he would need a job regardless. He opened his laptop, killed tabs and windows that he had been keeping alive, zombie-like, to mark his trail through the case. He dug up his résumé, swallowed horror at seeing his life condensed to a single page, at having to own up to his passion for useless pursuits. He sifted through listings. An artist in Hoboken needed someone to clean and type, a moving service needed a back and a pair of strong hands. Which part of his body could he lease. He was at it a few hours when his phone rang.

It was Derek.

"See?" Reddick said. "Sometimes a text just won't do."

"Enjoy your triumph. Honestly, I expected you to push me to voice mail. You're not back at work yet?"

"Yeah. About that." He told him about being fired, and his theory of Mrs. Leland's motives, and her offer.

"That sounds less like an offer and more like a threat."

"She said she had other ways of preventing me from talking, that this was the only way I could benefit in the process."

"I told you from the beginning—you were in over your head dealing with people like her."

"I wasn't expecting her to push back so hard."

"To me it seems like overkill—I can't see what she is so worried about that she would react that strongly. But take her at her word. She's considered how much her time is worth and decided that it's cheaper for her if you take the offer."

"So, what? That's it?"

"You could try and push for more money. See how much it actually means to her."

"You know I care about this."

"But you're thinking real hard about taking the cash."

"It's the kind of choice that seems clear until you actually have to make it. It isn't just that you have to weigh the money against your beliefs—it's that the money makes you mistrust the scale."

"That's nothing to be ashamed of. It's a lot of money for you."

"For you."

"Come on. You have to be real about where you are."

"Yeah. I'm not so great at that."

"Your problem is that you're a better doer than you are a thinker."

"I'm so glad you called. Really."

"It's nothing against you, man. Most people are, at least when they're young. The ratio flips when you get older but by then it's too late—you're already locked down by decisions you made when you were still lousy at making decisions. I was lucky. I had my mom to show me what good decisions, what thinking strategically, could do. I watched her scrape poverty off like old skin, and more importantly, I saw *how* she did it. She picked a spot and mapped out a path toward it. Good luck and hard work don't mean jack shit if you don't have your goals locked down tight."

"So you're saying take the money?"

"I'm saying you have to figure out what you want. I mean long-term, not just in this moment. Pick where you want to be in fifty years and lay every choice you make against that."

"That sounds great. But I don't have that kind of focus in me."

"It's not too late to learn."

"You take classes in this? Strategic thinking?"

"What do I keep saying to you, bro? UM is a good fucking school."

Reddick paused, then, "I've got a week."

"So use it. But listen—you want to know why I called or are you done with this?"

"The case?"

"I finally went through all the files you gave me."

"And?"

"I didn't see anything. It was all straightforward accounting stuff. A paper trail that doesn't go anywhere interesting."

Reddick walked to the window, watched shivering pedestrians hurry beneath the spider-web branches of leafless trees. "Nice to know I got myself fired for nothing."

"Sorry, man. You might like this, though—I also looked into Franky's Restoration Heights sale."

"And?"

"And he only created Tompkins Mac a week before the sale went through. Now, that doesn't necessarily mean anything—creating a LLC is pretty common for new landlords. It's what any advisor would recommend."

"But he isn't a new landlord."

"No, but even so, if he wanted to keep these assets separate, either from his personal assets or his company's, this is how he would go about it. Trust me when I say it's not suspicious on its own."

"On its own."

"Oh yeah. Because *three days* after the sale there is an assistant VP of Corren Capital onstage with the mayor announcing Restoration Heights—the first time the project became public."

Reddick paced back into his kitchen, his enthusiasm reigniting despite himself. "He knew it was coming. He bought those three properties knowing that he could flip them right back to Corren."

"For almost double what he paid."

"Buckley obviously told him it was about to happen. Isn't that insider trading?'

"Insider trading is only for securities, not real estate. There are disclosure laws, that sort of thing, and if there were any irregularities there could potentially be a lawsuit. But you would need a lot more than just good timing to make a case. Acting on information that only you have access to is pretty common with real estate—it's usually difficult to show that anything illegal actually happened."

"Wealthy people helping other wealthy people get wealthier."

"Right. Nothing to see here. Except."

"Except what?"

"Except that Tompkins Mac leveraged ninety-five percent of the deal."

"What does that mean?"

"It means Franky used a bank loan to cover almost the entire cost."

"Wait—that's a thing?"

"It's very, very rare—but not unheard of. Leveraging is a way to manage risk. Think about it like this: I want to make a bet. If I use all of my money, and the bet loses, all of my money is gone—I can't make any more bets."

"Or eat. Or pay your rent."

"Ha ha, assume that this money is separate okay? This is just what you have earmarked for investment."

Reddick thought of his checking account, scraped nearly to the bone on the first of every month. "Okay, right," he said.

"Now, if I get you to loan me half of it, and the bet loses, I still have half of my money. I have to pay you back but at least I can still make more bets—I'm still in the game. I'm not risking as much."

"Why would I let you bet with my money?"

"Because I'll pay you for it. That's what interest is. I pay you for the right to use some of your money instead of my own. Now for you to give me that loan, you have to be pretty sure that I can make those payments, on time, and when the term is up either repay the loan or refinance. Follow? Good. In the case of real estate, that means you need to be sure that the property that I want to buy—the bet—is going to generate enough revenue, through some combination of rents and resale value, for me to service that debt and ultimately repay the loan. I'm simplifying, but that's the basic calculus."

"What you're saying is that Franky's bet was almost entirely someone else's money."

"Exactly. But what's important is whose money it was—the bank. Serial real estate investors buy properties with other people's money all the time, but they are hitting up rich relatives or investment clubs or some other source for capital—not getting the bank to loan them ninety-five percent of the cost. That just isn't normal. Combine that with the timing and it's extremely suspicious. Because for a bank to put itself at that kind of risk, they're going to do their homework. Remember Franky only created his LLC a week before the sale—for a property inside the industry standard LTV—sorry, I mean, for a normal-sized loan—a bank could easily take two or three weeks to do a proper review. Throw in the increased risk and it simply doesn't make sense."

"What if they had the same inside information that he did? If they knew it was going to double in value in a couple weeks?"

"That dampens some of the risk, but still—what's their motivation? It wouldn't earn the bank more money, because, remember, the lender profits by charging the borrower for the loan, not by how successfully the borrower uses it. On a large scale, banks have made money from risky bets by bundling the loans and selling them to someone else—that was the subprime mortgage crisis in a nutshell—but this is a one-off. There is no obvious gain for the bank here. At least, not a legal one."

"Not a legal... You mean a bribe. To the banker making the loan."

"A bribe, a kickback, a verbal agreement to split the profits, whatever the arrangement. There would have to be something. It happens routinely in very hot markets—think Florida or Arizona right before the crisis—collusion between a banker and someone who wants to flip a property."

"And because Restoration Heights needed all that land."

"Those blocks were as hot as it gets. It all went down fast. Franky forms Tompkins Mac, gets the financing and makes the purchase in the span of a week, then two days later Restoration Heights is announced. No way does that happen without money changing hands. And money changing hands—unlike inside information—is very, very illegal."

"Do you know who gave him the loan?"

"I've got a few guys who owe me favors, so yeah, I found out. It was made at Bank United, downtown Brooklyn. The officer who signed off on it is named Mitchell Yang."

Reddick nearly dropped his phone. "That's the guy."

"Looks that way."

"No, I'm telling you. That's the guy. When I found all of this, the financial stuff, I saw a photo—Buckley, Franky and a guy named Mitchell. I didn't think anything of it. Then I met this girl the other night who used to date—still kind of dates—Franky. And what she said backs up everything you're saying. One—Franky's cash broke. So if he wanted in on Restoration Heights he would *have* to borrow the money. And two—because Franky tends to drag his feet on repaying his debts, people have gotten upset with him about not paying them back, including Buckley, and also a guy she didn't know—named Mitchell Yang."

"You're sure that's the name she said?"

"One hundred percent. She described him—it was definitely the same guy from the photo. So these three go way back. Could Franky still owe him money from that deal?"

"When did she hear this?'

"In the fall."

"No way he would have let it go that long—but if he's always strapped for cash he might have hit him up again. It could be a regular thing. But the sale, you know, that was three years ago."

Reddick paused, the time frame knocking something loose in his mind. "Three years. What month was it?"

"Give me a sec. August."

Reddick set his phone to speaker and pulled up his photos, searching until he found the image of Buckley's check stubs. The check Buckley wrote Franky, for one hundred eighty-seven thousand dollars, was dated August, three years ago.

"While I was in Buckley's study I also found a checkbook." He left his phone on speaker, tapped the image to send it.

"Yeah."

"I took photos of the check stubs. I'm sending you one."

"Hold up." A pause. "This is dated four days before the sale."

"It has to be connected, right? Maybe Buckley wanted in on this deal, too."

"He knew which properties Corren was targeting to make room for Restoration Heights. So if he wanted to make a little money for himself while he was at it—what's the math here?"

"You're asking me?" Reddick said.

"No, I'm thinking out loud. I've got the sale price—three point seven five. Five percent of that is…one hundred eighty-seven thousand."

"That check was the down payment." Reddick stopped, tried to put it together. "Three friends, school buddies. Each of them had a role to play. Buckley had the information, and supplied the little capital they actually needed. Mitchell secured the loans. But Buckley couldn't have his name on the paperwork, not with his connection to Corren."

"So that's where Franky comes in. Buckley channels the down payment through him. Now Franky is listed as the buyer, Buckley stays clean."

"It's more than that," Reddick said. "The whole plan was Franky's idea. I know it."

"Based on what?"

"What were the total profits here? What did they sell it for?"

"Corren paid six-point-seven-five. They pocketed three million clean."

"So let's say they split it evenly—what's a million dollars to Buckley? With his wealth—why risk doing anything dirty?"

"Because having money doesn't make you want it any less," Derek said. "In my experience it's the opposite."

"At Buckley's level, though—what's left to want? There are less than two dozen wealthier families in the world. A million in cash isn't going to change that, isn't even going to register. I've met him, I've spoken to him, to him and Franky both. I know how Franky treats him. This was his idea, I'm sure of it."

"What does Buckley get out of it, if not the money?"

"He's infatuated with Franky. He always has been. And Franky was probably as desperate for cash three years ago as he is now. So he concocts this plan—Buckley wouldn't say no, he's been letting him walk all over him for a decade now."

"Buckley Seward is that much of a mark?"

"For Franky he is. I need to talk to Mitchell Yang."

"Hold on a second. What were we just talking about? You need to set goals, make decisions off of them. If Mrs. Leland finds out you are still working on this she will pull her offer. You'll lose the money."

Reddick paused. "Fuck her money. What would I do with all that time off anyway?"

"If I'm being honest? You'd blow it playing basketball."

"Ha. I gotta run."

"Yeah, listen—I'll pick you up in like twenty minutes."

"You'll what?"

"Have you been outside today? It's freezing. I'm not taking the train."

"You're coming?"

"Come on, bro. You and I both know you won't understand a thing that banker says without me to translate. Give me twenty. Oh, and Reddick?"

"Yeah?"

"Dress nice."

★ ★ ★

Derek showed up in a slim charcoal suit, no tie. He looked like a different man, older and alert with power, as likely to be a Wharton classmate of Franky and Buckley's as to be helping Reddick pin them for fraud. Reddick had rummaged through his closet, discovered a pair of beige slacks, a pin-striped button-down he hadn't remembered he owned and a dark, narrow tie.

"You look like a fifth-grader going to church," Derek said.

He ditched the tie in the car. They found street parking in the nest of retail blocks east of Borough Hall, got out and walked until the jewelry windows and sneaker stores gave way to glossy high-rises. Bank United was wedged into the toe of a glass-and-steel tower. There was a pair of guards at the door and an air of mechanized bureaucracy from the women behind the counter. Derek asked for Mitchell Yang. Reddick stood behind him and tried to look less like a stain on someone's jacket.

Mitchell was an amplified version of his school photo, short and broad, with wide jowls and a rolling tide of oil-black hair. He invited them into his office. A framed Wharton diploma on one wall, the University of Pennsylvania's navy-and-blue shield on his mouse pad.

Derek shook his hand and introduced them as financial investigators, private contractors. He didn't give their real names.

"You should have just emailed." Mitchell looked skeptical, like he was deciding how far to play along. "I'm happy to help."

"I prefer face-to-face," Derek said. "I'm looking into the financing of some property in Bedford-Stuyvesant, particularly in the area northeast of Restoration Plaza."

"Are you talking about Restoration Heights?"

"I'd like to keep this conversation as narrow as possible. I want to focus on the specific properties my client is concerned about and not get pulled into the larger issues of that development."

"Okay, fine."

"We're here because we think you can help. There are some financial irregularities that my client would like cleared up, particularly regarding a loan that enabled three pieces of property in that area to be turned over."

Yang glanced at Reddick and back. "So how can I help you?"

"Tompkins Mac. I've got your signature on a loan they received from this bank three years ago."

"I can't say that I recall that name."

"Franky Dutton," Reddick said. "How about that one?"

Yang sat back in his chair, his face even. The name seemed to ground him. "Yeah, sure, I know Franky."

"You were schoolmates?"

"Different years. But yeah."

Derek jumped back in. "Did that personal relationship factor into your decision to extend him a loan that covered ninety-five percent of the value of the following properties on Tompkins Street?" He slid a list of the addresses across the desk. The banker looked them over casually.

"Only in the sense that it motivated him to come to me, as opposed to someone else. Business is built on relationships."

"Your relationship with him was strong enough that you not only felt comfortable financing that much of the purchase, it took you less than a week to review the sale."

"I won't discuss the details of our policies with you. But sure, the fact that I trust Franky helped speed things along. And that kind of leverage isn't unheard of."

"It's well above industry standard."

"In a market this solid we felt comfortable with our decision."

"You felt comfortable after a week of research?"

"I use my best judgment on all the loans I originate. And whether we underwrite or not isn't my call."

"You just passed the application down?" Reddick said. "Wink wink, nudge nudge, hey, guys, I know this is a little odd, but let it go? Or are there some falsified documents somewhere with your name on them?"

Mitchell shifted in his chair. "Who are you really? You haven't shown me an ID or a business card."

"What's the going rate for bank fraud? You get an even share of that three million?"

Reddick saw the number hit, a break in his frat boy composure. Mitchell blinked, pulled his indignant smile back into place—it wasn't enough to hide his sudden fear.

"Like shit you guys are investigators," he said.

"If you don't want to talk we could take this to your director," Derek said. "Or the CFPB."

"You wouldn't be in my office with this bullshit story if that's what you were going to do." He was seeping fear now—disproportionate to anything the two of them represented. "What do you want? Who sent you?"

"Nobody sent us," Reddick said.

"I told you people the first time—it's not my fault the deal went down that way."

"You people?"

"I made it square last spring. You said that would be the end of it."

"Made what square?" Reddick leaned forward, confused but eager. "Who did you talk to last year?"

"That fucking blonde cunt. Don't you know?"

"Hannah?" He hadn't suspected she would be involved here, on this side—had she gone behind Franky's back somehow?

"Like I would know her real name."

Reddick pulled Hannah's photo up on his phone and stabbed it at the banker's face. "Her?"

Mitchell squinted. "What? That's the wrong picture, buddy. I know that girl. That's Buckley's—that's my friend's girlfriend."

"And she's not the girl who came to see you?"

"Of course not. But look, I'll tell you what I told her—I'll zero this out once but you can't bleed me forever. I'm not defenseless. I have friends, too, alright?"

Reddick looked for another opening, wanted to keep him talking until he made sense—but Mitchell shut down.

"Now get the fuck out of here before I call security."

"Look," Reddick stood up. "Whatever your role here was, I don't care. I'm trying to help someone that I think got caught up in this deal—I'm talking a girl's life, so if you have an ounce of human compassion inside that doughy rich-kid fat fucking chest you'll tell me the straight truth." He held Hannah's photo up again. "You say you know this girl—that's who I'm trying to help. Did she come to your office? Did she try and blackmail you?"

Mitchell paused, let Reddick's vitriol slide off his skin like grease. "You have no idea what you are talking about."

Derek put his hand on his friend's shoulder. "Come on. Let's go."

Reddick scoured Mitchell's face for signs of a lie. The banker held firm. Reddick backed toward the door.

"If I see you in here again I'm calling security."

Derek raised his middle finger, then opened the office door.

"Wait," Reddick said.

"We have to go."

"No, wait." He swiped his phone, began tapping the keypad.

Mitchell buzzed his desk phone. "Tyrell, will you send security back to my office, please?"

"Seriously, man," Derek urged. "We can't be hanging out in here right now."

"I said wait."

Two large men in cheap suits came in. "Would you see these two out, please?" Yang said.

"Let's go," Derek snapped.

"Got it." Reddick lunged at Mitchell and the two suits followed him. He held the screen up. "What about her? Is this the woman that tried to—" he looked at the security guards "—that was in your office?"

"Get him out of here."

The guards put their hands on his shoulders and dragged him toward the door.

"Come on, Mitchell. Is this the damn woman or not?"

"We don't want this kind of trouble, man," Derek hissed.

"Mitchell," Reddick pleaded.

The banker hesitated, then gave a half shrug. "Sure it is. Like you don't know already."

The guards took Reddick out, one on each side. He tried to appear calm. Derek walked ahead of them without looking back. Once they were outside he waited at the nearest corner for Reddick to join him.

"You alright?"

Reddick glanced behind him, at the guards blocking the front door, glaring. "I'm fine."

"I realize I'm wearing a suit and all, but I can't have someone calling the cops on me." Derek's face was stern. "And not just because I'm worried about my career. You know what I'm saying?"

"I know, I'm sorry. I just had to show him one last photo."

Derek buttoned his coat, glanced around the sidewalks as if the police might yet be on their way. "So he said yes, finally? That it was Hannah that came to see him?"

Reddick unlocked the screen and handed him his phone. Derek looked at it.

"Cask? Isn't this that liquor store in Clinton Hill?"

"Yep." Reddick reached over and zoomed into a photo on the store's website, taken at a wine tasting. "And that's the owner, Mia. Who apparently blackmailed Mitchell Yang last spring."

TWENTY-ONE

"How did you know?"

They sat in Reddick's living room, on opposite ends of his couch, drinking coffees they had picked up on their way back. The conversation in the car had been quick, chaotic; Reddick hurling facts at his friend, details that in his excitement he wasn't sure whether he had withheld or not from earlier conversations. They had barely dug in before they were in front of Reddick's apartment so he invited him up. A dizzy energy bounded between them, a rush of discovery, still unformed but potent.

"I fell for it once already," Reddick said. "Confusing those two."

"They don't really look alike."

"Same gender, same hair. When the information is coming secondhand people are reduced to generalities."

"So you were on your guard against it this time. But even so, what made you think it could be Mia? There are more than two blonde women in Brooklyn."

"Because it couldn't be someone new. It couldn't be unrelated." The facts of the case were bending, closing themselves off. There was no room for new entries. "I already made that mistake once—letting myself believe that half of the case was a dead end. Trusting Ju'waun."

"You said his story checked out."

"The mugging, yeah. That happened. The whole Mia-for-Hannah confusion, too. But he played it coy about Hannah and Franky, like he had no idea about any of it. He didn't tell me any lies I could catch him in—he just didn't tell me everything. That's why he unloaded so much; he thought if he gave me enough information, then I would assume that it was all of it, and he was right." He thought about Ju'waun's final warning: *It's not at all like you think it is.*

"Maybe that's true," Derek said. "So Mia blackmailed Mitchell Yang last spring."

"Which prompted the argument that the girl I met at that party overheard. Mitchell wasn't upset about Franky not paying back some money he owed him, he was upset because the deal they did three years ago was causing him to be squeezed by Mia—presumably on behalf of the Genie."

"Right. But I'm still not sure how that connects to Hannah. I see two separate incidents—on the one hand a missing girl, on the other a real estate fraud."

Reddick thought back to his bifurcated map. "But they both involve the same two groups of people. How likely is it that these crooked finance assholes would be caught up with someone like the Genie even once, much less twice?"

"I guess that depends on how crooked they are."

"They have to be connected. Ju'waun was out with Hannah the night before she disappeared."

Derek leaned forward, rubbed the stubble at the nape of his neck. It was a side of him that Reddick hadn't seen before—

analytical, serious. He was taking Reddick's wild thrusts and turning them over, scrubbing them for consistency. "Unless he's telling the truth about that, too—what if he and Tyler just picked her up at a bar?"

"No way."

"Then what you've got is a chain. Buckley and Franky connect to Hannah, who went to that party with Ju'waun, who is dating Mia."

"And Mia tried to blackmail Mitchell Yang for dipping into Restoration Heights money with the help of Buckley and Franky. It isn't a chain, it's a circle."

"And someone took a piece out."

A piece with a name. "Hannah."

"There's your motive," Derek said. "If she's really the only link between the two groups—between Franky and Buckley on one side, the Genie and Mia on the other—then maybe someone wanted to sever that connection."

"And who would stand to gain by doing that?"

"Your man Franky, for one. If you think he would go that far to cover this up."

"He might." Lying to evict tenants, hurting a girl in a bar, bullying his hopeless best friend—yes, there were miles between any of those acts and murder. But if he was protecting himself, his business? People had killed for less. "He has a motive."

"He might, but I see two big problems with it. One, he didn't *need* to go after anyone—it would be difficult to prove he did anything wrong flipping those properties to Corren. You would need hard evidence, a voice mail or an email or something, and Franky undoubtedly knows that. Absent this evidence there was no reason to murder someone—much less Hannah, who seems like a pretty minor connection between the two parties. And two—why did Mia try to blackmail Yang?"

"Why target Hannah? I don't know. We don't know what she knew, what evidence she might have had. Maybe she did have an email or something like that. From what Marie said she seemed manipulative—maybe she was working a blackmail angle, too."

The alarm on Derek's phone began to buzz. "Shit, man. I've got to go. I'm looking at a place in the East Village today."

They stood up, clasped hands and bumped shoulders. Reddick thanked him.

"I think I'm almost there."

"I told you that you needed me," Derek said.

"Did I argue?"

"I heard it in your voice."

"I'll take all the help I can get." They clasped hands again, and Derek left.

Reddick went back to his room and began to restore the map. He packed the drawings away, stored his inks and other materials, aligned the pieces in their original shape. Hannah was joined in the center by Mitchell Yang, by the three men's plot, the quick fortune made off someone else's cash—all of the tendons he could find to connect Bed-Stuy and the Upper East Side, perhaps the only ones possible: money, exploitation, sex. A classic American cocktail of slumming and gentrification, with classic American victims. Was this it, was Hannah's story simply another iteration of that old one—one of the nation's few founding myths that has actually borne out to be true—that the powerful take from the weak, that there is nothing that cannot be sold—no home, no culture, no people—given the right offer?

He felt Hannah slipping away from him, into this. He felt himself losing his grip on the people involved to the swell of larger forces, the impersonal tug of social patterns. Ju'waun, Hannah, Franky, Buckley—they all had names, they were individuals making decisions—he couldn't let them become placeholders for theories about justice or history. He knew they were people because he had met them, they had behaviors, quirks, odors, affectations. They were all distinct. Class and race grouped people into circles where the likelihood for certain outcomes was radically different—but losing the sense that there were individuals inside those circles, that they were people with their own minds, meant surrendering entirely to an anonymous reading of history that he could not accept, that belied his own experience. These were two truths he could not reconcile.

Why Hannah? The answer was on the map. It had to be. He traced the lines radiating out from her name, murmuring a list of possible motivations. *Jealousy, revenge, secrecy, fear, entitlement, rage. Jealousy, revenge, secrecy. Jealousy revenge. Revenge.*

Revenge.

He picked up his phone and called Derek.

"Hey. I don't suppose you're stuck in traffic right now?"

"The BQE never quits, man. Why, what's up?"

"I was hoping you could check something for me. When you accessed those sales records, for Tompkins Mac—did you see who the seller was?"

"Yeah. I've got it on the seat next to me. Give me a sec." There was a rustle of fabric on leather seats, then he came back on. "Let me see. It was a private individual, a woman—I remember thinking how pissed I would be if it had been my mother. Not that she would have sold. Where is it. Oh yeah, here. Looks like…a…Jeannie Tucker."

"Jeannie Tucker?"

"Yeah, a local landlord. Like I said, it reminded me of my mother, so I did a quick search to see if she owned anything else. She has a couple other properties nearby."

"Feeling sentimental?"

"It's been known to happen."

"Do you have a list of those other properties?"

"Yeah."

"Is Cask on it?"

"Yeah. Holy shit. Yeah."

"How about a dry cleaners named Clean City?"

"That's on here, too. Who is she, Reddick?"

Jeannie. Genie.

"I've got to go."

"Reddick, what are you thinking? Who is she?" A pause, then, "Is Jeannie Tucker the Genie?"

"I've got to go *right now.*"

"Don't do anything stupid. Whatever you're thinking—don't do anything stupid."

But Reddick barely heard him—he was already hanging up.

He took that knowledge back to the map and ten minutes later he had it. He knew why Hannah disappeared, why Buckley reacted the way he did—the pieces sliding into place like gears.

He called Mrs. Leland. Thomas answered.

"Put her on the line."

"Good day, Reddick."

"Put her on the line, Thomas." There was a pause as he brought her the phone. "Mrs. Leland?"

"I hope you have come to the right conclusion, Reddick."

"I know where Hannah is."

She sighed. "I see. I'm disappointed that you won't see reason."

"I know who is behind this and I'm going there now. I only ask one thing. Check up on me. After all the work I did for you—you owe this to me. Make sure I come back. That's it. If I don't—call the police, and tell them what I'm about to tell you. Okay? Tell them and make sure it ends with me."

"You're being very dramatic. Buckley's fiancée is in Oregon."

"Buckley's fiancée isn't anywhere at all."

"So you are refusing my money?"

"With respect, Mrs. Leland—fuck your money." And then he told her what he knew, and where he was going.

"You don't have proof of any of this?"

"Clean City. Remember that. If I don't come back, you'll find all the proof you need there. Clean City."

He hung up and got his coat.

TWENTY-TWO

It was stuck on the end of a row of brick townhouses, squat and square, the roof a full floor lower than the rest of the block. It used to be some sort of garage. It was the kind of inconsequential building that you knew would be gone in five, ten years. The odd asymmetry of ending the block on a low note, like a bookend to keep the townhouses upright—not remotely enough character to survive what was coming. Just a corner you couldn't be bothered to notice.

The lobby was as he remembered. The outdated fliers, the lone chair, the shambled stack of magazines. The sense of a business without customers, plodding through numb days. No one behind the counter. He rang the bell. It was almost a minute before anyone showed—the same kid as last time shuffled disinterestedly to the counter.

"You think today is spring?"

"What?"

"Last time you was in here. You said you wanted to clean that coat, but you said you would wait until it was warm out."

"I did?"

"You said until spring."

Reddick gathered himself. "I'm not here about my coat."

"Yo, really."

"I need to see the Genie."

"We clean clothes, dude."

"What, is there a code or something? Do I say it three times fast? With my eyes closed?"

Patiently. "I have no idea what you are talking about."

"I'm talking about Jeannie Tucker. I'm talking about Hannah Granger. I'm talking about Sons of Cash Money and Mia and everyone else who runs errands for her. I'm talking about all the shit I already know, all the hoops I've jumped through to get this far. You think you can put me off? Take your shot."

He walked toward the low swinging doors at the end of the counter. The kid slid over to block him.

"The fuck, dude? You do not want this. You don't even know how much you do not want this."

Reddick clenched his jaw and pushed through the doors. The kid raised his arm to block his chest. Reddick slid past him.

"Yo. Yo, dude." Reddick felt his hand on his shoulder, trying to turn him, squeezing hard enough that he prepared to duck.

"TJ."

Reddick stopped, looked back. The kid's fist was poised to strike. Reddick stared at it blankly.

"TJ." Again, a woman's sandy contralto, twisting from the rear door. "You might as well let him in."

TJ let go of Reddick with an indifferent shove.

"Come on back," she said.

He went through the rear door into a refurbished garage.

The conversion was haphazard and incomplete. The concrete floor had been coated in thick varnish, oil stains trapped and preserved like fossils. The ghost of a rolling door survived in the outline of the new bricks that had filled it in. There were no windows to the outside. Pieces of unidentifiable machinery huddled in a corner, beneath a quilt of dust, beside worn metal cabinets. In the center of the room was a baggy sofa and matching chairs, cinnamon leather glistening like river stones. A large ashtray and an unlit joint rested on a table in front of them. A door to the right led to a small room, an add-on—interior windows revealed a table and chairs. A pyramid of money was piled on the table. Two men counted it. On the wall behind Reddick was an enormous flat-screen showing a live feed of the entrance to the cleaners, of the men counting money and of a handful of other rooms. The wall between the cleaners and the neighboring townhouse had been removed; a stairwell led to the upper floors next door.

The Genie sat on the leather couch, alone.

"So here I am, Reddick."

"You know my name."

Her hair was pulled into tight rows that brushed the nape of her long neck. She had a wide mouth and placid eyes. Below her angular shoulders she was solidly built, a heavy woman in her midsixties. Rich colors darted among the folds of her sweeping dress, the fabric fanned across the sofa, over her coiled legs. A pair of brown flats rested neatly on the floor beside her. Her voice tumbled from her chest, deep but rough.

"As much of my business as you have wormed into, I better know your name. Come sit down."

She nodded at one of the chairs. Reddick didn't move.

"I said come and sit down. You're here, aren't you? In my inner sanctum? The lair of the big bad monster you've been chasing. You'd better make the most of it. Summon whatever you've got left of that righteous rage."

"I can do this from back here."

"Why not be comfortable?"

"You wanted revenge."

She grinned, shifted in her seat. "I did. Tell me about it."

"You found out something was off with the financing. When Franky flipped the property so quickly you knew that you had been cheated and you went digging—I don't know how, but you found out about Mitchell, and Buckley. So you decided to make them pay. You found something you could use against Mitchell—or maybe you just threatened him—and you sent Mia, because you could trust her. So that's one down, two to go—how am I doing so far?"

"I said I would hear you out."

"Whatever you had on Mitchell wasn't enough to squeeze Franky or Buckley. You needed more information. You needed someone close to them. You needed Hannah."

The Genie reached for the joint and lit it. He was more afraid of what she would say than what she would do. He feared her knowledge, the clarity it would bring—he feared the stinging disappointment of resolution. This could end no other way—he had traced back along a web of connected actions, pursued some bleached fact from which everything else flowed, hidden by a gnarled and complicated logic—whatever he found could bring no satisfaction. The thing that comes first is the toughest thing to live with. It must be accepted without resort to explanation, without metaphysics or theory—a dumb mute stone of truth. Whatever she said was all he would have to sustain him.

"You probably feel brave," she said. "For coming here. This is your truth to power moment, right? You stand in front of me, you unravel this whole grand plot, and what do I do, exactly? What's my role?" She took a long pull from the joint, settled back into the couch and exhaled. "I provide you with satisfaction. I give you a moral clarity that you want so badly you believe you are willing to die for it. Because that's the next step, yeah? You make your speech, I confirm it—maybe fill in a little detail here and there, just to help the fit, just to actively engage in your truth-building, then I call in—I don't know, TJ or someone, and he puts a gun to your head and turns out the lights, and just before it all goes black you smile. I can see it. A nice cinematic smile. A close-up so that everybody knows you died with a martyr's peace. Because you found the *truth*." She smiled, and held out the joint. "Because you had courage, boy."

He waved away her offer.

"What's the matter? You turn down my chair. You turn down my smoke. White boys love this strain."

"I'm not here for your forgiveness."

"Come *on*, boy, I am fucking with you. Just sit down already."

"And I'm not here to die, in peace or otherwise. I let someone know where I was going, someone you can't touch—if I don't come back the cops will be at your door. They'll find all of this." He gestured at the counting room.

"Of course—you set a trap. For an extra layer of satisfaction during your close-up."

"Let me see her."

"Oh, I can't *wait* for this."

She picked up her phone, typed a brief message, then smoked quietly while they waited. He heard footsteps on the stairwell. A girl came down.

"Hannah. This is Reddick. He's been looking for you."

He had conflated the two versions of her—the reality was somewhere in between the girl in the photo and the girl in the alley. She had dyed her hair licorice black; the contrast diminished her magazine-cover cheekbones, pulled at the dark line of her slack mouth. She was shorter than he remembered, her skin rougher, her features less refined. He realized how alike her face was to his—not for any specific resemblance but in their disjointed Americanness, their odd motley of incongruent pieces. They each carried a history of incompatible parts.

"Yeah? Have we met?" Sober, her voice lost some of its nasal whine, its bratty-girl caricature.

It was the proof he wanted, the confirmation of what he saw in the map. Getting it unnerved him. "Yes. Two weeks ago. Almost two weeks ago."

"Jeannie, what did you want?" she asked.

"This. I wanted exactly this."

"It was a Sunday night," Reddick said. "You were outside without a coat. Drunk. There was a party in my building and you had come out for, I don't know, air, a cigarette. We went into the alley together. I was taking out my garbage. Your phone—someone texted you. And you left."

It was as bare a telling as he had managed yet. He saw how spare it was, how ordinary. A glancing encounter in a city composed entirely of glancing encounters. Standing in front of her now he couldn't articulate what in that moment had moved him, couldn't separate it from any number of other incidents that had passed by unnoticed. He couldn't connect the body in front of him to the person he had been chasing.

Hannah laughed, a husky, boyish sound that rolled from her chest, a register lower than her speaking voice. "I'm sorry, dude, but I don't remember that at all. I must've been pretty fucked-up."

"Yeah."

She laughed some more, enthralled with the comedy of

her lost memories. "I probably had some pills. This was Saturday?"

"Sunday. Two Sundays ago."

The timing finally registered on her face, a flash of caution. "Where was this?"

"Bed-Stuy. Near Restoration Heights."

She frowned. "Are you sure that was even me?"

"You went missing the next day. Buckley was frantic."

"Buckley?" Suddenly panicked. "What the fuck, Jeannie? Who the fuck is this?"

"You want to tell her, Reddick, or should I?"

"I don't know if I have anything left to say."

The Genie laughed. "Did you come here to speak truth to power, or to have power speak the truth to you?"

"I just needed to see. To know I was right."

"You want to fill me in here?" Hannah asked.

"Why don't you both sit down."

Reddick, finally, obeyed. He and Hannah went to opposite chairs, forming a triangle with the Genie at the apex. Hannah picked up the Genie's smoldering joint.

"Hannah, you were incautious. I told you to stay inside until we got paid."

"I wanted to celebrate. That job took, like, eight months—you never said it could go so long. It felt like I was getting out of jail."

Reddick thought of the Sewards' house, the lavish art. "Was it really that bad?"

"It's hard to be something you aren't. Harder than you think."

"You would have had everything."

She sneered at him. "I couldn't stick it out for the long haul, and with his lawyers I wasn't gonna leave that marriage any richer than I came in. It wasn't that I minded being somebody's beard, or having to pretend I wanted to fuck him. Honestly I just hated being around all that faggy art."

"I've tried to give her culture," the Genie said. "But some lessons won't be learned."

"I learned enough to make him believe in me, to get his snobby parents on my side. I learned enough that he didn't mind me fucking around so long as I never brought up Tony."

Beard. Tony. Reddick was a step behind. "Tony—you mean Anthony Leland, the state senator?"

Hannah shrugged indifferently. "Buckley's one true love. Everyone knew it, both mothers, the staff." She rolled her eyes. "Ugh, the staff. You should have heard them go on, like they were watching *Romeo and Juliet*." She dropped her voice an octave, reeled in her loose vowels. "'Oh, if only Buckles and Tony could be together, isn't it just tragic?'"

The lifestyle blogs, the images of the two men at work or play—how could he have missed it? They were lovers. Buckley was trapped beneath a lie. It explained the power of Franky's grip. Their college liaison had been cruel play for him—but for Buckley it was a glimpse of freedom, of a life compatible with his instincts. It also explained the urgency behind Mrs. Leland's involvement—because here was a scandal worth fearing. Her son could shake off ties to a corrupt development, could outlast allegations of some role in the disappearance of his friend's fiancée—but a male lover would bury his ambitions. He was married, he had a family and he had picked the wrong political party. Sarah's words came back to him—*the only people who care about a little cocksucking are Republican politicians.*

"You could have spoiled it," the Genie chided. "You let Franky see you with two of *my* boys."

"I told him I picked them up at a bar," Hannah said. "Franky is so stuck on himself that as long as I went home with him he wouldn't bother to question anything. It's not like I was ever going to see him again and I was entitled to one last decent piece of ass. As a reward for time served."

"It was such an obvious con," Reddick said. "I don't know how it took me so long to see it."

"Those motherfuckers owed me money," the Genie snapped. "A whole lot of fucking money."

"Franky, Mitchell, Buckley—they took you for a ride with that deal," Reddick said. "Why did you sell? Why do you all always sell to these arrogant developers when you know they don't care about the neighborhood?"

"'You all,'" she sneered. "The mysteries of the black heart, right? You want me to speak for my people."

"I didn't mean it like that."

"*You all* never do. I know why I sold. Yeah? I know what *my* reasons are. You want that and I'll tell you. You want something else, you want to understand the motivations of a people? I've got some sorry news. There is no *people*. That's the hard lesson this country taught me. It is the heart of my success. You want this to be a community but it's only a territory. Individuals stuck in the same place, battered by the same forces. Of course they respond the same way. If the building you're standing in is on fire, then you'll try to get out, and everyone standing in there with you will try to get out, too—but that doesn't make you a community, just a bunch of individuals trying not to burn alive. Behaving rationally. That's why I sold. Because it was rational. I bought those buildings when I was twenty years old, when I still carried a gun—when you didn't go out in this neighborhood alone. I bought all three properties for sixty-five thousand dollars and my boys shook their heads, told me I was wasting money, that I was parroting my callow West Indian neighbors who thought they could buy their way into respectability. Who prostrated themselves before the false idol of honest work. You run girls, my crew said, you run drugs—why would you want to be a landlord. That's what we got Jews for." She looked to see if Reddick laughed. He didn't. She sighed and continued. "I ran my first girls out of one of those buildings. I grew weed, stacked money and bricks of anything I could move. Fifteen, twenty years of that and I realized the properties were worth more legit. By then I had buildings all over Bed-Stuy and Clinton Hill—some in parts that had turned straight, some in parts that stayed rough. Mostly older tenants, on borrowed time. The day was going to come when someone showed up with a barrel full of money and I was only waiting on the right time to cash out. The money they were throwing at us—are still throwing—that's money you have to be a goddamned fool to turn down. Clean-ass white money, too. Clean as Buckley's and Franky's. Why should I care what happens to this neighborhood. History? This is just a place where I earn a living. When I help people, when I lend them a hand—it's only because we're all stuck in the same inferno. But there comes a time when you got to get yourself out."

"Then he flipped it for twice as much."

"I never had good luck. I work hard, I have a generous spirit, but I never had good luck. I thought that was all it was. But months went by, years, and I watched the towers come up, and the stories rolled in about the money they paid for that land, the holdouts getting triple the old market value. Those towers were like two stakes in my heart. Not like for those fool protesters—but because I knew I had been swindled.

"Franky's name was the only one on the paperwork but I knew he had friends. Inside information—that's that white game, everybody knows it. But I like games, too. And I figured I could make this right. So I sent Mia after him. She's retired now but in her time she was unstoppable. I knew she could make him talk. A few dates and he admitted the whole thing to her. *Bragged* is the better word. She found out who his partners were, went to that fat banker first, and barely had to whisper *fraud* before he talked—never mind that she had no proof. He's crooked all the way down. But I'm fair. I pride myself in that. So I let Mitchell keep a little something—a quarter of the million he made off my properties, to take the sting out of my proposition."

"But you still needed money from the other two."

"I had a problem—how could Franky make things right if he was broke? The money he took from me was long spent. Then Mia told me who the third man in their little conspiracy was—Buckley Seward. *Seward*. I recognized that name. Unlike Hannah I appreciate culture—I've been to our timid Brooklyn Museum, which begs for attention in the looming shadow of her Manhattan sisters. You go to museums? You see names branded on galleries, on hallways. But the Sewards—they got an entire *wing*. So I thought, this boy can help his friend out. There is more than enough Seward money to cover Franky's share. The question was how to get to him."

"You sent Hannah to find something you could squeeze him with."

"I'd already used my best girl on Franky."

"Hey," Hannah said.

"It's the truth, girl. Smart, ambitious and tits the size of your face. When I let her open that store I lost a weapon. You aren't without talents, though."

Hannah frowned and took another hit from the joint.

"She's better at playing the Sewards' type anyway. She seems uncouth now but classy is her specialty. Look at those perfect teeth." Hannah, obliging, smiled.

"You rented an apartment for her, set up a fake identity."

The Genie waved her hands, dismissed the effort. "I already owned an apartment in the city, from back when I thought the island was the path to legitimate money. I gave her a new last name, a hometown on the other side of the country so it wouldn't look suspicious that they hadn't met her folks."

"Then you got her into that reception, had her approach his dad."

"I did my research this time. Flatter his vain father, submit to his regal mother—at first that was just to catch his interest. I didn't think she would have to go so far. I didn't think she would have to get engaged to the son of a bitch—but then, I didn't know about Tony. My bad luck showing up again. I thought it might blow the whole plan up—how could she get close if Buckley preferred a manlier shoulder to cry on? But give Hannah credit—she played it smart, she made his situation work for us. Because his parents wanted Tony sidelined, wanted their son to have a proper wife, wanted a mother for their grandkids, and my girl made sure they knew she was ripe for the job. Once they were on her side the boy couldn't say no for long."

"When he went to look for her that morning—you left him a blackmail note," Reddick said. "That's why he was so shaken when he came back."

"Not a note. An email." The Genie turned to Hannah. "Did you delete that file?"

"I still have it." She typed for a moment, summoned an audio recording and held the phone out, the speaker toward Reddick. He heard a conversation, two voices. It took a moment for him to recognize one as Hannah. Her enunciation was cleaner, more precise, unmistakably upper middle class, private college. The second voice was Buckley.

"What were you fighting about?"

"I don't want to get into it, honestly. Franky can be terribly frustrating."

"Buckles. You've been so tense lately. Don't you think you might feel better if we talked about it?"

There was a pause, a rustle of clothes. Reddick glanced at Hannah. She was grinning, a starlet basking in her Oscar reel.

"You're right, Hannie." A long, heavy sigh. "It's this money I gave him."

"Is he refusing to pay you back?"

"It's not like that. It wasn't a loan, it was for a deal. For this idea he had that I should never have gone along with."

"I don't understand."

"It was three years ago, before Restoration Heights was announced—I don't want to bore you."

"I want to help."

"Okay, but I hope it isn't difficult for you to follow. So back then, Franky and a friend of ours, Mitchell, had this idea, to flip some properties that were inside the territory we had marked off for Restoration Heights. They wanted to buy before we announced, then sell to it Corren afterwards. I'd told them Corren was in a hurry. I was in their strategic meetings, I knew they wanted momentum to push it past the local resistance. Market value would double for everything inside the zone once Corren started buying. Franky's plan didn't seem so bad, a little cash on the side."

"So what was wrong about it?"

"Mitchell approved all the financing, then got a third of the profits—it would be very easy for a lawyer to make the case that we paid Mitchell to approve our loan. That's illegal, Hannie. Then last year some local thug squeezed Mitchell because of it—Franky confessed the whole thing to some, I don't know—*escort*—that he was with, and she told her boss. At least, that's what Mitchell claims. How could Franky be so stupid. They tried to keep it from me but Mitchell finally told me, warned me, and I confronted Franky about it tonight. It's all so sordid—I'm sorry to drag you into this."

"My poor Buckles—it's okay. The more I know, the more I can help you."

The Genie waved her finger and Hannah stopped the playback.

"It goes on like that, the fool babbling more details, blaming Franky for the very thing he was in the act of doing—the irony is my favorite part. I sent him an email with my demands, with this attached to it. It was important that he knew exactly what he was being punished for, that I wasn't using anything against him that he hadn't earned. Once that was done I let Hannah decide how she wanted to leave."

Hannah exhaled a small cloud of dank smoke. "I've always been partial to Irish goodbyes."

Reddick turned to her. "I barely recognized your voice."

"Accents are my thing. I can do South Boston, rich Boston, Long Island, Ohio, pretty much whatever you want." She shrugged haphazardly. "I always liked pretending."

"That recording was enough, then? To force him to play along?"

"He paid me three days ago," the Genie said. "Whether it was his fear of being exposed, or the intensity of his shame at being so thoroughly, so easily duped—in the end it doesn't matter. Because he paid in full."

"Him putting me off—he was just trying to cover his tracks."

"You didn't make it easy. Blind as you were—you got my people so worked up thinking you were going to expose Mia and Ju'waun, as if I didn't already know what those two were doing. If she wants to play star-crossed lover to Tyler's wannabe cousin I couldn't care less—but I like to cultivate a certain reputation, to keep everyone in line, so when your drunk accomplice started asking questions of some of my boys, I guess it was only natural that they got amped up. Once Ju'waun told me who you were really after, I knew it would come to this. I read you before I saw you—I understood who you were from your barest description. Earnest and lost, desperate to attach yourself to something that matters, too dumb and too stubborn to end up anywhere other than sitting across from me."

"Jeannie, why are we telling this guy all of this?"

"Because he did a rare thing, Hannah. He earned it. He spent the last nine days burying himself alive, one shovel at a time, trying to find out what happened to that poor blonde girl who wanted to kiss him in an alley."

"I wanted to kiss him?"

"Trying to *save* her, you believe that?"

Reddick felt his body sink into the generous leather. He had uncovered a plot without villains. There was no one to accept the blame—just a network of escalating grievances, of desolate people, of injuries repaid in kind. He had thought it was revenge, but revenge is always personal, always intuitive—an expression of emotion, like tears. There was nothing like that here. Only cold business and patterns of exploitation, a cycle in which all the names were replaceable. There was nothing to expose, no one who needed saving, who needed justice. There was, finally, no Hannah. Just some girl with her name and her face.

The Genie leaned forward. "Now you know. The question is, what are you going to do about it?"

"I told you. I just came to see. To know for sure."

"You could go to the police."

He thought about Clint and his detective friend—the biases they would bring, which crimes they would investigate and which they would ignore, who would suffer most. If he took every name from his map and threw them into the mill of justice, he knew who would emerge unscathed, and why. There was no way to tell anyone without picking a side.

"Or you could go to the press. Add all of this to the case against Restoration Heights. Buckley Seward's little scheme to rip off a poor old black woman. Try to direct the blaze of outrage to your pet cause. You know you can't stop it. Maybe you believe you could contain it."

"There's no way to do that without exposing you."

"Probably not."

"I don't think you would let me."

"What would I do to stop you? I'm not a murderer, Reddick. I'm a businesswoman. If you haven't learned that by now, I wonder what all of this was for."

"So I can go?"

"Answer me first. What are you going to do?"

He stood up. "I think you know."

The Genie smiled. Hannah was back on her phone, thumb scrolling for a diversion with more meaning or interest than the person passing a few feet from her body.

"You think there is nothing you could prove."

"It's worse than that. There's nothing I care about proving."

He turned and walked out, back through the rows of hanging clothes sheathed in plastic. TJ was nowhere to be found. Reddick smashed the bell on the counter, the one-note ring echoing like a brief scream in the small lobby. He hit it again, violently, then two more times in quick succession, and then again, repeatedly hammering the thin metal until the panicked ringing was beaten into a broken, arid click. He snatched it up and slung it at the wall, was rewarded with one final despairing chime before he walked outside.

The clouds were low and thick, shifting in the damp wind.

A spring he couldn't feel yet was gathering. He wandered, dazed. He reached into his pocket and removed his phone. There were seven messages, all from Derek, descending from concern to fear and finally a plea. *I'm coming back. Just call me and let me know you haven't gotten yourself killed.* He looked up and saw that he was standing in front of the entrance to the G stop at Bedford Avenue. A rush hour train had just arrived. Bodies streamed up from the tunnel, almost all of them white, young, home from a long day wrestling the city. They flowed east and west into the arteries of their new neighborhood, the spoils of their bloodless conquest. He stood on the corner, watched them all come—faces like his, skin like his, speaking a language he never learned. He slipped his phone into his pocket. He was surrounded by them, consumed—you can look and look but you'll never see the difference.

★ ★ ★ ★ ★

ACKNOWLEDGMENTS

I am deeply indebted to Kate Garrick, who made this possible and who not only understands where I'm from but also understands why that matters. I also owe a huge thanks to John Glynn of Hanover Square Press for his enthusiasm and insight, and for having the vision to bring out the best in this book. Thank you to all my readers for their honest feedback, Rachael, Ben, Ivanny and especially Eli. I am a better writer for their candor. Thank you to Brian and Mark for their primer on the NYPD and gangs, to Ray for helping me unknot the tangle of Brooklyn real estate, to Josie and Agnes for helping me get this book out of my apartment and into the world, and to everyone at the Bedford-Stuyvesant YMCA, my home-away-from-home, for treating me like family.

Most importantly, I'd like to thank my wife, Holly Frisbee, for her optimism, her relentless belief and her unwavering love through all those years when we had nothing but those things to sustain us. We did it, darling.